PUCK OF POOK'S HILL

Rudyard Joseph Kipling was born in Bombay in 1865. His father, John Lockwood Kipling, was the author and illustrator of *Beast and Man in India* and his mother, Alice, was the sister of Lady Burne-Jones. In 1871 Kipling was brought home from India and spent five unhappy years with a foster family in Southsea, an experience he later drew on in *The Light That Failed* (1890). The years he spent at the United Services College, a school for officers' children, are depicted in *Stalky and Co.* (1899) and the character of Beetle is something of a self-portrait. It was during his time at the college that he began writing poetry and *Schoolboy Lyrics* was published privately in 1881. In the following year he started work as a journalist in India, and while there produced a body of work, stories, sketches and poems – notably *Plain Tales from the Hills* (1888) – which made him an instant literary celebrity when he returned to England in 1889. *Barrack Room Ballads* (1892) contains some of his most popular pieces, including 'Mandalay', 'Gunga Din' and 'Danny Deever'. In this collection Kipling experimented with form and dialect, notably the cockney accent of the soldier poems, but the influence of hymns, music-hall songs, ballads and public poetry can be found throughout his verse.

In 1892 he married an American, Caroline Balestier, and from 1892 to 1896 they lived in Vermont, where Kipling wrote *The Jungle Book*, published in 1894. In 1901 came *Kim* and in 1902 the *Just So Stories*. Tales of every kind – including historical and science fiction – continued to flow from his pen, but *Kim* is generally thought to be his greatest long work, putting him high among the chroniclers of British expansion.

From 1902 Kipling made his home in Sussex, but he continued to travel widely and caught his first glimpse of warfare in South Africa, where he wrote some excellent reportage on the Boer War. However, many of the views he expressed were rejected by anti-imperialists who accused him of jingoism and love of violence. Though rich and successful, he never again enjoyed the literary esteem of his early years. With the onset of the Great War his work became a great deal more sombre. The stories he subsequently wrote, *A Diversity of Creatures* (1917), *Debits and Credits* (1926) and *Limits and Renewals* (1932) are now thought by many to contain some of his finest writing. The death of his only son in 1915 also contributed to a new inwardness of vision.

Kipling refused to accept the role of Poet Laureate and other civil honours, but he was the first English writer to be awarded the Nobel Prize, in 1907. He died in 1936 and his autobiographical fragment *Something of Myself* was published the following year.

Sarah Wintle is a lecturer in English literature at University College London.

Rudyard Kipling

PUCK
OF POOK'S HILL

EDITED,
WITH AN INTRODUCTION AND NOTES,
BY SARAH WINTLE

PENGUIN BOOKS

PENGUIN BOOKS

Published by the Penguin Group
27 Wrights Lane, London w8 5tz, England
Viking Penguin Inc., 40 West 23rd Street, New York, New York 10010, USA
Penguin Books Australia Ltd, Ringwood, Victoria, Australia
Penguin Books Canada Ltd, 2801 John Street, Markham, Ontario, Canada l3r 1b4
Penguin Books (NZ) Ltd, 182–190 Wairau Road, Auckland 10, New Zealand

Penguin Books Ltd, Registered Offices: Harmondsworth, Middlesex, England

First published 1906
Published in Penguin Books 1987
3 5 7 9 10 8 6 4

Introduction and notes copyright © Sarah Wintle, 1987
All rights reserved

Made and printed in Great Britain by
Richard Clay Ltd, Bungay, Suffolk
Typeset in Lasercomp Ehrhardt

Contents

PUCK OF POOK'S HILL

Introduction

The subject matter and preoccupations of children's literature change in the same way as those of writing for adults. In both cases the changes relate in part to changes in social concerns and behaviour. Kipling's niece, the popular novelist Angela Thirkell, tells in her memoir *Three Houses* of the games she used to play with her cousin Josephine. One of their favourites, when they were only six years old, was Cavaliers and Roundheads, although they also played Knights of the Round Table and Crusaders. The two girls were valiant royalist knights and Kipling himself sometimes joined in as a thrillingly bold and bad Oliver Cromwell. Such children would, when a few years older, have little difficulty with either the history or the ethos of *Puck of Pook's Hill*.

As a book for children, *Puck* is now less popular than the *Jungle Books* or the eminently readable *Just So Stories*. History, particularly of the chivalric and politically conservative kind that this book expounds, is no longer the stuff children's games are made from, although the children's historical novelist Rosemary Sutcliff has testified to the influence on her own writings of her childhood reading of *Puck*. Yet this was never entirely a children's book. On 8 October 1906, the month in which it was published in book form, George Wyndham, a forty-three-year-old Member of Parliament, former government minister and man of letters (he was later admired by T. S. Eliot), sat alone in his study and wrote to his sister:

I read *Puck of Pook's Hill* yesterday and I will be bound to say that nobody has enjoyed it more than I did. It will – I daresay – strike you from the children, governess, tea-time, fairy-tale point of view . . . But anyway that is only the envelope of his letter. His letter – what he meant – was written to me. Because I am alone in my Tower. So I thanked him.

7

Wyndham, that same day, wrote an enthusiastic letter of thanks to Kipling, citing in particular the Roman stories.

What the book might mean for adults will be the subject of this introduction. The local Sussex preoccupations, especially, involved Kipling in some fairly recondite reading. This antiquarian aspect is dealt with in the notes to each story which, in keeping with Kipling's obvious didactic intention, I have made quite full. Yet the history of *Puck* is neither pedantic nor academic. Kipling did not hesitate to invent – very plausibly – when he needed to. In the book he has imaginatively transformed the localized Sussex childhood of his own two children to present, with adult knowingness, his own version of the myth of England and the English countryside. This myth, because it has to do with origins and beginnings, often involves ideas of both childhood and history. Form and content in *Puck* are a great deal more closely and fruitfully entwined than Wyndham's envelope-and-letter image indicates.

II

The first few years of the twentieth century were particularly significant for Kipling, both with regard to his private life and his political opinions and beliefs. In September 1902 he moved with his family to Batemans, the house near Burwash, Sussex, where he was to live – when not on his travels – until his death in 1936; 1902 was also the year the Anglo-Boer War ended. In 1897 Kipling had met Cecil Rhodes and Alfred Milner, two key figures in South African affairs at this time, and from 1900 until 1908 he and his family wintered regularly in the Cape. Rhodes had a house built for them in the grounds of his own house, The Woolsack, and even at one point gave them a lion cub. Kipling wrote a story about this cub for his two children, John and Elsie, in which they appear for the first time as Dan and Una. Dan, from the Old Testament Book of Daniel, and Una, from Book I of Spenser's *Faerie Queene*, are names with impeccably leonine credentials. Kipling's admiration of Rhodes, who had fantastic dreams of a world-wide Anglo-Saxon empire, and his experiences in the Boer War as a journalist and semi-official raiser of troop morale, were important factors in the formation of the imperial vision of his middle years.

Kim, Kipling's last Indian story, was published in 1901. He did not then turn to South Africa for his prime literary subject and inspiration, but rather. to England, and the Sussex countryside in particular. He and his family had lived since 1897 in the village of Rottingdean, near Brighton, where his maternal aunt Georgiana and her husband, the Pre-Raphaelite painter Edward Burne-Jones, had had a house for some years. Kipling's views on Sussex were at first unenthusiastic. He was impatient with the slowness and inefficiency of the local workmen building him a drill-shed in which he could drill a small company of volunteers – part of his personal contribution to the South African campaign, and to a general stiffening of the English will. He wrote to Rhodes that, 'England is a stuffy little place, mentally, morally and physically'. (Carrington, *Kipling*, 1955, p. 383) Besides, Josephine, his elder daughter, died, aged seven, in 1899, and Rottingdean became painfully suffused with memories of her. The move to Batemans seems to have effected a remarkable change of mind and mood as he indicated in a letter to an American friend:

Then we discovered England which we had never done before . . . and went to live in it. England is a wonderful land. It is the most marvellous of all foreign countries that I have ever been in. It is made up of trees and green fields and mud and the gentry, and at last I'm one of the gentry. (Carrington, p. 383)

Kipling's elation might seem to have run away with his logic, for members of the gentry in the sense he indicates here are unlikely to be foreign. However in the story, 'An Habitation Enforced', published in 1905, he constructed a tale showing just how the foreign might become native, Americans – with suitable antecedents – become Sussex squires. One of the literary advantages of such naturalized natives is that they are self-conscious about their status and so better able to voice its essence than those who are simply born to it. The three narrators of the major historical tales in *Puck* are natives of this kind, settlers rather than indigenous inhabitants – a Norman knight, a Roman centurion, native born but of Roman 'stock', and a Spanish Jew. In this, their position corresponds to that of the Indian-born author, himself a 'foreigner' come to make his home in Sussex. His sedulous cultivation of the language of belonging in *Puck* is a major part of the artful reconstruction of a particular fiction of England and Englishness which underpins the book and carries the connection between the stories.

Batemans then, and what Kipling could describe as 'the stuffy little valley where she stood', was a key precipitating factor in the imaginative composition of the book in which that particular small place is recomposed into the heart of England. In his autobiography *Something of Myself* Kipling devotes the whole of chapter seven to the early days at Batemans, and what he found there. The local inhabitants are

artists and craftsmen, either in stone or in timber, or wood-cutting or drain-laying or – which is a gift – the aesthetic disposition of dirt; persons of contrivance who could conjure with any sort of material.

Contrivance, conjuring, craft: through such characteristic code words he almost too easily acknowledges their dignity and worth, and at the same time assimilates himself as craftsman to their world. One cannot help observing that his ideas seem to have changed somewhat since his encounter with the builders of the drill-shed. Among these 'artists and craftsmen' is a poacher and tree-expert, the utterer of the phrase, 'Have it as you're minded. I dunno as I should if I was you,' who is transformed into the eternal countryman, Hobden, in *Puck* and related poems like 'The Land'. Hobdens remain forever the same in the valley, and only those who come and go are subject to the demands of history.

An ancient peasant life rich in craft and cunning was not all that the Kiplings found at Batemans. They dug up Roman, Jacobean and Cromwellian objects in the grounds and were astonished by the ancient logs which underpinned the foundations of the mill. Kipling, with the aid of 'Sir William Willcocks, who had designed the Assouan Dam – a trifling affair on the Nile', converted this mill to turn a dynamo for domestic electricity. In addition, 'every foot of that little corner was alive with ghosts and shadows', the ghosts and shadows which are magicked up into brilliant and unghostly life to tell the stories which are written on the land about the land itself:

> See you the dimpled track that runs,
>   All hollow through the wheat?
> O that was where they hauled the guns
>   That smote King Philip's fleet. (p. 41)

This is a landscape which, to the initiated, the diviners of its secrets, tells a nation's history and which Puck and his magic will reveal. The 'stuffy little valley', when you settle in it and learn its language, is an enchanted and resonant place.

The imaginative origins of a work as thematically rich as *Puck* are likely to be multiple. Kipling, in *Something of Myself*, tells of how a cousin, Ambrose Poynter, suggested that he should write a Roman story with a hero named Parnesius, and tells too of several false starts to other stories about subjects as diverse as Baltic pirates and Daniel Defoe. In fact, he was thinking of writing something on the last days of the Romans in Britain as early as 1897 when he consulted Edward Burne-Jones about the best books on the subject. Burne-Jones recommended the last volume of the German historian Theodore Mommsen's massive *History of Rome*, and the volume of Bohn's Library which contained the early British histories of Geoffrey of Monmouth, Nennius and Gildas – as well as an eighteenth-century forgery, the *Chronicle of Richard of Cirencester*, which Kipling used for some details in the Roman stories. 1897 is the year in which Kipling, prompted by what he saw as the unthinking complacency of late-Victorian England, wrote his most famous imperialist poem, 'Recessional':

Far-called, our navies melt away;
On dune and headland sinks the fire;
Lo, all our pomp of yesterday
Is one with Nineveh and Tyre!
Judge of the Nations, spare us yet,
Lest we forget – lest we forget!

Puck echoes and develops the message of 'Recessional' in noting the fragility of empire as well as its orientation towards not forgetting – remembering for a purpose is, after all, one version of what it means to write history. The story, 'A Centurion of the Thirtieth', is prefaced by a poem which Kipling later chose to introduce his collection, *Songs from Books* (1913):

Cities and Thrones and Powers,
Stand in Time's eye,
Almost as long as flowers,
Which daily die:
But, as new buds put forth,
To glad new men,
Out of the spent and unconsidered Earth,
The Cities rise again.

'Cities and Thrones and Powers' may include Nineveh and Tyre, but in the context of the book it indicates Rome in particular, the dying days of whose empire are powerfully depicted in the central stories. *Puck* is concerned with the last days of one imperial power and the early history of another. Warnings of decline are countered by the stress on beginnings and youth – 'new buds put forth' – and a bleak cyclical view of history is balanced against a more local and hopeful view of individual human powers and responsibilities.

Comparisons of the British and Roman empires were rather less common, even in the heady days of late-nineteenth-century imperialism, than one might suppose. It may be that the shadow of decline and fall lay too heavily over the connection. Nonetheless, one of Cecil Rhodes's favourite quotations was from the *Meditations* of the Stoic emperor-philosopher, Marcus Aurelius: 'Remember always that you are a Roman'; a phrase that neatly connects imperial pretensions with an expression of the kind of public-school stoicism which seems to have constituted the ethical code of many imperial servants, and which Kipling manages to make almost moving in these stories. English-Roman analogies were most often made by historians and aspiring pro-consuls with classical educations; the centrality of the three Roman stories in *Puck* answers to the centrality of the imperial idea in the work as a whole.

The Victorian imperialist, James Froude, made a particularly interesting use of the parallel near the beginning of his book, *Oceana*:

Horace had seen in Rome what we are now witnessing in England – fields deserted, the people crowding into cities. He noted the growing degeneracy. He foretold the inevitable consequences.

The decline of Rome was linked to the idea of urban corruption, cosmopolitanism and the consequent physical degeneration of the inhabitants of cities. Froude himself thought that this was unlikely to happen to the British empire, because any superfluous, undersized and degenerate urban English could be shipped off to people the open, green spaces of Australia or South Africa, where the combination of hard work and fresh air, 'in some of the fairest spots upon the globe', would soon restore them to rude, Anglo-Saxon good health. Froude, however, was writing before the Boer War, and the horror generated by the discovery that many recruits to the army, particularly those from the large, urban areas, were physically undersized and unfit for military service. Imperial decline, it seemed, was quite far gone, and the miserable British military performance in the first year of the war did nothing to counteract this perception. The British finally won the war, thanks in no small measure to their degenerate English recruits as well as to the aid of healthier contingents from other parts of the empire, and Kipling thought that the whole episode would teach the nation 'no end of a lesson; it will do us no end of good'.

This phrase is the refrain from the poem, 'The Lesson', written at the end of the war. The real lesson to be learned, in

Kipling's view, was that a redirection of the national will, through a renewed examination of what the nation might ideally consist of, was necessary. Late nineteenth- and early twentieth-century attempts to define, redeem or re-energize the imperial idea through redefining the nation were often made through particular applications of essentially rural ideas of England and Englishness. Only the countryside, for example, could provide healthy soldiers to guard the imperial territories. True Englishmen, this line of thought suggests, are always countrymen, or, as Hal o' the Draft puts it in *Puck*, 'What can town folk know of the nature of housen – or land?' (p. 170) The land is home and England. However, the notion that the heart of England is not the metropolitan centre but some village somewhere in the soft, southern half of the country has itself recently been taken as a symptom of decline. The idea can be interpreted as a sign of a fundamental unwillingness to accept an industrially and commercially based modern society, and therefore an indication of a merely nostalgic and even lazy conservatism. *Puck*, with its imperialist and conservative leanings, and its concern with soldiers, the countryside and children who will, as the final poem suggests, pledge themselves to the nation, is a central text as far as these ideas and this debate is concerned.

III

Kipling's choice of Puck as the coordinating figure of his narrative seems to have been suggested by a performance by John and Elsie of parts of *A Midsummer Night's Dream* in the old quarry at Batemans. This play was often celebrated as the most English of Shakespeare's works with its rich writing about fairies, honeysuckle and musk roses; it was also a play which was considered particularly suitable as an introduction to Shakespeare for children, because of the fairies. Fairy stories, under the influence of serious folklorists like Andrew Lang – an acquaintance of Kipling's – made something of a comeback as children's literature towards the end of the nineteenth century. Such stories were then considered to record, in a relatively pure form, our cultural infancy, and thus to speak to those in the same stage of their individual lives.

This revival, it is worth noting, was given added impetus, albeit in a slightly different direction, by the resounding success of Barrie's play *Peter Pan* at the end of 1904. This work resembles *Puck* insofar as it combines elements of fairy-tale with elements of the boys' adventure story deriving from Ballantyne's *The Coral Island* and Stevenson's *Treasure Island*. Such books lie behind the story, 'The Knights of the Joyous Venture', in *Puck*, just as the more narrowly historical kind of boys' fiction is suggested by some of the other tales. The adventures of the young pairs of friends, Richard and Hugh, Parnesius and Pertinax, Harry and Sebastian, might well be entitled, following the popular historical novels of G. H. Henty, 'With William to Hastings', or 'With Maximus on the Wall'. Kipling's account of human behaviour, however, is rather more challenging, and besides, Henty did not write about fairies.

Folklore and fairy-tale were thus a matter of serious concern. The figure of Puck himself is treated at some length in an article by the President of the Folklore Society, the publisher Alfred Nutt, which appeared in *Folklore*, the Society's journal, in 1897. Kipling did not join the Folklore Society until 1911, and was then an inactive member. However, he may well have met Nutt or come across his writings through his Burne-Jones connections, for although there is no conclusive evidence he read Nutt's article, the correspondences between the article and *Puck* are striking and illuminating. The article is entitled, 'The Fairy Mythology of English Literature; its Origin and Nature', and it takes Shakespeare as its starting point. Nutt argues that we can recover from *A Midsummer Night's Dream* the 'elements of a conception of life and nature older than the most ancient recorded utterance of earth's most ancient races'. Fairy beliefs are part of an 'antique religion of the soil', and fairies are rustic creatures, 'rude and coarse and earthy', not as Puck, who might be thinking of *Peter Pan*, puts it: 'little buzzflies with butterfly wings and gauze petticoats'. Puck and Oberon are rightly brought together by Shakespeare, for there is a long-standing connection between Arthurian literature and the fairy world,

Introduction

exemplified in the medieval romance, *Huon of Bordeaux* –
referred to in 'Weland's Sword', as well as in the first story in
the sequel to *Puck, Rewards and Fairies*. Both kinds of story,
according to Nutt, are in essence Celtic, and their central characters are the 'dispossessed immortals of an Irish Pantheon'. Puck
tells Dan and Una that the English fairies are old Gods, and
have to do 'with ancient country rites'. His phrase, 'People of
the Hills' is an adaptation of the Celtic *aes sidhe*, 'people of the
fairy hillocks'.

Nutt, however, takes his argument further; the fairy creed
was, he thinks, 'common to all the Aryan-speaking people of
Europe, to the ancestors of Greeks, Romans and Slavs as well
as to the ancestors of Celts and Teutons'. Hence the parallel
pointed out by the Elizabethan writer, Thomas Nashe, between
elves and Robin Goodfellow – another name for Puck – and
classical fauns and satyrs is 'valid and illuminating'. Parnesius,
the Roman centurion, calls Puck, 'Faun', and Puck speaks Latin
like a native – although he also appears to speak Hebrew. Nutt
also refers to a tract published in 1628 which, like *A Midsummer
Night's Dream*, celebrates Puck's abilities as a shape changer;
this apparently relates him to Merlin and Dionysius. Be that as
it may, Kipling's Puck becomes, in some strangely powerful
moments, a horse, a bull and a 'magnificent old dog fox':

'Oh, Mus' Reynolds, Mus' Reynolds!' said Hobden, under his
breath. 'If I knowed all was inside your head, I'd know something
wuth knowin'. Mus' Dan an' Miss Una, come along o' me while I lock
up my liddle hen-house.' (p. 164)

Hobden, man of the soil and half-believer in fairies, never
encounters or talks to Puck *in propria persona*, nor does he meet
the major historical heroes. As an adult, he cannot be allowed to
share the children's secret – so secret that even Dan and Una
must be magicked into forgetfulness before re-encountering
the normal world of parents and governesses. Nonetheless,
Hobden's privileged status as a son of the soil means that he
does unknowingly meet Puck in the guise of his old and almost
certainly dead friend Tom Shoesmith, in the most locally

folkloric of all the tales, 'Dymchurch Flit'. The fairies' departure is a fairly well-known fairy motif, but there is a moment in this story which is a good illustration of the width of Kipling's reading, and of his imaginative use of it to connect the local with his grand historical scheme. When the fairies climb into the boat which will take them across the channel to safety, there occurs a characteristic touch of descriptive precision:

That boat she sunk lower an' lower, but all the Widow could see in it was her boys movin' hampered-like to get at the tackle.   (p. 192)

This observation and part of the surrounding narrative appear to have been borrowed from a passage in *The Gothic War* by the sixth-century Byzantine historian, Procopius. The passage is known to Celtic scholars as a particularly late reference to Celtic religious beliefs. Procopius describes how the Armoricans – the inhabitants of Brittany – would be woken by a low voice and a knocking at the door in order that they might ferry the souls of the dead over to the island of Britain. When they went to the harbour they would find boats, apparently empty, sunk to the gunwales. One common explanation of fairy origins was that they were souls of the dead, an explanation which accounts for Puck's disguise as the dead Tom Shoesmith in this story. Hobden's wife is a descendant of the widow herself and so the borrowing from the historian indicates the ancient descent and immemorial continuities imagined by Kipling for his embodiment of Sussex man as well as for his fairy spokesman.

Dan and Una alone are able to speak to Puck, to the historical characters and to Hobden with equal ease, and this is not only because children, fairies and peasants go together as primitive originals but because they are a particular kind of child. They, unlike their fictional parents, know Hobden's secrets, his reasons for advising their father not to grub up the old tree stump which is his best place for rabbit snares. As children they are almost classless, not yet incorporated into the adult structures that dictate who may say what to whom. Kipling needs them in order to make Hobden fully articulate. Yet the children are also owners of the land, its legal heirs, in a way that

Hobden, whatever his customary rights, is not. It is this fact
that makes possible Puck's gift of seizin in 'Weland's Sword', a
gift which will enable them to make the place their own in a
more than material sense. One kind of ownership is dependent
on the other.

The whole book is about initiation, the preparing of Dan and
Una, children of 'one of the gentry', to take, as the final poem
puts it, their 'place,/As men and women with [their] race'. (p.
210) The children take possession of a life's task through the
acquisition of knowledge about and understanding of a place
and its inhabitants and its history. The valley contains an old
forge; Batemans itself was probably built by a Sussex ironmaster in the days when the Weald with its plentiful supply of
charcoal produced much of England's iron. At the end of the
valley Weland Smith, in the first story, forges a sword on which
he inscribes, in secret runic code, the plot the rest of the book
will unfold. This plot is the story of the forging of a race and
its imperial destiny, a process which is both learned about and
in part re-enacted by the children.

Imperial possessions are at first frontier countries before
they are brought under the rule of the law. The frontier –
Hadrian's Wall – is the central image of the Roman stories,
and it is there that Parnesius and Pertinax grow up:

'Where are the Captains of the Wall?'
We said we were those men.
'But you are old and grey-haired,' he cried. 'Maximus said that they
were boys.'
'Yes, that was true some years ago,' said Pertinax. 'What is our fate
to be, you fine and well-fed child?' (p. 162)

The Norman stories too trace the journey of two young men
from an eager and untried youth to a disillusioned and politically tested maturity, wittily turning the boy's adventure story
upside-down in the process, for when Richard and Hugh encounter gorillas and gold in equatorial Africa they are well on
into middle age. This story too is a journey to a future frontier,
to the 'gold coast' later to be taken under British rule, but the

earlier story, 'Young Men at the Manor', is a frontier story too, involving the defence of newly-won English territory against marauding bands of Normans, the acquisition of cunning in the task of reconciling Saxon and Norman, and thus the welding together of a new nation.

For Dan and Una that same valley, however small and even 'stuffy' it might seem to an adult, is still a frontier, a place to be explored and taken possession of, both in fact and imagination. They fish for trout, secretly, in the brook hidden by the dense growth of 'willow, hazel, and guelder-rose' along its banks, and they are familiar with its natural history, the distribution of trout and kingfishers, just as the frontiersman of the colonial imagination knows the secret ways and the hunting grounds of his territory. The children, however, do more than fish and birdwatch; their games of imaginative pretence involve the transformation of the valley into a number of historical versions of the world's wild places:

That day they intended to discover the North Cape like 'Othere, the old sea-captain', in the book of verses which Una had brought with her; but on account of the heat they changed it to a voyage up the Amazon and the sources of the Nile. (p. 79)

On the same page we learn that they often call their boat the *Golden Hind* or *The Long Serpent*. Another part of the valley transforms into Volaterrae, an Etruscan stronghold in the days before the Romans had conquered even their Italian territories.

Dan and Una's colonial adventures are quite innocent – they involve, naturally enough, no bloodshed, violence, cunning tricks or crafty dealing. The territory they explore and make their own is not only a wild place, but also an Eden or a paradise. Early colonizers of the new world often thought they had discovered paradise, and sometimes celebrated the innocent goodness of the primitive inhabitants they found there. Later, this innocence was construed as childishness; primitives, men without history, or men who had not yet entered history, were living as all men lived in the early days, or childhood, of the human race. Thus, there need be no present inhabitants of Dan and Una's Edenic territory because they themselves are the natives, innocent inhabitants and owners of an original paradise, or paradise of origins. Take a slightly wider view, of course, and there is a native population, represented by Hobden and his son the Bee Boy who is 'not quite right in the head' – a simpleton, or yet another version of the primitive. In relation to these natives, as we have seen, Dan and Una revert to being their father's children, for whom history and hardship, cunning and craft wait just round the corner.

Once the frontier is held, the new settlers must get to know the natives and their customs. Alfred Nutt in a later article in *Folklore* published in 1899, an article much preoccupied with both England's imperial responsibilities and its Celtic and Teutonic heritage, argues for the practical uses of folklore in the administration of overseas territories, and builds much of his argument on the analogy with Rome. The 'English race', he suggests, has transmitted to the modern world 'much of the ancient customary wisdom of the Teutonic-speaking peoples', and so,

England, preserving, elaborating the native customs of one of the component elements of our mixed race, has reared a structure of institutions not unworthy to be set by the side of the Roman, and destined to control the fortunes of even wider realms and more numerous populations.

The Romans themselves, he points out, were willing to learn about, and from, the customs and institutions of their subject peoples. Kipling's Pertinax is interested in the Pict religion, and so is this kind of imperial folklorist. Much of the pioneering work in the collecting of folklore in the late nineteenth and early twentieth centuries was done by leisured ladies who talked to their servants. Dan and Una, when they listen in the oast house to the story of 'Dymchurch Flit' and the Bee Boy's heritage, are learning about the natives of their valley in a way that rehearses and ratifies their future status just as much as does their listening to the more obviously political stories of adventure and rule.

IV

In early-twentieth-century writing about imperialism the combining of *imperium* – the exercise of power through military rule – and *libertas* – freedom – was often seen as problematic and involved distinctions between the settled, white, Anglo-Saxon dominions – South Africa, Australia – and the areas with large native populations, India above all. South Africa, of course, was unique in being both a settled territory and a land with a large indigenous population, but the latter's freedom was regrettably not a matter of prime concern to most of those interested in ideas of empire. Kipling is concerned with both power and freedom in *Puck*, but his imperial interests had shifted with his South African experience to the white empire and his narrative structure with its separation of the Roman and Norman stories allows him to keep the two notions from clashing. The conservative political ideology of the English countryside, connected with ownership of land and the figure of the sturdy yeoman, propounds ideas of freedom and custom. These ideas are often historically justified by appeals to ancient Saxon law and thus to continuities with the Teutonic past, continuities which are also embodied in Magna Charta. The first four stories in *Puck* are stories of settlement and along with the last, a story of Magna Charta, are particularly concerned with ideas of law, liberty and race as well as being closely tied in with the land. Parnesius, after all, only spent one night at the valley forge on his way to the Wall, where his life, as has often been remarked, is reminiscent of that of a subaltern on the North-west Frontier.

Weland, the central character of the initial story, is a figure from Nordic or Teutonic mythology who turns up in Anglo-Saxon literature, Walter Scott's novel *Kenilworth* – Scott was a pioneering folklorist – and in a curious work by Thomas Hughes, *The Scouring of the White Horse*, which mixes Anglo-Saxonizing, folklore and muscular Christianity. There is a copy of this work in Kipling's study at Batemans. Hughes, the author of the better-known *Tom Brown's Schooldays*, was a friend of Charles Kingsley. Kingsley in 1864 published *The Roman and the Teuton*, a series of lectures he had given at Oxford on the dying days of one imperial race and the infancy of another. Kipling had not necessarily read this work, but it elaborates in a particularly clear fashion some ideas about the imperial destiny of the English which, imaginatively transformed, underlie both the formal pattern of the stories and the significance of the children in *Puck*.

Kingsley announced his subject in the first lecture which stressed the childishness, above all the boyishness, of the early Teutons: 'To the strange and complicated education which God appointed for this race and by which he has fitted it to become, at least for many centuries henceforth, the ruling race of the world, I wish to call your attention . . .' Later in the same lecture Kingsley discriminates between English and continental Teutonism and the distinction leads him into a fantasy of rural Saxon life which suggests the virtues of a country childhood for races and nations as well as individuals:

Happy for us Englishmen, that we were forced to seek our adventure here, in this lovely isle; to turn aside from the great stream of Teutonic immigration; and settle here, each man on his forest clearing, to till the ground in comparative peace, keeping unbroken the old Teutonic laws, unstained the old Teutonic faith and virtue, cursed neither with poverty nor riches, but fed with food sufficient for us. To us indeed, after long centuries peace brought sloth, and sloth foreign invaders and bitter woes: but better so, than that we should have cast away alike our virtue and our lives, in that mad quarrel over the fairy gold of Rome.

Here part of the preparation for the imperial task seems to be both the idyllic life of the sturdy independent Teutonic yeoman in the early days of the nation's history and the subsequent and bracing 'bitter woe' of the Norman Conquest. Kingsley's attitude to 'the fairy gold of Rome' corresponds in part too, as we shall see, to the role of treasure in *Puck*.

Kipling makes his version of Weland the only pagan god – in the original stories he is not a god – who becomes, and deserves to become, English; in the manuscript he is even described as a 'gentleman', which goes to show how Kipling improved his text in revising it. Weland arrives as part of a successive wave of immigration – Puck mentions Phoenicians (inaccurately), Gauls, Jutes, Danes and Frisians – each wave bringing its own gods. Most of these, after some high-handed behaviour, leave, 'because they couldn't get on with the English for one reason or another'. (Who, it might be asked, are 'the English' if not Gauls, Jutes, Danes and Frisians?) Only Weland stays and 'honestly worked for his living after he came down in the world' (p. 51). This honest life of Kingsley-like yeomanly independence and virtue earns him, in the end, release and the right to play a part in England's story: 'You may remember that I was not a gentle God in my Day and my Time and my Power. I shall never be released till some human being truly wishes me well' (p. 54). Such insistent use of triplets and parallels throughout the early stories – it is particularly marked in the first two – stresses their ritualistic, mythic and initiatory aspect, both for the history Weland initiates and for the initiation of the children; 'By Right of Oak, Ash, and Thorn are you free to come and go and look and know where I shall show or best you please' (p. 48). The language at these early crucial points in the narrative is highly charged.

It is the Saxon Hugh, Norman-educated novice, lord of the manor and descendant of Cerdic of Wessex, who frees Weland through his courtesy and thus receives the gift of the sword which he will pass on to the Norman knight. Hugh, who carries his fishing rod over his shoulder like a spear, is a model knight in his chivalry and so claims literary descent from Walter Scott's Ivanhoe, another chivalric Saxon who is connected with Cerdic and friendly with Normans. In *Ivanhoe*, Scott was concerned to examine the relations between conqueror and conquered, and of both with the Jews. The last, climactically awkward story in *Puck* is also concerned with the place of the Jews in the reign of King John, and Kipling's Kadmiel has not escaped the influence of Scott's Isaac, who in his turn descends from Shakespeare's Shylock.

The immediate source for the Norman stories was not Kingsley or Scott but the massive five-volume *History of the*

Introduction

Norman Conquest (1870–76) by E. A. Freeman, who included some hard remarks about the accuracy of Scott's historical imagination in his text. The scope of this work, from the early Teutonic invasions to Magna Charta and the coronation of Edward I, 'the first King of the new stock who deserved to be called an Englishman, the first King in whom the blood of Cerdic and Woden had swallowed up the blood of Norman Dukes and Angevin Counts', is close to that of the Weland's sword narrative in *Puck*. Freeman argues that although the conquest was 'the great turning point in the English nation', it is not the beginning of English history, for, 'The conquered did not become Normans but the Conquerors did become English men.' The beginning for Freeman, as for Kingsley, and here too Kipling follows them, lay with those first invasions and this event, interpreted as the making of a race as well as of a legal and institutional inheritance, determined not only what happened to the Norman invaders in the eleventh century but also the nature of nineteenth-century Englishmen. Freeman, however, did not regard the Normans with much favour, for he was an ardent believer in the supreme value of England's Saxon and Teutonic heritage and believed too in the sacrosanctness of nations. Thus, logically enough, and unlike other Teutonists like Kingsley, he disapproved of empire as involving a violation of national identities.

The Norman stories in *Puck* stress the legal and customary continuities obviously enough, but they also relate to the immediate imperial theme. Kipling wrote to George Wyndham in reply to his letter of thanks: 'I swear I didn't mean to write parables – much – but when situations are so ludicrously, or terribly, parallel what can one do?' This applies most obviously to the Roman stories with their subaltern-like centurions and charismatic but flawed leader. But the Norman stories provide an analogue to what was, or what should be, happening in South Africa. There, Englishman and Boer, like Norman and Saxon, might learn to farm together as Kipling suggests in his poem, 'The Settler'. The figure of Aquila even seems to owe something to Kipling's admired Lord Roberts. Both men are small and ride horses of a particular colour, Roberts greys and Aquila

24

roans. *The Friend*, the paper for which Kipling wrote in South Africa, was bilingual in English and Afrikaans and had been set up by Roberts and Milner to hold out a hand of imperial friendship to the Boers. Aquila, at the betrothal of the Norman Richard to the Saxon Ælueva, makes a speech 'in what he swore was good Saxon' (p. 74). The third Norman story even anticipates the Roman stories that follow it by including a 'Recessional'-like note of warning. The old men at Pevensey: Aquila, Richard and Hugh, are shown guarding Pevensey Castle not only against a threatened invasion from the continent but also from traitors who pretend to serve their king but who scheme to let in the invaders. Ruling classes must always guard against rottenness at the core.

Weland's story starts a process of defining Englishness, with its reference to the pagan gods who left because they couldn't get on with the English. This hint of exclusiveness takes a racial tinge in, interestingly, the Roman stories. Empires lead to all sorts of racial mixings and cosmopolitanism which is acknowledged in the description of Roman Bath where you meet:

fortune-tellers, and goldsmiths, and merchants, and philosophers, and feather-sellers, and ultra-Roman Britons, and ultra-British Romans, and tame tribesmen pretending to be civilized, and Jew lecturers, and – oh, everybody interesting.   (p. 122)

Parnesius-like, the Indian Kipling is enchanted with such exotic human variety, but we might remember Froude's warning that urban degeneration, often allied in nineteenth-century minds with cosmopolitanism, was a prime cause of Rome's decline. Parnesius's father thinks that Rome's decline started when Rome forsook her gods and became tolerant, and reminds Parnesius that they are 'people of the Old Stock' (p. 124). The stories and the poem, 'The Little People', suggest that the Picts are inferior to both the Romans of the old empire and the Teutonic invaders – founders of the new empire. All this, of course, is unhistorical nonsense and only countered by the sympathetic portrayal of Allo – significantly, a horse-coper, like Majub Ali in *Kim*. The inhabitants of Parnesius's villa on the Isle of

Wight were almost certainly British Celts, and Roman citizenship was widely extended in the later years of the empire. The stories preserve distinctions, like those between Roman legionnaries and foreign auxiliaries, which had become blurred many years before.

The last story, 'The Treasure and the Law', is the most obvious attempt in the book to extend the notion of Englishness and to modify its exclusiveness by making a Jew instrumental in the formulation of Magna Charta, customarily considered one of the crucial documents in the story of England and Englishness. Kipling, however, had in addition a topical reason for writing about Jews and Englishness and this again has to do with South Africa. Kipling was moved by Cecil Rhodes's imperial vision, which would extend the virtues of Anglo-Saxon rule and settlement over vast territories, but he must also have been aware of Rhodes's deep involvement with the owners of the South African gold and diamond mines and their great finance houses. This side of South African life was partly dominated by Jews, men like Barney Barnato from the East End or Sir Alfred Beit from Germany. During the Boer War the pro-war party might claim to be fighting for high principles of civilization, but the left, pro-Boer faction based its case on a discernment of the commercial interests that lay behind the high imperial principles, a suspicion of international finance and, allied with these, anti-Semitism. Any honest evaluation of what was going on in South Africa would have to acknowledge the importance of gold, diamonds and money, as well as frontier farming.

The poem which prefaces the story is a suspiciously guileless celebration of the sinister idea that 'Israel' has some predetermined and organic sympathy with gold – Jews can 'snuff' it out, feel its presence in their blood, and so run a kind of secret world economy. Kipling's story takes up the idea of a Jewish conspiracy – men who meet at night to decide the fate of kingdoms – and sets it against the figure of Kadmiel, the solitary, prophetic Jew, whose virtue is established by his Old Testament origins; like Moses, he is a law-giver and will drown an army of horsemen in the sea. Kipling seems to be trying to

reclaim Jewish virtue, and incorporate its religiously auth-
enticated idea of law into that already sanctioned by the Saxon
heritage. However, the story is more oddly complicated and
even more muddled than this account suggests.

Kadmiel appears to be a member of a Freemason-like
brotherhood and so in Kipling's eyes a member of an elect and
specially virtuous body of men, the details of whose com-
panionship must always remain secret. Freemasonry and virtue
are linked in the Roman stories, where Mithraism is presented
as an analogue to Freemasonry. It is not clear in the text of the
story whether Kadmiel's secret society is related to the secret
meetings the Jews held in his father's house in Spain. In any
case, Jewish conspiracy theory and Freemasonry were connected
in nineteenth-century anti-Semitic writing. Cecil Rhodes was
obsessed all his life with the idea of a secret body of virtuous
and powerful men who would run a world empire. George
Wyndham, in the letter to his sister quoted at the beginning of
this introduction, talked of 'a masonic grip of secret fraternity'
– a grip which clasped together readers of *Puck* – and in a later
letter to his mother, commented on a meeting he attended to
plan the 1910 election campaign for the Conservatives: '. . . I
can only say this to you and Papa. All that I am from you – the
largeness and the precision – I have been allowed to say in this
utterly secret private body of persons who know and care and
dare.' The language makes them sound like Dan and Una, but
in fact this 'utterly secret private' group included Lord Curzon,
a Viceroy of India, Arthur Balfour, a former Prime Minister,
and F. E. Smith, a future Lord Chancellor. Wyndham's letters
are on occasion unpleasantly anti-Semitic, especially about
those he sees as having bought their way into politics.

Kipling, then, has to discriminate between secret societies
and, in his story, Kadmiel is implicitly transferred from one
secret body, which is deliberately not evaluated in any overt
fashion, to another, comprising those who have affected England's destiny. The price of his transfer is that he should deny
what has been set up as the dominant characteristic of his race,
his affinity with, and love of, gold, for it is by sacrificing his
cousin's hoard of treasure that Kadmiel accomplishes his end,

even if he does then go back to lending money on next season's crops. Yet this sacrificial act cannot entirely redeem Kadmiel from the taint of his Jewishness. He is presented as an isolated and unloved figure; even Puck is not entirely at ease with him, and his outlandish exoticism seems to associate him with the pheasants which are being so busily slaughtered around him: 'Kadmiel turned on him with a sweep and a whirr of his spicy-scented gown' (p. 198). One of the men shooting pheasants is 'young Mr Meyer', who gets away with peppering a beater by giving the chap a sovereign, an episode which could be read as illustrating the assimilation of the Jews into the traditional hunting and shooting heart of English society. Thirteenth-century Kadmiel is surprised that a twentieth-century Jew who harms an Englishman is not lynched. However, in the telling, the episode defeats itself. Meyer is not a good shot; he gets over-excited – very un-English – and will shoot at rabbits. He wears yellow gaiters too, to match the yellowish fur on Kadmiel's gown, just as Scott's Isaac, in the fifth chapter of *Ivanhoe*, is described as wearing 'a high square yellow cap of a peculiar fashion, assigned to his nation to distinguish them from Christians'.

This apparent attempt to assimilate young Mr Meyer into the pheasant-shooting gentry might be another way of severing the links with gold, and having him swallowed up by the all-powerful and money-free essence of England. However, in spite of the letter quoted at the beginning of this introduction, Kipling's attitude to the traditional Tory gentry and their ideas was always ambivalent. The story, 'Below the Mill Dam' (1902), satirizes what he saw as nostalgic pigheadedness on the part of the Balfourite Conservatives over the question of technological progress. His famously outspoken poem, 'The Islanders', is an attack on what he saw as dereliction of duty over military service and the defence of the island and its empire. The poem has this to say about the recreational predilections of the upper-class:

Will ye pitch some white pavilion, and busily even the odds,
With nets and hoops and mallets, with rackets and bats and rods?

Introduction

Will the rabbit war with your foeman – the red deer horn them
for hire?
Your kept cock-pheasant keep you? – he is master of many a
shire.

When a slaughtered pheasant falls near Dan and Una, Puck
and Kadmiel, it spatters on the ground like a shell. Meyer's
place in the shooting party may illustrate the growth of toler-
ance, but Kipling also sees it as a symptom of decadence.

A number of the South African–Jewish 'randlords' did buy
English country houses; it is doubtful whether Kipling
approved on any grounds. Kadmiel is neither landowner nor
soldier, and his twentieth-century analogue, who may be the
first and is a sort of parody of the second, is presented as
comic. The contradictions implicit in Kipling's treatment of
the idea of the Jew shows up both his own unresolved feelings
about the question and the difficulties that inevitably emerge
when the rural myth of England is forced to confront – however
obliquely – economics and modernity.

The gold which Kadmiel throws into the English Channel is
of course the material gains of the 'joyous venture' of Sir
Richard and Sir Hugh. This entertainingly told expedition to
Africa could be seen, somewhat crudely, as paradigmatic of
colonial exploitation. In return for a few trinkets and the defeat
of a troupe of gorillas, the adventurers leave behind a grateful
native population and bring back a boatload of treasure. Interestingly, they do not know what to do with their gold. Thorkild of
Borkum, a flamboyant barbarian, would have used it to decorate
his ship; it turns the more responsible Richard and Hugh into
sad old men, and all they can do with it is to hide it in the tidal
well of Pevensey Castle.

Kipling was proud of this invention; some years after the
book was published a similar well was discovered at Pevensey
and Kipling claimed this validated his historical intuition.
Kipling tells us that Aquila had it dug for drinking water but it
was flooded from the sea. In fact, tidal wells off private
chambers, as this one is, would have been used as privies. The
coincidence of this fact with Freud's observation, in his 1908

paper, 'Character and Anal Eroticism', of the symbolic relation of faeces and treasure or money prompts further playful speculation. Kadmiel, when he ferries the gold out to sea, is not only 'buying' English liberty, but flushing out a dirty secret. The joke is that Kipling's 'intuition' has brought him dangerously near the insights of a greater writer on empire, Joseph Conrad. *Heart of Darkness*, a book, like *Puck*, concerned with secrets, is unsparing in its analysis of the corrupt commercialism which lies near the heart of imperialism, and in *Nostromo*, the name of wealthy Costaguana, with its rich silver mine, is derived from sea-gull droppings.

V

Kipling, somewhat childishly, liked secrets, secret societies, secret languages, secret crafts, for they all seemed to him to underwrite the significance of their content or concerns, as well as offering a desired sense of belonging. Becoming a gentleman at Batemans and being a patriot are both versions of belonging, although they do not necessarily have anything to do with secrecy. This is certainly true of patriotism of a jingoistic kind, with which Kipling is so often identified, but there is another conception of patriotism which sees it as a feeling to be kept secret, and as rightly accompanied by feelings of modesty and even shame. There is an episode in *Stalky and Co.* in which a vulgar Tory MP addresses the school cadet-corps:

... in a raucous voice he cried aloud little matters like the hope of Honour and dream of Glory, that boys do not discuss even with their most intimate equals ... He profaned the most secret places of their souls with outcries and gesticulations.

Kipling adds, significantly, that the peroration of this speech went down later, 'with overwhelming success at a meeting of electors'. The final insult comes when the man waves a large Union Jack at his audience; 'that horror', the boys think, but the corps sergeant, not being officer class, is 'touched to the quick'. The passage is concerned to distinguish between the coarse jingoism of the masses and the secret, profounder and deeper emotions felt by officers and gentlemen. In their case, the outward symbol of the flag is replaced by memories of talismanic objects and sacred country places engraved on the soul in early childhood.

For the upper classes, patriotism is knowledge of a shared secret, shared by a group like that which Rhodes fantasized about, or Wyndham wrote of. The power of this secret comes from its deep roots in common childhood experiences as well as the way it is felt to legitimate adult activities of more powerful and even suspect kinds. Some of the boys listening to the empty words of the 'jelly-bellied flag-flapper' think of 'an old sword in a passage, or above a breakfast-room table, seen and fingered by stealth since they could walk'. Such a sword, hung in the intimate recesses of a home, unremarked upon, yet 'fingered by stealth' in some childish rite, is offered as far more meaningful than the Union Jack, which is part of a glaringly public and adult system of signs.

Dan and Una's life in the valley is hidden from grown-ups; they have a 'private gap in the fence' (p. 118), and the stories they hear are secret too, articulations of what the silent landscape holds. Puck always magics them into forgetting what they have heard with leaves of oak, ash and thorn, and here the secrets deepen. Oak, ash and thorn sound like trees which appear in ancient folklore; they are in fact the names of three letters from the runic alphabet. The plots of the stories the children hear are inscribed in runic letters on Weland's sword. They indicate a secret code, the interpretation of which the children are privileged to learn, but which remains a secret in their hearts rather than their minds; knowledge so deep that it becomes unconscious.

Kipling was interested in the process by which children learn to read and write, and in the origins of writing – the archetype of all secret codes. Two of the later *Just So Stories* are concerned with these topics – the earlier ones are emphatically designed for reading aloud – and the alphabet invented is runic. Learning to read and write is a crucial moment in a child's incorporation into the adult world, and can thus be seen as a step away from childish closeness to the oral, the concrete and the material. Runes, significantly, are nearly always found engraved on things: swords, cups, stones. Puck initiates the children into hearing stories told to them by the protagonists, stories which, if they are written at all, are written on the land, not in books. Children's books are often mentioned in the text, but only to be supplemented by a kind of real presence – a Norman knight whose helmet knocks audibly against his saddle-bow, or a Roman centurion with a horsehair plume that rasps on his shoulders and who carries a blood-stained letter from his emperor round his neck.

Yet the book, with its insistent emphasis on the inevitability of growing up and living with self-conscious virtue in a morally and politically tough world, cannot rest in, or even continually turn back to, the language of the concrete and material. Other languages are acquired and used, and bring with them their own particular kinds of belonging: to an adult world of personal responsibility and loyalty, to a nation or place and its destiny. These adult languages carry the major share of the narrative burden. Yet the responsibilities delineated in the stories are for the most part about protecting, guarding or holding a place – a frontier, a country, a manor, a valley – and the language of place, if not the language of responsibility, is close to that of children, even when it reflects the feelings of adults: 'The knight lifted his arms as though he would hug the whole dear valley, and Swallow, hearing the chink of his chain-mail, looked up and whinnied softly' (p. 70). The language of patriotism is itself allied to the language of kinship as the final poem in *Puck*, 'The Children's Song', shows clearly enough:

> Land of our Birth, our faith, our pride,
> For whose dear sake our fathers died;
> O Motherland, we pledge to thee,
> Head, heart, and hand through the years to be!   (p. 210)

Parnesius led a happy family childhood at his home in the Isle of Wight; Sir Richard's children played pirates on the valley stream, just as Dan and Una used to; Harry Dawe is Burwash-born and bred, and his mother lived at Little Lindens just up from the valley; Hobden has only once been out of the county. The land that is guarded by grown men with craft and cunning, as Kipling felt his contemporary England should be guarded, has for all of them a shared significance. It is the place where they grew up or where their children grow up, and so a place too of wives and mothers. Only Una, we might note, hears Parnesius's account of his family life and it is Dan who walks on the sword-side of Sir Richard's horse, the sword in question being of course that forged by Weland. For the male narrators the land is their past and the seed of the future; the present is usually working for it somewhere else.

The last story again fails to fit the pattern. Kadmiel's childhood is urban and foreign, and he has no children of his own. He is, as a reference in the text makes clear, not only like Moses but also like the Wandering Jew, an exile from all normal, human ties. He is without friends and his story is without love. Love in this book is always indicated either by a shared adventure or by some material thing; the sword Hugh gives to Richard, the letter Maximus writes to his captains, shared baked potatoes, a valley you would like to hug, or squares of turf you can hand from one person to another. Kadmiel neither cultivates, guards nor owns any land. What he does is alter a text in the interests of justice and the future. His version of history, or the version implicitly suggested by his action, is prophetic, even apocalyptic; it suggests that England will become a promised land of freedom for everybody. His action forecasts the undoing, through a piece of writing, of the child-centred and territorially based exclusivities – of insiders, secret-sharers, initiates, land-owners and immemorial land-dwellers – so carefully established in the previous nine. The cost of this undoing is radical; Kadmiel quarrels with, or even betrays, his only relative in England and goes to live in Bury St Edmunds, where, a few years before the date of Magna Charta, as Kipling knew, many Jews were massacred in a savage outbreak of anti-Semitism, prompted, it seems, by the Crusades. If growing up means leaving secrets behind – the secret treasure is cast out –

then the costs are shown to be great. Kipling himself thought that this last story was perhaps too dark and heavy for its context.

Puck of Pook's Hill adumbrates a particularly rich version of the early-twentieth-century myth of England, as far as feelings about landscape, history and empire are concerned. Kipling's inspired use of writing for and about children leads him to expose the psychic deep-rootedness of the myth as well as how it is embedded in a certain kind of life, southern and middle-class in particular. It is, however, Kipling's imperialism and the related stress on military virtues that preserve his vision of England from the creeping nostalgia for a lost and innocent past that is almost endemic to the myth. Whatever most of us may now think about Kipling's politics, and they cannot be ignored, they did at least ensure in this case an intense and enlivening commitment to the making of connections between the myth, history and contemporary event and an acknowledgement that the pressures of history are unrelenting. None of his hero-narrators returns home; Kadmiel's isolation is extreme, but it finds an answering echo in most of the other stories. The strength of *Puck of Pook's Hill* is that it is a contemplation of inevitable loss as well as a celebration of a long continuity.

Acknowledgements

I should like to thank the following of my colleagues in the English Department, University College London for their help: John Dodgson, Dan Jacobson, Kathryn Metzenthin, Venetia Newall, Elizabeth Palmer, Kenneth Palmer and David Trotter. Anne Oxenham of the Map Library also gave valuable advice.

Select Bibliography

Biography

Charles Carrington, *Kipling: His Life and Work*, London, 1955
Angus Wilson, *The Strange Ride of Rudyard Kipling*, London, 1977

Criticism

Jacqueline Bratton, 'Of England, Home and Duty; The Image of England in Victorian and Edwardian Juvenile Fiction', in *Imperialism and Popular Culture*, ed. John M. Mackenzie, Manchester, 1986
Roger Lancelyn Green, *Kipling and the Children*, London, 1965
(ed.), *Kipling: The Critical Heritage*, London, 1971
Mary Lascelles, *The Story-teller Retrieves the Past*, Oxford, 1980
A. L. Rivet, *Rudyard Kipling's Roman Britain: Fact and Fiction*, Keele, 1976
Andrew Rutherford (ed.), *Kipling's Mind and Art*, Edinburgh, 1964
Joyce Tompkins, *The Art of Rudyard Kipling*, London, 1959

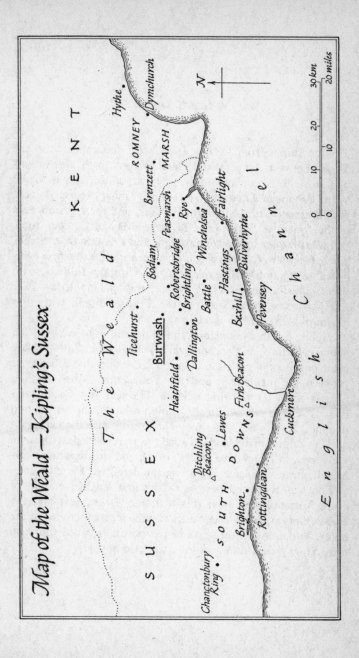

Map of the Weald—Kipling's Sussex

N

30 km
20 miles
0   10   20
0   10

KENT

The Weald

SUSSEX

ROMNEY
MARSH

Hythe
Dymchurch
Brenzett
Bodiam
Peasmarsh
Robertsbridge
Rye
Winchelsea
Brightling
Fairlight
Ticehurst
Battle
Hastings
Burwash
Bexhill
Bulverhythe
Dallington
Pevensey
Heathfield
Firle Beacon

Chanctonbury
Ring

Ditchling
Beacon
Lewes
SOUTH DOWNS
Cuckmere
Brighton
Rottingdean

English Channel

A Note on the Text

The ten stories from *Puck of Pook's Hill* first appeared in the *Strand* between January and October 1906, with illustrations by Claude A. Shepperson. The first four stories also appeared in the American *Ladies Home Journal*, January to April 1906, with illustrations by Charlotte Harding, and the remaining six in the American *McClure's Magazine*, May to October 1906, with illustrations by André Castaigne and Frederic Dorr Steele. The collection of ten stories and sixteen poems was first published in 1906 by Macmillan in the Uniform Edition, with twenty illustrations by H. R. Millar, and by Doubleday, Page and Company, New York, in the Trade Edition, with four illustrations by Arthur Rackham.

Kipling donated the manuscript of the stories to the Bodleian Library, Oxford, on the condition that no one be allowed to use it for purposes of collation. There are considerable differences between the manuscript and the *Strand* text, which Kipling revised again for the first edition. The text was finally (and lightly) revised for the Sussex edition of 1937, the last edition to appear in Kipling's lifetime. The poems, with the exception of 'The Runes on Weland's Sword', were reprinted, with some variations, in *Songs from Books* (1913), and in subsequent collected editions of verse, including the definitive *Verse* (1940).

The text reprinted here is of the first English edition of 1906. Variations between this text, the *Strand* text and the Sussex edition, which are of critical interest, are included in the notes. Variations in the texts of the poems between the 1906 text, *Songs from Books* and *Verse* are also noted.

PUCK OF POOK'S HILL

⁅ Weland's Sword ⁆

Puck's Song [1]

See you the dimpled track that runs,
  All hollow through the wheat?
O that was where they hauled the guns
  That smote King Philip's fleet. [2]

See you our little mill that clacks,
  So busy by the brook?
She has ground her corn and paid her tax
  Ever since Domesday Book.

See our stilly woods of oak
  And the dread ditch beside?
O that was where the Saxons broke,
  On the day that Harold died. [3]

See you the windy levels spread
  About the gates of Rye?
O that was where the Northmen fled,
  When Alfred's ships came by. [4]

See you our pastures wide and lone,
  Where the red oxen [5] browse?
O there was a City thronged and known,
  Ere London boasted a house.

And see you, after rain, the trace
  Of mound and ditch and wall?
O that was a Legion's camping-place,
  When Caesar sailed from Gaul. [6]

And see you marks that show and fade,
  Like shadows on the Downs?
O they are the lines the Flint Men made,
  To guard their wondrous towns.

Trackway and Camp and City lost,
　　Salt Marsh where now is corn;
Old Wars, old Peace, old Arts that cease,
　　And so was England born!

She is not any common Earth,
　　Water or wood or air,
But Merlin's Isle of Gramarye,[7]
　　Where you and I will fare.

Weland's Sword

The children were at the Theatre, acting to Three Cows as much as they could remember of *Midsummer Night's Dream*. Their father had made them a small play out of the big Shakespeare one, and they had rehearsed it with him and with their mother till they could say it by heart. They began where Nick Bottom the weaver comes out of the bushes with a donkey's head on his shoulder, and finds Titania Queen of the Fairies asleep. Then they skipped to the part where Bottom asks three little fairies to scratch his head and bring him honey, and they ended where he falls asleep in Titania's arms. Dan was Puck and Nick Bottom, as well as all three Fairies. He wore a pointy-eared cloth cap for Puck, and a paper donkey's head out of a Christmas cracker – but it tore if you were not careful – for Bottom. Una was Titania, with a wreath of columbines and a foxglove wand.

The Theatre lay in a meadow called the Long Slip.[1] A little mill-stream, carrying water to a mill two or three fields away, bent round one corner of it, and in the middle of the bend lay a large old fairy Ring of darkened grass, which was the stage. The mill-stream banks, overgrown with willow, hazel, and guelder-rose, made convenient places to wait in till your turn came; and a grown-up who had seen it said that Shakespeare himself could not have imagined a more suitable setting for his play. They were not, of course, allowed to act on Midsummer Night itself, but they went down after tea on Midsummer Eve, when the shadows were growing, and they took their supper – hard-boiled eggs, Bath Oliver biscuits,[2] and salt in an envelope – with them. Three Cows had been milked and were grazing steadily with a tearing noise that one could hear all down the meadow; and the noise of the mill at work sounded like bare feet running on hard ground. A cuckoo sat on a gate-post singing his broken June tune, 'cuckoo-cuk', while a busy kingfisher

43

crossed from the mill-stream to the brook which ran on the other side of the meadow. Everything else was a sort of thick, sleepy stillness smelling of meadow-sweet and dry grass.

Their play went beautifully. Dan remembered all his parts – Puck, Bottom, and the three Fairies – and Una never forgot a word of Titania – not even the difficult piece where she tells the Fairies how to feed Bottom with 'apricocks, ripe figs, and dewberries',[3] and all the lines end in 'ies'. They were both so pleased that they acted it three times over from beginning to end before they sat down in the unthistly centre of the Ring to eat eggs and Bath Olivers. This was when they heard a whistle among the alders on the bank, and they jumped.

The bushes parted. In the very spot where Dan had stood as Puck they saw a small, brown, broad-shouldered, pointy-eared person with a snub nose, slanting blue eyes, and a grin that ran right across his freckled face. He shaded his forehead as though he were watching Quince, Snout, Bottom, and the others rehearsing *Pyramis and Thisbe*, and in a voice as deep as Three Cows asking to be milked, he began:

> 'What hempen homespuns have we swaggering here,
> So near the cradle of our fairy Queen?'

He stopped, hollowed one hand round his ear, and, with a wicked twinkle in his eye, went on:

> 'What, a play toward; I'll be auditor,
> An actor too, perhaps, if I see cause.'[4]

The children looked and gasped. The small thing – he was no taller than Dan's shoulder – stepped quietly into the Ring.

'I'm rather out of practice,' said he; 'but that's the way my part ought to be played.'

Still the children stared at him – from his dark blue cap, like a big columbine flower, to his bare, hairy feet. At last he laughed.

'Please don't look like that. It isn't *my* fault. What else could you expect?' he said.

'We didn't expect anyone,' Dan answered, slowly. 'This is our field.'

'Is it?' said their visitor, sitting down. 'Then what on Human

Earth made you act *Midsummer Night's Dream* three times over, *on* Midsummer Eve, *in* the middle of a Ring, and under – right *under* one of my oldest hills in Old England? Pook's Hill – Puck's Hill – Puck's Hill – Pook's Hill! [5] It's as plain as the nose on my face.'

He pointed to the bare, fern-covered slope of Pook's Hill that runs up from the far side of the mill-stream to a dark wood. Beyond that wood the ground rises and rises for five hundred feet, till at last you climb out on the bare top of Beacon Hill, to look over the Pevensey Levels and the Channel and half the naked South Downs.

'By Oak, Ash, and Thorn!' he cried, still laughing. 'If this had happened a few hundred years ago you'd have had all the People of the Hills out like bees in June!'

'We didn't know it was wrong,' said Dan.

'Wrong!' The little fellow shook with laughter. 'Indeed, it isn't wrong. You've done something that Kings and Knights and Scholars in old days would have given their crowns and spurs and books to find out. If Merlin himself had helped you, you couldn't have managed better! You've broken the Hills – you've broken the Hills! It hasn't happened in a thousand years.'

'We – we didn't mean to,' said Una.

'Of course you didn't! That's just why you did it. Unluckily the Hills are empty now, and all the People of the Hills are gone. I'm the only one left. I'm Puck, the oldest Old Thing in England, very much at your service if – if you care to have anything to do with me. If you don't, of course you've only to say so, and I'll go.'

He looked at the children and the children looked at him for quite half a minute. His eyes did not twinkle any more. They were very kind, and there was the beginning of a good smile on his lips.

Una put out her hand. 'Don't go,' she said. 'We like you.'

'Have a Bath Oliver,' said Dan, and he passed over the squashy envelope with the eggs.

'By Oak, Ash, and Thorn,' cried Puck, taking off his blue cap, 'I like you too. Sprinkle a plenty salt on the biscuit, Dan, and I'll eat it with you. That'll show you the sort of person *I* am. Some of us' – he went on, with his mouth full – 'couldn't abide Salt, or Horse-shoes over a door, or Mountain-ash berries, or Running Water, or Cold Iron, or the sound of Church Bells. But I'm Puck!'

He brushed the crumbs carefully from his doublet and shook hands.

'We always said, Dan and I,' Una stammered, 'that if it ever happened we'd know ex-actly what to do; but – but now it seems all different somehow.'

'She means meeting a fairy,' said Dan. '*I* never believed in 'em – not after I was six, anyhow.'

'I did,' said Una. 'At least, I sort of half believed till we learned "Farewell Rewards". Do you know "Farewell Rewards and Fairies"?' [6]

'Do you mean this?' said Puck. He threw his big head back and began at the second line:

> 'Good housewives now may say,
> For now foul sluts in dairies
>   Do fare as well as they;
> For though they sweep their hearths no less

('Join in, Una!')

>   Than maids were wont to do,
> Yet who of late for cleanliness
>   Finds sixpence in her shoe?'

The echoes flapped all along the flat meadow.

'Of course I know it,' he said.

'And then there's the verse about the Rings,' said Dan. 'When I was little it always made me feel unhappy in my inside.'

'"Witness those rings and roundelays," do you mean?' boomed Puck, with a voice like a great church organ.

>   'Of theirs which yet remain,
> Were footed in Queen Mary's days
>   On many a grassy plain.
> But since of late Elizabeth,
>   And later James came in,
> Are never seen on any heath
>   As when the time hath been.

'It's some time since I heard that sung, but there's no good beating about the bush: it's true. The People of the Hills have all left. I saw them come into Old England and I saw them go. Giants, trolls, kelpies, brownies, goblins, imps; wood, tree, mound, and water spirits; heath-people, hill-watchers, treasure-guards, good people, little people, pishogues, leprechauns, night-riders, pixies, nixies, gnomes, and the rest – gone, all gone! I came into England with Oak, Ash, and Thorn, and when Oak, Ash, and Thorn are gone I shall go too.'

Dan looked round the meadow – at Una's oak by the lower gate, at the line of ash trees that overhang Otter Pool where the mill-stream spills over when the mill does not need it, and at the gnarled old white-thorn where Three Cows scratched their necks.

'It's all right,' he said; and added, 'I'm planting a lot of acorns this autumn too.'

'Then aren't you most awfully old?' said Una.

'Not old – fairly long-lived, as folk say hereabouts. Let me see – my friends used to set my dish of cream for me o' nights when Stonehenge was new. Yes, before the Flint Men made the Dewpond under Chanctonbury Ring.' [7]

Una clasped her hands, cried 'Oh!' and nodded her head.

'She's thought a plan,' Dan explained. 'She always does like that when she thinks a plan.'

'I was thinking – suppose we saved some of our porridge and put it in the attic for you. They'd notice if we left it in the nursery.'

'Schoolroom,' said Dan, quickly, and Una flushed, because they had made a solemn treaty that summer not to call the schoolroom the nursery any more.

'Bless your heart o' gold!' said Puck. 'You'll make a fine considering wench some market-day. I really don't want you to put out a bowl for me; but if ever I need a bite, be sure I'll tell you.'

He stretched himself at length on the dry grass, and the children stretched out beside him, their bare legs waving happily in the air. They felt they could not be afraid of him any more than of their particular friend old Hobden the hedger. He did not bother them with grown-up questions, or laugh at the donkey's head, but lay and smiled to himself in the most sensible way.

'Have you a knife on you?' he said at last.

Dan handed over his big one-bladed outdoor knife, and Puck began to carve out a piece of turf from the centre of the Ring.

'What's that for – Magic?' said Una, as he pressed up the square of chocolate loam that cut like so much cheese.

'One of my little magics,' he answered, and cut another. 'You see, I can't let you into the Hills because the People of the Hills have gone; but if you care to take seizin [8] from me, I may be able to show you something out of the common here on Human Earth. You certainly deserve it.'

'What's taking seizin?' said Dan, cautiously.

'It's an old custom the people had when they bought and sold land. They used to cut out a clod and hand it over to the buyer, and you weren't lawfully seized of your land – it didn't really belong to you – till the other fellow had actually given you a piece of it – like this.' He held out the turves.

'But it's our own meadow,' said Dan, drawing back. 'Are you going to magic it away?'

Puck laughed. 'I know it's your meadow, but there's a great deal more in it than you or your father ever guessed. Try!'

He turned his eyes on Una.

'I'll do it,' she said. Dan followed her example at once.

'Now are you two lawfully seized and possessed of all Old England,' began Puck, in a sing-song voice. 'By Right of Oak, Ash, and Thorn are you free to come and go and look and know where I shall show or best you please. You shall see What you shall see and you shall hear What you shall hear, though It shall have happened three thousand year; and you shall know neither Doubt nor Fear. Fast! Hold fast all I give you.'

The children shut their eyes, but nothing happened.

'Well?' said Una, disappointedly opening them. 'I thought there would be dragons.'

'Though It shall have happened three thousand year,' said Puck, and counted on his fingers. 'No; I'm afraid there were no dragons three thousand years ago.'

'But there hasn't happened anything at all,' said Dan.

'Wait awhile,' said Puck. 'You don't grow an oak in a year –
and Old England's older than twenty oaks. Let's sit down again
and think. *I* can do that for a century at a time.'

'Ah, but you're a fairy,' said Dan.

'Have you ever heard me use that word yet?' said Puck,
quickly.[9]

'No. You talk about "the People of the Hills", but you never
say "fairies",' said Una. 'I was wondering at that. Don't you
like it?'

'How would you like to be called "mortal" or "human being"
all the time?' said Puck; 'or "son of Adam" or "daughter of
Eve"?'

'I shouldn't like it at all,' said Dan. 'That's how the Djinns
and Afrits talk in the *Arabian Nights*.'[10]

'And that's how *I* feel about saying – that word that I don't
say. Besides, what you call *them* are made-up things the People
of the Hills have never heard of – little buzzflies with butterfly
wings and gauze petticoats,[11] and shiny stars in their hair, and a
wand like a school-teacher's cane for punishing bad boys and
rewarding good ones. *I* know 'em!'

'We don't mean that sort,' said Dan. 'We hate 'em too.'

'Exactly,' said Puck. 'Can you wonder that the People of the
Hills don't care to be confused with that painty-winged, wand-
waving, sugar-and-shake-your-head set of impostors? Butterfly
wings, indeed! I've seen Sir Huon[12] and a troop of his people
setting off from Tintagel Castle[13] for Hy-Brasil[14] in the teeth
of a sou'-westerly gale, with the spray flying all over the Castle,
and the Horses of the Hill wild with fright. Out they'd go in a
lull, screaming like gulls, and back they'd be driven five good
miles inland before they could come head to wind again. Butter-
fly-wings! It was Magic – Magic as black as Merlin could make
it, and the whole sea was green fire and white foam with
singing mermaids in it. And the Horses of the Hill picked their
way from one wave to another by the lightning flashes! *That*
was how it was in the old days!'

'Splendid,' said Dan, but Una shuddered.

'I'm glad they're gone, then; but what made the People of
the Hills go away?' Una asked.

'Different things. I'll tell you one of them some day – the thing that made the biggest flit of any,' said Puck. 'But they didn't all flit at once. They dropped off, one by one, through the centuries. Most of them were foreigners who couldn't stand our climate. *They* flitted early.'

'How early?' said Dan.

'A couple of thousand years or more. The fact is they began as Gods. The Phoenicians brought some over when they came to buy tin; and the Gauls, and the Jutes, and the Danes, and the Frisians, and the Angles brought more when they landed. They were always landing in those days, or being driven back to their ships, and they always brought their Gods with them. England is a bad country for Gods. Now, *I* began as I mean to go on. A bowl of porridge, a dish of milk, and a little quiet fun with the country folk in the lanes was enough for me then, as it is now. I belong here, you see, and I have been mixed up with people all my days.[15] But most of the others insisted on being Gods, and having temples, and altars, and priests, and sacrifices of their own.'

'People burned in wicker baskets?'[16] said Dan. 'Like Miss Blake tells us about?'

'All sorts of sacrifices,' said Puck. 'If it wasn't men, it was horses, or cattle, or pigs, or metheglin – that's a sticky, sweet sort of beer. *I* never liked it. They were a stiff-necked, extravagant set of idols, the Old Things. But what was the result? Men don't like being sacrificed at the best of times; they don't even like sacrificing their farm-horses. After a while men simply left the Old Things alone, and the roofs of their temples fell in, and the Old Things had to scuttle out and pick up a living as they could. Some of them took to hanging about trees, and hiding in graves and groaning o' nights. If they groaned loud enough and long enough they might frighten a poor countryman into sacrificing a hen, or leaving a pound of butter for them. I remember one Goddess called Belisama.[17] She became a common wet water-spirit somewhere in Lancashire. And there were hundreds of other friends of mine.[18] First they were Gods. Then they were People of the Hills, and then they flitted to other places because they couldn't get on with the English for one reason or another. There was only one Old Thing, I remember, who honestly worked for his living after he came down in the world. He was called Weland,[19] and he was a smith to some Gods. I've forgotten their names, but he used to make them swords and spears. I think he claimed kin with Thor of the Scandinavians.'

'*Heroes of Asgard* Thor?'[20] said Una. She had been reading the book.

'Perhaps,' answered Puck. 'None the less, when bad times came, he didn't beg or steal. He worked; and I was lucky enough to be able to do him a good turn.'

'Tell us about it,' said Dan. 'I think I like hearing of Old Things.'

They rearranged themselves comfortably, each chewing a grass stem. Puck propped himself on one strong arm and went on:

'Let's think! I met Weland first on a November afternoon in a sleet storm, on Pevensey Level –'

'Pevensey? Over the hill, you mean?' Dan pointed south.

'Yes; but it was all marsh in those days, right up to Horsebridge and Hydeneye. I was on Beacon Hill – they called it Brunanburgh[21] then – when I saw the pale flame that burning thatch makes, and I went down to look. Some pirates – I think they must have been Peofn's men – were burning a village on the Levels, and Weland's image – a big, black wooden thing with amber beads round its neck – lay in the bows of a black thirty-two-oar galley that they had just beached. Bitter cold it was! There were icicles hanging from her deck and the oars were glazed over with ice, and there was ice on Weland's lips. When he saw me he began a long chant in his own tongue, telling me how he was going to rule England, and how I should smell the smoke of his altars from Lincolnshire to the Isle of Wight. *I* didn't care! I'd seen too many Gods charging into Old England to be upset about it. I let him sing himself out while his men were burning the village, and then I said (I don't know what put it into my head), "Smith of the Gods," I said, "the time comes when I shall meet you plying your trade for hire by the wayside."'

51

'What did Weland say?' said Una. 'Was he angry?'

'He called me names and rolled his eyes, and I went away to wake up the people inland. But the pirates conquered the country, and for centuries Weland was a most important God. He had temples everywhere – from Lincolnshire to the Isle of Wight, as he said – and his sacrifices were simply scandalous. To do him justice, he preferred horses to men; but men *or* horses, I knew that presently he'd have to come down in the world – like the other Old Things. I gave him lots of time – I gave him about a thousand years – and at the end of 'em I went into one of his temples near Andover [22] to see how he prospered. There was his altar, and there was his image, and there were his priests, and there were the congregation, and everybody seemed quite happy, except Weland and the priests. In the old days the congregation were unhappy until the priests had chosen their sacrifices; and so would *you* have been. When the service began a priest rushed out, dragged a man up to the altar, pretended to hit him on the head with a little gilt axe, and the man fell down and pretended to die. Then everybody shouted: "A sacrifice to Weland! A sacrifice to Weland!"'

'And the man wasn't really dead?' said Una.

'Not a bit. All as much pretence as a dolls' tea-party. Then they brought out a splendid white horse, and the priest cut some hair from its mane and tail and burned it on the altar, shouting, "A sacrifice!" That counted the same as if a man and a horse had been killed. I saw poor Weland's face through the smoke, and I couldn't help laughing. He looked so disgusted and so hungry, and all he had to satisfy himself was a horrid smell of burning hair. Just a dolls' tea-party!

'I judged it better not to say anything then ('twouldn't have been fair), and the next time I came to Andover, a few hundred years later, Weland and his temple were gone, and there was a Christian bishop in a church there. None of the People of the Hills could tell me anything about him, and I supposed that he had left England.' Puck turned; lay on the other elbow, and thought for a long time.

'Let's see,' he said at last. 'It must have been some few years later – a year or two before the Conquest, I think – that I came back to Pook's Hill here, and one evening I heard old Hobden talking about Weland's Ford.'

'If you mean old Hobden the hedger, he's only seventy-two. He told me so himself,' said Dan. 'He's a intimate friend of ours.'

'You're quite right,' Puck replied. 'I meant old Hobden's ninth great-grandfather. He was a free man and burned charcoal hereabouts. I've known the family, father and son, so long that I get confused sometimes. Hob of the Dene was my Hobden's name, and he lived at the Forge cottage. Of course, I pricked up my ears when I heard Weland mentioned, and I scuttled through the woods to the Ford just beyond Bog Wood yonder.' He jerked his head westward, where the valley narrows between wooded hills and steep hop-fields.

'Why, that's Willingford Bridge,' said Una. 'We go there for walks often. There's a kingfisher there.'

'It was Weland's Ford [23] then, dear. A road led down to it from the Beacon on the top of the hill – a shocking bad road it was – and all the hillside was thick, thick oak-forest, with deer in it. There was no trace of Weland, but presently I saw a fat old farmer riding down from the Beacon under the greenwood tree. His horse had cast a shoe in the clay, and when he came to the Ford he dismounted, took a penny out of his purse, laid it on a stone, tied the old horse to an oak, and called out: "Smith, Smith, here is work for you!" Then he sat down and went to sleep. You can imagine how *I* felt when I saw a white-bearded, bent old blacksmith in a leather apron creep out from behind the oak and begin to shoe the horse. It was Weland himself. I was so astonished that I jumped out and said: "What on Human Earth are you doing here, Weland?"'

'Poor Weland!' sighed Una.

'He pushed the long hair back from his forehead (he didn't recognize me at first). Then he said: "*You* ought to know. You foretold it, Old Thing. I'm shoeing horses for hire. I'm not even Weland now," he said. "They call me Wayland-Smith."'

'Poor chap!' said Dan. 'What did you say?'

'What could I say? He looked up, with the horse's foot on his lap, and he said, smiling, "I remember the time when I wouldn't have accepted this old bag of bones as a sacrifice, and now I'm glad enough to shoe him for a penny."

'"Isn't there any way for you to get back to Valhalla,[24] or wherever you come from?" I said.

'"I'm afraid not," he said, rasping away at the hoof. He had a wonderful touch with horses. The old beast was whinnying on his shoulder. "You may remember that I was not a gentle God in my Day and my Time and my Power. I shall never be released till some human being truly wishes me well."

'"Surely," said I, "the farmer can't do less than that. You're shoeing the horse all round for him."

'"Yes," said he, "and my nails will hold a shoe from one full moon to the next. But farmers and Weald clay," said he, "are both uncommon cold and sour."

'Would you believe it, that when that farmer woke and found his horse shod he rode away without one word of thanks? I was so angry that I wheeled his horse right round and walked him back three miles to the Beacon, just to teach the old sinner politeness.'

'Were you invisible?' said Una. Puck nodded, gravely.

'The Beacon was always laid in those days ready to light, in case the French landed at Pevensey; and I walked the horse about and about it that lee-long[25] summer night. The farmer thought he was bewitched – well, he *was*, of course – and began to pray and shout. *I* didn't care! I was as good a Christian as he any fair-day in the County, and about four o'clock in the morning a young novice came along from the monastery that used to stand on the top of Beacon hill.'

'What's a novice?' said Dan.

'It really means a man who is beginning to be a monk, but in those days people sent their sons to a monastery just the same as a school. This young fellow had been to a monastery in France for a few months every year, and he was finishing his studies in the monastery close to his home here. Hugh was his name, and he had got up to go fishing hereabouts. His people owned all this valley. Hugh heard the farmer shouting, and asked him what in the world he meant. The old man spun him a wonderful tale about fairies and goblins and witches; and I *know* he hadn't seen a thing except rabbits and red deer all that night. (The People of the Hills are like otters – they don't show except when they choose.) But the novice wasn't a fool. He looked down at the horse's feet, and saw the new shoes fastened as only Weland knew how to fasten 'em. (Weland had a way of turning down the nails that folks called the Smith's Clinch.)

'"H'm!" said the novice. "Where did you get your horse shod?"

'The farmer wouldn't tell him at first, because the priests never liked their people to have any dealings with the Old Things. At last he confessed that the Smith had done it. "What did you pay him?" said the novice. "Penny," said the farmer, very sulkily. "That's less than a Christian would have charged," said the novice. "I hope you threw a 'Thank you' into the bargain." "No," said the farmer; "Wayland-Smith's a heathen." "Heathen or no heathen," said the novice, "you took his help, and where you get help there you must give thanks." "What?" said the farmer – he was in a furious temper because I was walking the old horse in circles all this time – "What, you young jackanapes?" said he. "Then by your reasoning I ought to say 'Thank you' to Satan if he helped me?" "Don't roll about up there splitting reasons with me," said the novice. "Come back to the Ford and thank the Smith, or you'll be sorry."

'Back the farmer had to go. I led the horse, though no one saw me, and the novice walked beside us, his gown swishing through the shiny dew and his fishing-rod across his shoulders spear-wise. When we reached the Ford again – it was five o'clock and misty still under the oaks – the farmer simply wouldn't say "Thank you". He said he'd tell the Abbot that the novice wanted him to worship heathen gods. Then Hugh the novice lost his temper. He just cried, "Out!" put his arm under the farmer's fat leg, and heaved him from his saddle on to the turf, and before he could rise he caught him by the back of the neck and shook him like a rat till the farmer growled, "Thank you, Wayland-Smith."'

'Did Weland see all this?' said Dan.

'Oh, yes, and he shouted his old war-cry when the farmer

thudded on to the ground. He was delighted. Then the novice turned to the oak tree and said, "Ho! Smith of the Gods, I am ashamed of this rude farmer; but for all you have done in kindness and charity to him and to others of our people, I thank you and wish you well." Then he picked up his fishing-rod – it looked more like a tall spear than ever – and tramped off down your valley.'

'And what did poor Weland do?' said Una.

'He laughed and he cried with joy, because he had been released at last, and could go away. But he was an honest Old Thing. He had worked for his living and he paid his debts before he left. "I shall give that novice a gift," said Weland. "A gift that shall do him good the wide world over and Old England after him.[26] Blow up my fire, Old Thing, while I get the iron for my last task." Then he made a sword – a dark grey, wavy-lined sword – and I blew the fire while he hammered. By Oak, Ash, and Thorn, I tell you, Weland was a Smith of the Gods! He cooled that sword in running water twice, and the third time he cooled it in the evening dew, and he laid it out in the moonlight and said Runes[27] (that's charms) over it, and he carved Runes of Prophecy on the blade. "Old Thing," he said to me, wiping his forehead, "this is the best blade that Weland ever made. Even the user will never know how good it is. Come to the monastery."

'We went to the dormitory where the monks slept, we saw the novice fast asleep in his cot, and Weland put the sword into his hand, and I remember the young fellow gripped it in his sleep. Then Weland strode as far as he dared into the Chapel and threw down all his shoeing tools – his hammer, and pincers, and rasps – to show that he had done with them for ever. It sounded like suits of armour falling, and the sleepy monks ran in, for they thought the monastery had been attacked by the French. The novice came first of all, waving his new sword and shouting Saxon battle-cries. When they saw the shoeing-tools they were very bewildered, till the novice asked leave to speak, and told what he had done to the farmer, and what he had said to Wayland-Smith, and how, though the dormitory light was burning, he had found the wonderful rune-carved sword in his cot.

'The Abbot shook his head at first, and then he laughed and said to the novice: "Son Hugh, it needed no sign from a heathen God to show me that you will never be a monk. Take your sword, and keep your sword, and go with your sword, and be as gentle as you are strong and courteous. We will hang up the Smith's tools before the Altar," he said, "because, whatever the Smith of the Gods may have been in the old days, we know that he worked honestly for his living and made gifts to Mother Church." Then they went to bed again, all except the novice, and he sat up in the garth [28] playing with his sword. Then Weland said to me by the stables: "Farewell, Old Thing; you had the right of it. You saw me come to England, and you see me go. Farewell!"

'With that he strode down the hill to the corner of the Great Woods – Woods Corner, you call it now – to the very place where he had first landed – and I heard him moving through the thickets towards Horsebridge for a little, and then he was gone. That was how it happened. I saw it.'

Both children drew a long breath.

'But what happened to Hugh the novice?' said Una.

'And the sword?' said Dan.

Puck looked down the meadow that lay all quiet and cool in the shadow of Pook's Hill. A corncrake jarred in a hay-field near by, and the small trouts of the brook began to jump. A big white moth flew unsteadily from the alders and flapped round the children's heads, and the least little haze of water-mist rose from the brook.

'Do you really want to know?' Puck said.

'We do,' cried the children. 'Awfully!'

'Very good. I promised you that you shall see What you shall see, and you shall hear What you shall hear, though It shall have happened three thousand year; but just now it seems to me that, unless you go back to the house, people will be looking for you. I'll walk with you as far as the gate.'

'Will you be here when we come again?' they asked.

'Surely, sure-ly,' said Puck. 'I've been here some time already. One minute first, please.'

He gave them each three leaves – one of Oak, one of Ash, and one of Thorn.

'Bite these,' said he. 'Otherwise you might be talking at home of what you've seen and heard, and – if I know human beings – they'd send for the doctor. Bite!'

They bit hard, and found themselves walking side by side to the lower gate. Their father was leaning over it.

'And how did your play go?' he asked.

'Oh, splendidly,' said Dan. 'Only afterwards, I think, we went to sleep. It was very hot and quiet. Don't you remember, Una?'

Una shook her head and said nothing.

'I see,' said her father.

'Late – late in the evening Kilmeny came home,
  For Kilmeny had been she could not tell where,
  And Kilmeny had seen what she could not declare.[29]

But why are you chewing leaves at your time of life, daughter? For fun?'

'No. It was for something, but I can't azactly remember,' said Una.

And neither of them could till –

A Tree Song [1]

Of all the trees that grow so fair,
   Old England to adorn,
Greater are none beneath the Sun,
   Than Oak, and Ash, and Thorn.
Sing Oak, and Ash, and Thorn, good Sirs
   (All of a Midsummer morn)!
Surely we sing no little thing,
   In Oak, and Ash, and Thorn!

Oak of the Clay lived many a day,
   Or ever Æneas [2] began;
Ash of the Loam was a lady at home,
   When Brut was an outlaw man;
Thorn of the Down saw New Troy Town [3]
   (From which was London born);
Witness hereby the ancientry
   Of Oak, and Ash, and Thorn!

Yew that is old in churchyard mould,
   He breedeth a mighty bow;
Alder for shoes do wise men choose,
   And beech for cups also.
But when ye have killed, and your bowl is spilled,
   And your shoes are clean outworn,
Back ye must speed for all that ye need,
   To Oak, and Ash, and Thorn!

Ellum [4] she hateth mankind, and waiteth
   Till every gust be laid,
To drop a limb on the head of him,
   That anyway trusts her shade:
But whether a lad be sober or sad,
   Or mellow with ale from the horn,
He will take no wrong when he lieth along
   'Neath Oak, and Ash, and Thorn!

Oh, do not tell the Priest our plight,
   Or he would call it a sin;

But – we have been out in the woods all night,
  A-conjuring Summer in!
And we bring you news by word of mouth –
  Good news for cattle and corn –
Now is the Sun come up from the South,
  With Oak, and Ash, and Thorn!

Sing Oak, and Ash, and Thorn, good Sirs
  (All of a Midsummer morn)!
England shall bide till Judgment Tide,
  By Oak, and Ash, and Thorn!

Young Men at the Manor

They were fishing, a few days later, in the bed of the brook that for centuries had cut deep into the soft valley soil. The trees closing overhead made long tunnels through which the sunshine worked in blobs and patches. Down in the tunnels were bars of sand and gravel, old roots and trunks covered with moss or painted red by the irony water; foxgloves growing lean and pale towards the light; clumps of fern and thirsty shy flowers who could not live away from moisture and shade. In the pools you could see the wave thrown up by the trouts as they charged hither and yon, and the pools were joined to each other – except in flood time, when all was one brown rush – by sheets of thin broken water that poured themselves chuckling round the darkness of the next bend.

This was one of the children's most secret hunting-grounds, and their particular friend, old Hobden the hedger, had shown them how to use it. Except for the click of a rod hitting a low willow, or a switch and tussle among the young ash-leaves as a line hung up for the minute, nobody in the hot pasture could have guessed what game was going on among the trouts below the banks.

'We's got half-a-dozen,' said Dan, after a warm, wet hour. 'I vote we go up to Stone Bay and try Long Pool.'

Una nodded – most of her talk was by nods – and they crept from the gloom of the tunnels towards the tiny weir that turns the brook into the mill-stream. Here the banks are low and bare, and the glare of the afternoon sun on the Long Pool below the weir makes your eyes ache.

When they were in the open they nearly fell down with astonishment. A huge grey horse, whose tail-hairs crinkled the glassy water, was drinking in the pool, and the ripples about his muzzle flashed like melted gold. On his back sat an old, white-haired man dressed in a loose glimmery gown of chain-mail. He was bare-headed, and a nut-shaped iron helmet hung at his saddle-bow. His reins were of red leather five or six inches deep, scalloped at the edges, and his high padded saddle with its red girths was held fore and aft by a red leather breastband and crupper.

'Look!' said Una, as though Dan were not staring his very eyes out. 'It's like the picture in your room – "Sir Isumbras at the Ford".' [1]

The rider turned towards them, and his thin, long face was just as sweet and gentle as that of the knight who carries the children in that picture.

'They should be here now, Sir Richard,' said Puck's deep voice among the willow-herb.

'They are here,' the knight said, and he smiled at Dan with the string of trouts in his hand. 'There seems no great change in boys since mine fished this water.'

'If your horse has drunk, we shall be more at ease in the Ring,' said Puck; and he nodded to the children as though he had never magicked away their memories a week before.

The great horse turned and hoisted himself into the pasture with a kick and a scramble that tore the clods down rattling.

'Your pardon!' said Sir Richard to Dan. 'When these lands were mine, I never loved that mounted men should cross the brook except by the paved ford. But my Swallow here was thirsty, and I wished to meet you.'

'We're very glad you've come, sir,' said Dan. 'It doesn't matter in the least about the banks.'

He trotted across the pasture on the sword side of the mighty horse, and it was a mighty iron-handled sword that swung from Sir Richard's belt. Una walked behind with Puck. She remembered everything now.

'I'm sorry about the Leaves,' he said, 'but it would never have done if you had gone home and told, would it?'

'I s'pose not,' Una answered. 'But you said that all the fair–People of the Hills had left England.'

'So they have; but I told you that you should come and go and look and know, didn't I? The knight isn't a fairy. He's Sir Richard Dalyngridge,[2] a very old friend of mine. He came over

62

with William the Conqueror, and he wants to see you particularly.'

'What for?' said Una.

'On account of your great wisdom and learning,' Puck replied, without a twinkle.

'Us?' said Una. 'Why, I don't know my Nine Times – not to say it dodging, and Dan makes the most *awful* mess of fractions. He can't mean *us!*'

'Una!' Dan called back. 'Sir Richard says he is going to tell what happened to Weland's sword. He's got it. Isn't it splendid?'

'Nay – nay,' said Sir Richard, dismounting as they reached the Ring, in the bend of the mill-stream bank. 'It is you that must tell me, for I hear the youngest child in our England today is as wise as our wisest clerk.' He slipped the bit out of Swallow's mouth, dropped the ruby-red reins over his head, and the wise horse moved off to graze.

Sir Richard (they noticed he limped a little) unslung his great sword.

'That's it,' Dan whispered to Una.

'This is the sword that Brother Hugh had from Wayland-Smith,' Sir Richard said. 'Once he gave it me, but I would not take it; but at the last it became mine after such a fight as never christened man fought. See!' He half drew it from its sheath and turned it before them. On either side just below the handle, where the Runic letters shivered as though they were alive, were two deep gouges in the dull, deadly steel. 'Now, what Thing made those?' said he. 'I know not, but you, perhaps, can say.'

'Tell them all the tale, Sir Richard,' said Puck. 'It concerns their land somewhat.'

'Yes, from the very beginning,' Una pleaded, for the knight's good face and the smile on it more than ever reminded her of 'Sir Isumbras at the Ford'.

They settled down to listen, Sir Richard bare-headed to the sunshine, dandling the sword in both hands, while the grey horse cropped outside the Ring, and the helmet on the saddle-bow clinged softly each time he jerked his head.

'From the beginning, then,' Sir Richard said, 'since it concerns your land, I will tell the tale. When our Duke came out of Normandy to take his England, great knights (have ye heard?) came and strove hard to serve the Duke, because he promised them lands here, and small knights followed the great ones. My folk in Normandy were poor; but a great knight, Engerrard of the Eagle – Engenulf de Aquila [3] – who was kin to my father, followed the Earl of Mortain, [4] who followed William the Duke, and I followed De Aquila. Yes, with thirty men-at-arms out of my father's house and a new sword, I set out to conquer England three days after I was made knight. I did not then know that England would conquer me. We went up to Santlache [5] with the rest – a very great host of us.'

'Does that mean the Battle of Hastings – Ten Sixty-Six?' Una whispered, and Puck nodded, so as not to interrupt.

'At Santlache, over the hill yonder' – he pointed south-eastward towards Fairlight – 'we found Harold's men. We fought. At the day's end they ran. My men went with De Aquila's to chase and plunder, and in that chase Engerrard of the Eagle was slain, and his son Gilbert took his banner and his men forward. This I did not know till after, for Swallow here was cut in the flank, so I stayed to wash the wound at a brook by a thorn. There a single Saxon cried out to me in French, and we fought together. I should have known his voice, but we fought together. For a long time neither had any advantage, till by pure ill-fortune his foot slipped and his sword flew from his hand. Now I had but newly been made knight, and wished, above all, to be courteous and fameworthy, so I forbore to strike and bade him get his sword again. "A plague on my sword," said he. "It has lost me my first fight. You have spared my life. Take my sword." He held it out to me, but as I stretched my hand the sword groaned like a stricken man, and I leaped back crying, "Sorcery!"

(The children looked at the sword as though it might speak again.)

'Suddenly a clump of Saxons ran out upon me and, seeing a Norman alone, would have killed me, but my Saxon cried out that I was his prisoner, and beat them off. Thus, see you, he

saved my life. He put me on my horse and led me through the
woods ten long miles to this valley.'

'To here, d'you mean?' said Una.

'To this very valley. We came in by the Lower Ford under
the King's Hill yonder' – he pointed eastward where the valley
widens.

'And was that Saxon Hugh the novice?' Dan asked.

'Yes, and more than that. He had been for three years at the
monastery at Bec by Rouen, where' – Sir Richard chuckled –
'the Abbot Herluin [6] would not suffer me to remain.'

'Why wouldn't he?' said Dan.

'Because I rode my horse into the refectory, when the scholars
were at meat, to show the Saxon boys we Normans were not
afraid of an abbot. It was that very Saxon Hugh tempted me to
do it, and we had not met since that day. I thought I knew his
voice even inside my helmet, and, for all that our Lords fought,
we each rejoiced we had not slain the other. He walked by my
side, and he told me how a Heathen God, as he believed, had
given him his sword, but he said he had never heard it sing
before. I remember I warned him to beware of sorcery and
quick enchantments.' Sir Richard smiled to himself. 'I was very
young – very young!

'When we came to his house here we had almost forgotten
that we had been at blows. It was near midnight, and the Great
Hall was full of men and women waiting news. There I first
saw his sister, the Lady Ælueva, of whom he had spoken to us
in France. She cried out fiercely at me, and would have had me
hanged in that hour, but her brother said that I had spared his
life – he said not how he saved mine from the Saxons – and
that our Duke had won the day; and even while they wrangled
over my poor body, of a sudden he fell down in a swoon from
his wounds.

'"This is *thy* fault," said the Lady Ælueva to me, and she
kneeled above him and called for wine and cloths.

'"If I had known," I answered, "he should have ridden and
I walked. But he set me on my horse; he made no complaint; he
walked beside me and spoke merrily throughout. I pray I have
done him no harm."

'"Thou hast need to pray," she said, catching up her underlip. "If he dies, thou shalt hang."

'They bore off Hugh to his chamber; but three tall men of the house bound me and set me under the beam of the Great Hall with a rope round my neck. The end of the rope they flung over the beam, and they sat them down by the fire to wait word whether Hugh lived or died. They cracked nuts with their knife-hilts the while.'

'And how did you feel?' said Dan.

'Very weary; but I did heartily pray for my schoolmate Hugh his health. About noon I heard horses in the valley, and the three men loosed my ropes and fled out, and De Aquila's men rode up. Gilbert de Aquila [7] came with them, for it was his boast that, like his father, he forgot no man that served him. He was little, like his father, but terrible, with a nose like an eagle's nose and yellow eyes like an eagle. He rode tall war-horses – roans, which he bred himself – and he could never abide to be helped into the saddle. He saw the rope hanging from the beam and laughed, and his men laughed, for I was too stiff to rise.

'"This is poor entertainment for a Norman knight," he said, "but, such as it is, let us be grateful. Show me, boy, to whom thou owest most, and we will pay them out of hand."'

'What did he mean? To kill 'em?' said Dan.

'Assuredly. But I looked at the Lady Ælueva where she stood among her maids, and her brother beside her. De Aquila's men had driven them all into the Great Hall.'

'Was she pretty?' said Una.

'In all my long life I have never seen woman fit to strew rushes before my Lady Ælueva,' the knight replied, quite simply and quietly. 'As I looked at her I thought I might save her and her house by a jest.

'"Seeing that I came somewhat hastily and without warning," said I to De Aquila, "I have no fault to find with the courtesy that these Saxons have shown me." But my voice shook. It is – it was not good to jest with that little man.

'All were silent awhile, till De Aquila laughed. "Look, men – a miracle," said he. "The fight is scarce sped, my father is not yet buried, and here we find our youngest knight already set down in his Manor, while his Saxons – ye can see it in their fat faces – have paid him homage and service! By the Saints," he said, rubbing his nose, "I never thought England would be so easy won! Surely I can do no less than give the lad what he has taken. This Manor shall be thine, boy," he said, "till I come again, or till thou art slain. Now, mount, men, and ride. We follow our Duke into Kent to make him King of England."

'He drew me with him to the door while they brought his horse – a lean roan, taller than my Swallow here, but not so well girthed.

'"Hark to me," he said, fretting with his great war-gloves. "I have given thee this Manor, which is a Saxon hornets' nest, and I think thou wilt be slain in a month – as my father was slain. Yet if thou canst keep the roof on the hall, the thatch on the barn, and the plough in the furrow till I come back, thou shalt hold the Manor from me; for the Duke has promised our Earl Mortain all the lands by Pevensey,[8] and Mortain will give me of them what he would have given my father. God knows if thou or I shall live till England is won; but remember, boy, that here and now fighting is foolishness and" – he reached for the reins – "craft and cunning is all."

'"Alas, I have no cunning," said I.

'"Not yet," said he, hopping abroad, foot in stirrup, and poking his horse in the belly with his toe. "Not yet, but I think thou hast a good teacher. Farewell! Hold the Manor and live. Lose the Manor and hang," he said, and spurred out, his shield-straps squeaking behind him.

'So, children, here was I, little more than a boy, and Sant-lache fight not two days old, left alone with my thirty men-at-arms, in a land I knew not, among a people whose tongue I could not speak, to hold down the land which I had taken from them.'

'And that was here at home?' said Una.

'Yes, here. See! From the Upper Ford, Weland's Ford, to the Lower Ford, by the Belle Allée, west and east it ran half a league. From the Beacon of Brunanburgh behind us here, south and north it ran a full league – and all the woods were full of broken men from Santlache, Saxon thieves, Norman plunderers, robbers, and deer-stealers. A hornets' nest indeed!

'When De Aquila had gone, Hugh would have thanked me for saving their lives; but the Lady Ælueva said that I had done it only for the sake of receiving the Manor.

'"How could I know that De Aquila would give it me?" I said. "If I had told him I had spent my night in your halter he would have burned the place twice over by now."

'"If any man had put *my* neck in a rope," she said, "I would have seen his house burned thrice over before *I* would have made terms."

'"But it was a woman," I said; and I laughed, and she wept and said that I mocked her in her captivity.

'"Lady," said I, "there is no captive in this valley except one, and he is not a Saxon."

'At this she cried that I was a Norman thief, who came with false, sweet words, having intended from the first to turn her out in the fields to beg her bread. Into the fields! She had never seen the face of war!

'I was angry, and answered, "This much at least I can disprove, for I swear" – and on my sword-hilt I swore it in that place – "I swear I will never set foot in the Great Hall till the Lady Ælueva herself shall summon me there."

'She went away, saying nothing, and I walked out, and Hugh limped after me, whistling dolorously (that is a custom of the English), and we came upon the three Saxons that had bound me. They were now bound by my men-at-arms, and behind them stood some fifty stark and sullen churls of the House and the Manor, waiting to see what should fall. We heard De Aquila's trumpets blow thin through the woods Kentward.

'"Shall we hang these?" said my men.

'"Then my churls will fight," said Hugh, beneath his breath; but I bade him ask the three what mercy they hoped for.

'"None," said they all. "She bade us hang thee if our master died. And we would have hanged thee. There is no more to it."

'As I stood doubting a woman ran down from the oak wood above the King's Hill yonder, and cried out that some Normans were driving off the swine there.

'"Norman or Saxon," said I, "we must beat them back, or they will rob us every day. Out at them with any arms ye have!" So I loosed those three carles and we ran together, my men-at-arms and the Saxons with bills and bows which they had hidden in the thatch of their huts, and Hugh led them. Half-way up the King's Hill we found a false fellow from Picardy – a sutler[9] that sold wine in the Duke's camp – with a dead knight's shield on his arm, a stolen horse under him, and some ten or twelve wastrels[10] at his tail, all cutting and slashing at the pigs. We beat them off, and saved our pork.[11] One hundred and seventy pigs we saved in that great battle.' Sir Richard laughed.

'That, then, was our first work together, and I bade Hugh tell his folk that so would I deal with any man, knight or churl, Norman or Saxon, who stole as much as one egg from our valley. Said he to me, riding home: "Thou hast gone far to conquer England this evening." I answered: "England must be thine and mine, then. Help me, Hugh, to deal aright with these people. Make them to know that if they slay me De Aquila will surely send to slay them, and he will put a worse man in my place." "That may well be true," said he, and gave me his hand. "Better the devil we know than the devil we know not, till we can pack you Normans home." And so, too, said his Saxons; and they laughed as we drove the pigs downhill. But I think some of them, even then, began not to hate me.'

'I like Brother Hugh,' said Una, softly.

'Beyond question he was the most perfect, courteous, valiant, tender, and wise knight that ever drew breath,' said Sir Richard, caressing the sword. 'He hung up his sword – this sword – on the wall of the Great Hall, because he said it was fairly mine, and never he took it down till De Aquila returned, as I shall presently show. For three months his men and mine guarded the valley, till all robbers and nightwalkers learned there was nothing to get from us save hard tack[12] and a hanging. Side by side we fought against all who came – thrice a week sometimes we fought – against thieves and landless knights looking for good manors. Then we were in some peace, and I made shift by Hugh's help to govern the valley – for all this valley of yours

was my Manor – as a knight should. I kept the roof on the hall
and the thatch on the barn, but ... The English are a bold
people. His Saxons would laugh and jest with Hugh, and Hugh
with them, and – this was marvellous to me – if even the
meanest of them said that such and such a thing was the Custom
of the Manor, then straightway would Hugh and such old men
of the Manor as might be near forsake everything else to debate
the matter – I have seen them stop the mill with the corn half
ground – and if the custom or usage were proven to be as it was
said, why, that was the end of it, even though it were flat
against Hugh, his wish and command. Wonderful!'

'Aye,' said Puck, breaking in for the first time. 'The Custom
of Old England was here before your Norman knights came,
and it outlasted them, though they fought against it cruel.'

'Not I,' said Sir Richard. 'I let the Saxons go their stubborn
way, but when my own men-at-arms, Normans not six months
in England, stood up and told me what was the custom of the
country, *then* I was angry. Ah, good days! Ah, wonderful people!
And I loved them all.'

The knight lifted his arms as though he would hug the whole
dear valley, and Swallow, hearing the chink of his chain-mail,
looked up and whinnied softly.

'At last,' he went on, 'after a year of striving and contriving
and some little driving, De Aquila came to the valley, alone and
without warning. I saw him first at the Lower Ford, with a
swineherd's brat on his saddle-bow.

'"There is no need for thee to give any account of thy
stewardship," said he. "I have it all from the child here." And
he told me how the young thing had stopped his tall horse at
the Ford, by waving of a branch, and crying that the way was
barred. "And if one bold, bare babe be enough to guard the
Ford in these days, thou hast done well," said he, and puffed
and wiped his head.

'He pinched the child's cheek, and looked at our cattle in the
flat by the river.

'"Both fat," said he, rubbing his nose. "This is craft and
cunning such as I love. What did I tell thee when I rode away,
boy?"

'"Hold the Manor or hang," said I. I had never forgotten it.

'"True. And thou hast held." He clambered from his saddle and with sword's point cut out a turf from the bank and gave it me where I kneeled.'

Dan looked at Una, and Una looked at Dan.

'That's seizin,'[13] said Puck, in a whisper.

'"Now thou art lawfully seized of the Manor, Sir Richard," said he – 'twas the first time he ever called me that – "thou and thy heirs for ever. This must serve till the King's clerks write out thy title on a parchment. England is all ours – if we can hold it."

'"What service shall I pay?" I asked, and I remember I was proud beyond words.

'"Knight's fee, boy, knight's fee!"[14] said he, hopping round his horse on one foot. (Have I said he was little, and could not endure to be helped to his saddle?) "Six mounted men or twelve archers thou shalt send me whenever I call for them, and – where got you that corn?" said he, for it was near harvest, and our corn stood well. "I have never seen such bright straw. Send me three bags of the same seed yearly, and furthermore, in memory of our last meeting – with the rope round thy neck – entertain me and my men for two days of each year in the Great Hall of thy Manor."

'"Alas!" said I, "then my Manor is already forfeit. I am under vow not to enter the Great Hall." And I told him what I had sworn to the Lady Ælueva.'

'And hadn't you ever been into the house since?' said Una.

'Never,' Sir Richard answered smiling. 'I had made me a little hut of wood up the hill, and there I did justice and slept . . . De Aquila wheeled aside, and his shield shook on his back. "No matter, boy," said he. "I will remit the homage for a year."'

'He meant Sir Richard needn't give him dinner there the first year,' Puck explained.

'De Aquila stayed with me in the hut, and Hugh, who could read and write and cast accounts, showed him the Roll of the Manor, in which were written all the names of our fields and men, and he asked a thousand questions touching the land, the

71

timber, the grazing, the mill, and the fish-ponds, and the worth of every man in the valley. But never he named the Lady Ælueva's name, nor went he near the Great Hall. By night he drank with us in the hut. Yes, he sat on the straw like an eagle ruffled in her feathers, his yellow eyes rolling above the cup, and he pounced in his talk like an eagle, swooping from one thing to another, but always binding fast. Yes; he would lie still awhile, and then rustle in the straw, and speak sometimes as though he were King William himself, and anon he would speak in parables and tales, and if at once we saw not his meaning he would yerk [15] us in the ribs with his scabbarded sword.

'"Look you, boys," said he, "I am born out of my due time. Five hundred years ago I would have made all England such an England as neither Dane, Saxon, nor Norman should have conquered. Five hundred years hence I should have been such a councillor to Kings as the world hath never dreamed of. 'Tis all here," said he, tapping his big head, "but it hath no play in this black age. Now Hugh here is a better man than thou art, Richard." He had made his voice harsh and croaking, like a raven's.

'"Truth," said I. "But for Hugh, his help and patience and long-suffering, I could never have kept the Manor."

'"Nor thy life either," said De Aquila. "Hugh has saved thee not once, but a hundred times. Be still, Hugh!" he said. "Dost thou know, Richard, why Hugh slept, and why he still sleeps, among thy Norman men-at-arms?"

'"To be near me," said I, for I thought this was truth.

'"Fool!" said De Aquila. "It is because his Saxons have begged him to rise against thee, and to sweep every Norman out of the valley. No matter how I know. It is truth. Therefore Hugh hath made himself an hostage for thy life, well knowing that if any harm befell thee from his Saxons thy Normans would slay him without remedy. And this his Saxons know. Is it true, Hugh?"

'"In some sort," said Hugh, shamefacedly; "at least, it was true half a year ago. My Saxons would not harm Richard now. I think they know him; but I judged it best to make sure."

'Look, children, what that man had done – and I had never guessed it! Night after night had he lain down among my men-at-arms, knowing that if one Saxon had lifted knife against me his life would have answered for mine.

'"Yes," said De Aquila. "And he is a swordless man." He pointed to Hugh's belt, for Hugh had put away his sword – did I tell you? – the day after it flew from his hand at Santlache. He carried only the short knife and the long-bow. "Swordless and landless art thou, Hugh; and they call thee kin to Earl Godwin." [16] (Hugh was indeed of Godwin's blood.) "The Manor that was thine is given to this boy and to his children for ever. Sit up and beg, for he can turn thee out like a dog, Hugh."

'Hugh said nothing, but I heard his teeth grind, and I bade De Aquila, my own overlord, hold his peace, or I would stuff his words down his throat. Then De Aquila laughed till the tears ran down his face.

'"I warned the King," said he, "what would come of giving England to us Norman thieves. Here art thou, Richard, less than two days confirmed in thy Manor, and already thou hast risen against thy overlord. What shall do to him, *Sir* Hugh?"

'"I am a swordless man," said Hugh. "Do not jest with me," and he laid his head on his knees and groaned.

'"The greater fool thou," said De Aquila, and all his voice changed; "for I have given thee the Manor of Dallington up the hill this half-hour since," and he yerked at Hugh with his scabbard across the straw.

'"To me?" said Hugh. "I am a Saxon, and, except that I love Richard here, I have not sworn fealty [17] to any Norman."

'"In God's good time, which because of my sins I shall not live to see, there will be neither Saxon nor Norman in England," said De Aquila. "If I know men, thou art more faithful unsworn than a score of Normans I could name. Take Dallington, and join Sir Richard to fight me tomorrow, if it please thee!"

'"Nay," said Hugh. "I am no child. Where I take a gift, there I render service"; and he put his hands between De Aquila's, and swore to be faithful, and, as I remember, I kissed him, and De Aquila kissed us both.

'We sat afterwards outside the hut while the sun rose, and De Aquila marked our churls going to their work in the fields, and talked of holy things, and how we should govern our manors in time to come, and of hunting and of horse-breeding, and of the King's wisdom and unwisdom; for he spoke to us as though we were in all sorts now his brothers. Anon a churl stole up to me – he was one of the three I had not hanged a year ago – and he bellowed – which is the Saxon for whispering – that the Lady Ælueva would speak to me at the Great House. She walked abroad daily in the Manor, and it was her custom to send me word whither she went, that I might set an archer or two behind and in front to guard her. Very often I myself lay up in the woods and watched on her also.

'I went swiftly, and as I passed the great door it opened from within, and there stood my Lady Ælueva, and she said to me: "Sir Richard, will it please you enter your Great Hall?" Then she wept, but we were alone.'

The knight was silent for a long time, his face turned across the valley, smiling.

'Oh, well done!' said Una, and clapped her hands very softly. 'She was sorry, and she said so.'

'Aye, she was sorry, and she said so,' said Sir Richard, coming back with a little start. 'Very soon – but *he* said it was two full hours later – De Aquila rode to the door, with his shield new scoured (Hugh had cleansed it), and demanded entertainment, and called me a false knight, that would starve his overlord to death. Then Hugh cried out that no man should work in the valley that day, and our Saxons blew horns, and set about feasting and drinking, and running of races, and dancing and singing; and De Aquila climbed upon a horse-block and spoke to them in what he swore was good Saxon, but no man understood it. At night we feasted in the Great Hall, and when the harpers and the singers were gone we four sat late at the high table. As I remember, it was a warm night with a full moon, and De Aquila bade Hugh take down his sword from the wall again, for the honour of the Manor of Dallington, and Hugh took it gladly enough. Dust lay on the hilt, for I saw him blow it off.

74

'She and I sat talking a little apart, and at first we thought the harpers had come back, for the Great Hall was filled with a rushing noise of music. De Aquila leaped up; but there was only the moonlight fretty [18] on the floor.

'"Hearken!" said Hugh. "It is my sword," and as he belted it on the music ceased.

'"Over Gods, forbid that I should ever belt blade like that," said De Aquila. "What does it foretell?"

'"The Gods that made it may know. Last time it spoke was at Hastings, when I lost all my lands. Belike it sings now that I have new lands and am a man again," said Hugh.

'He loosed the blade a little and drove it back happily into the sheath, and the sword answered him low and crooningly, as – as a woman would speak to a man, her head on his shoulder.

'Now that was the second time in all my life I heard this Sword sing . . .'

'Look!' said Una. 'There's mother coming down the Long Slip. What will she say to Sir Richard? She can't help seeing him.'

'And Puck can't magic us this time,' said Dan.

'Are you sure?' said Puck; and he leaned forward and whispered to Sir Richard, who, smiling, bowed his head.

'But what befell the sword and my brother Hugh I will tell on another time,' said he, rising. 'Ohé, Swallow!'

The great horse cantered up from the far end of the meadow, close to mother.

They heard mother say: 'Children, Gleason's old horse has broken into the meadow again. Where did he get through?'

'Just below Stone Bay,' said Dan. 'He tore down simple flobs of the bank! We noticed it just now. And we've caught no end of fish. We've been at it all the afternoon.'

And they honestly believed that they had. They never noticed the Oak, Ash, and Thorn leaves that Puck had slyly thrown into their laps.

Sir Richard's Song [1]

I followed my Duke ere I was a lover,
    To take from England fief [2] and fee;
But now this game is the other way over –
    But now England hath taken me!

I had my horse, my shield and banner,
    And a boy's heart, so whole and free;
But now I sing in another manner –
    But now England hath taken me!

As for my Father in his tower,
    Asking news of my ship at sea;
He will remember his own hour –
    Tell him England hath taken me!

As for my Mother in her bower,
    That rules my Father so cunningly;
She will remember a maiden's power –
    Tell her England hath taken me!

As for my Brother in Rouen city,
    A nimble and naughty page is he;
But he will come to suffer and pity –
    Tell him England hath taken me!

As for my little Sister waiting
    In the pleasant orchards of Normandie;
Tell her youth is the time for mating –
    Tell her England hath taken me!

As for my Comrades in camp and highway,
    That lift their eyebrows scornfully;
Tell them their way is not my way –
    Tell them England hath taken me!

Kings and Princes and Barons faméd,
    Knights and Captains in your degree;
Hear me a little before I am blaméd –
    Seeing England hath taken me!

76

Young Men at the Manor

Howso great man's strength be reckoned,
There are two things he cannot flee;
Love is the first, and Death is the second –
And Love, in England, hath taken me!

The Knights of the Joyous Venture

Harp Song of the Dane Women

What is a woman that you forsake her,
And the hearth-fire and the home-acre,
To go with the old grey Widow-maker?

She has no house to lay a guest in —
But one chill bed for all to rest in,
That the pale suns and the stray bergs nest in.

She has no strong white arms to fold you,
But the ten-times-fingering weed to hold you
Bound on the rocks where the tide has rolled you.

Yet, when the signs of summer thicken,
And the ice breaks, and the birch-buds quicken,
Yearly you turn from our side, and sicken —

Sicken again for the shouts and the slaughters —
You steal away to the lapping waters,
And look at your ship in her winter quarters.

You forget our mirth, and talk at the tables,
The kine in the shed and the horse in the stables —
To pitch her sides and go over her cables!

Then you drive out where the storm-clouds swallow:
And the sound of your oar-blades falling hollow,
Is all we have left through the months to follow.

Ah, what is Woman that you forsake her,
And the hearth-fire and the home-acre,
To go with the old grey Widow-maker?

The Knights of the Joyous Venture

It was too hot to run about in the open, so Dan asked their friend, old Hobden, to take their own dinghy from the pond and put her on the brook at the bottom of the garden. Her painted name was the *Daisy*, but for exploring expeditions she was the *Golden Hind*[1] or the *Long Serpent*,[2] or some such suitable name. Dan hiked and howked[3] with a boat-hook (the brook was too narrow for sculls), and Una punted with a piece of hop-pole. When they came to a very shallow place (the *Golden Hind* drew quite three inches of water) they disembarked and scuffled her over the gravel by her tow-rope, and when they reached the overgrown banks beyond the garden they pulled themselves up stream by the low branches.

That day they intended to discover the North Cape like 'Othere, the old sea-captain',[4] in the book of verses which Una had brought with her; but on account of the heat they changed it to a voyage up the Amazon and the sources of the Nile. Even on the shaded water the air was hot and heavy with drowsy scents, while outside, through breaks in the trees, the sunshine burned the pasture like fire. The kingfisher was asleep on his watching-branch, and the blackbirds scarcely took the trouble to dive into the next bush. Dragon-flies wheeling and clashing were the only things at work, except the moor-hens and a big Red Admiral, who flapped down out of the sunshine for a drink.

When they reached Otter Pool the *Golden Hind* grounded comfortably on a shallow, and they lay beneath a roof of close green, watching the water trickle over the flood-gates down the mossy brick chute from the mill-stream to the brook. A big trout – the children knew him well – rolled head and shoulders at some fly that sailed round the bend, while once in just so often the brook rose a fraction of an inch against all the wet

79

pebbles, and they watched the slow draw and shiver of a breath of air through the tree-tops. Then the little voices of the slipping water began again.

'It's like the shadows talking, isn't it?' said Una. She had given up trying to read. Dan lay over the bows, trailing his hands in the current. They heard feet on the gravel-bar that runs half across the pool and saw Sir Richard Dalyngridge standing over them.

'Was yours a dangerous voyage?' he asked, smiling.

'She bumped a lot, sir,' said Dan. 'There's hardly any water this summer.'

'Ah, the brook was deeper and wider when my children played at Danish pirates. Are you pirate-folk?'

'Oh, no. We gave up being pirates years ago,' explained Una. 'We're nearly always explorers now. Sailing round the world, you know.'

'Round?' said Sir Richard. He sat him in the comfortable crotch of an old ash-root on the bank. 'How can it be round?'

'Wasn't it in your books?' Dan suggested. He had been doing geography at his last lesson.

'I can neither write nor read,' he replied. 'Canst *thou* read, child?'

'Yes,' said Dan, 'barring the very long words.'

'Wonderful! Read to me, that I may hear for myself.'

Dan flushed, but opened the book and began – gabbling a little – at 'The Discoverer of the North Cape'.

> 'Othere, the old sea captain,
> Who dwelt in Helgoland,
> To Alfred, lover of truth,
> Brought a snow-white walrus tooth,
> That he held in his right hand.'

'But – but – this I know! This is an old song! This I have heard sung! This is a miracle,' Sir Richard interrupted. 'Nay, do not stop!' He leaned forward, and the shadows of the leaves slipped and slid upon his chain-mail.

'I ploughed the land with horses,
But my heart was ill at ease,
For the old sea-faring men
Came to me now and then
With their Sagas of the Seas.'

His hand fell on the hilt of the great sword. 'This is truth,' he cried, 'for so did it happen to me,' and he beat time delightedly to the tramp of verse after verse.

'"And now the land," said Othere,
"Bent southward suddenly,
And I followed the curving shore,
And ever southward bore
Into a nameless sea."'

'A nameless sea!' he repeated. 'So did I – so did Hugh and I.'

'Where did you go? Tell us,' said Una.

'Wait. Let me hear all first.' So Dan read to the poem's very end.

'Good,' said the knight. 'That is Othere's tale – even as I have heard the men in the Dane ships sing it. Not in those same valiant words, but something like to them.'

'Have you ever explored North?' Dan shut the book.

'Nay. My venture was South. Farther South than any man has fared, Hugh and I went down with Witta and his heathen.' He jerked the tall sword forward, and leaned on it with both hands; but his eyes looked long past them.

'I thought you always lived here,' said Una, timidly.

'Yes; while my Lady Ælueva lived. But she died. She died. Then, my eldest son being a man, I asked De Aquila's leave that he should hold the Manor while I went on some journey or pilgrimage – to forget. De Aquila, whom the Second William had made Warden of Pevensey in Earl Mortain's place, was very old then, but still he rode his tall, roan horses, and in the saddle he looked like a little white falcon. When Hugh, at Dallington over yonder, heard what I did, he sent for my second son, whom being unmarried he had ever looked upon as his own child, and, by De Aquila's leave, gave him the Manor of Dallington to hold till he should return. Then Hugh came with me.'

'When did this happen?' said Dan.

'That I can answer to the very day, for as we rode with De Aquila by Pevensey – have I said that he was Lord of Pevensey and of the Honour of the Eagle? – to the Bordeaux ship that fetched him his wines yearly out of France, a Marsh man ran to us crying that he had seen a great black goat which bore on his back the body of the King, and that the goat had spoken to him. On that same day Red William our King, the Conqueror's son, died of a secret arrow while he hunted in a forest.[5] "This is a cross matter," said De Aquila, "to meet on the threshold of a journey. If Red William be dead I may have to fight for my lands. Wait a little."

'My Lady being dead, I cared nothing for signs and omens, nor Hugh either. We took that wine-ship to go to Bordeaux; but the wind failed while we were yet in sight of Pevensey, a thick mist hid us, and we drifted with the tide along the cliffs to the west. Our company was, for the most part, merchants returning to France, and we were laden with wool and there were three couple of tall hunting-dogs chained to the rail. Their master was a knight of Artois.[6] His name I never learned, but his shield bore gold pieces on a red ground, and he limped, much as I do, from a wound which he had got in his youth at Mantes siege.[7] He served the Duke of Burgundy against the Moors in Spain,[8] and was returning to that war with his dogs. He sang us strange Moorish songs that first night, and half persuaded us to go with him. I was on pilgrimage to forget – which is what no pilgrimage brings. I think I would have gone, but . . .

'Look you how the life and fortune of man changes! Towards morning a Dane ship, rowing silently, struck against us in the mist, and while we rolled hither and yon Hugh, leaning over the rail, fell outboard. I leaped after him, and we two tumbled aboard the Dane, and were caught and bound ere we could rise. Our own ship was swallowed up in the mist. I judge the Knight of the Gold Pieces muzzled his dogs with his cloak, lest they should give tongue and betray the merchants, for I heard their baying suddenly stop.

'We lay bound among the benches till morning, when the Danes dragged us to the high deck by the steering-place, and their captain – Witta, he was called – turned us over with his foot. Bracelets of gold from elbow to armpit he wore, and his red hair was long as a woman's, and came down in plaited locks on his shoulder. He was stout, with bowed legs and long arms. He spoiled us of all we had, but when he laid hand on Hugh's sword and saw the runes on the blade hastily he thrust it back. Yet his covetousness overcame him and he tried again and again, and the third time the Sword sang loud and angrily, so that the rowers leaned on their oars to listen. Here they all spoke together, screaming like gulls, and a Yellow Man, such as I have never seen, came to the high deck and cut our bonds. He was yellow – not from sickness, but by nature – yellow as honey, and his eyes stood endwise in his head.'

'How do you mean?' said Una, her chin on her hand.

'Thus,' said Sir Richard. He put a finger to the corner of each eye, and pushed it up till his eyes narrowed to slits.

'Why, you look just like a Chinaman!' cried Dan. 'Was the man a Chinaman?'

'I know not what that may be. Witta had found him half dead among ice on the shores of Muscovy.⁹ *We* thought he was a devil. He crawled before us and brought food in a silver dish which these sea-wolves had robbed from some rich abbey, and Witta with his own hands gave us wine. He spoke a little in French, a little in South Saxon, and much in the Northman's tongue. We asked him to set us ashore, promising to pay him better ransom than he would get price if he sold us to the Moors – as once befell a knight of my acquaintance sailing from Flushing.

'"Not by my father Guthrum's head," said he. "The Gods sent ye into my ship for a luck-offering."

'At this I quaked, for I knew it was still the Danes' custom to sacrifice captives to their gods for fair weather.

'"A plague on thy four long bones!" said Hugh. "What profit canst thou make of poor old pilgrims that can neither work nor fight?"

'"Gods forbid I should fight against thee, poor Pilgrim with the Singing Sword," said he. "Come with us and be poor no more. Thy teeth are far apart, which is a sure sign thou wilt travel and grow rich."

' "What if we will not come?" said Hugh.

' "Swim to England or France," said Witta. "We are midway between the two. Unless ye choose to drown yourselves no hair of your head will be harmed here aboard. We think ye bring us luck, and I myself know the runes on that Sword are good." He turned and bade them hoist sail.

'Hereafter all made way for us as we walked about the ship, and the ship was full of wonders.'

'What was she like?' said Dan.

'Long, low, and narrow, bearing one mast with a red sail, and rowed by fifteen oars a-side,' the knight answered. 'At her bows was a deck under which men might lie, and at her stern another shut off by a painted door from the rowers' benches. Here Hugh and I slept, with Witta and the Yellow Man, upon tapestries as soft as wool. I remember' – he laughed to himself – 'when first we entered there a loud voice cried, "Out swords! Out swords! Kill, kill!" Seeing us start Witta laughed, and showed us it was but a great-beaked grey bird with a red tail. He sat her on his shoulder, and she called for bread and wine hoarsely, and prayed him to kiss her. Yet she was no more than a silly bird. But – ye knew this?' He looked at their smiling faces.

'We weren't laughing at you,' said Una. 'That must have been a parrot. It's just what Pollies do.'

'So we learned later. But here is another marvel. The Yellow Man, whose name was Kitai, had with him a brown box. In the box was a blue bowl with red marks upon the rim, and within the bowl, hanging from a fine thread, was a piece of iron no thicker than that grass stem, and as long, maybe, as my spur, but straight. In this iron, said Witta, abode an Evil Spirit which Kitai, the Yellow Man, had brought by Art Magic out of his own country that lay three years' journey southward. The Evil Spirit strove day and night to return to his country, and therefore, look you, the iron needle pointed continually to the South.' [10]

'South?' said Dan, suddenly, and put his hand into his pocket.

'With my own eyes I saw it. Every day and all day long, though the ship rolled, though the sun and the moon and the stars were hid, this blind Spirit in the iron knew whither it would go, and strained to the South. Witta called it the Wise Iron, because it showed him his way across the unknowable seas.' Again Sir Richard looked keenly at the children. 'How think ye? Was it sorcery?'

'Was it anything like this?' Dan fished out his old brass pocket-compass, that generally lived with his knife and key-ring. 'The glass has got cracked, but the needle waggles all right, sir.'

The knight drew a long breath of wonder. 'Yes, yes. The Wise Iron shook and swung in just this fashion. Now it is still. Now it points to the South.'

'North,' said Dan.

'Nay, South! There is the South,' said Sir Richard. Then they both laughed, for naturally when one end of a straight compass-needle points to the North, the other must point to the South.

'Té,' said Sir Richard, clicking his tongue. 'There can be no sorcery if a child carries it. Wherefore does it point South – or North?'

'Father says that nobody knows,' said Una.

Sir Richard looked relieved. 'Then it may still be magic. It was magic to *us*. And so we voyaged. When the wind served we hoisted sail, and lay all up along the windward rail, our shields on our backs to break the spray. When it failed, they rowed with long oars; the Yellow Man sat by the Wise Iron, and Witta steered. At first I feared the great white-flowering waves, but as I saw how wisely Witta led his ship among them I grew bolder. Hugh liked it well from the first. My skill is not upon the water; and rocks, and whirlpools such as we saw by the West Isles of France, where an oar caught on a rock and broke, are much against my stomach. We sailed South across a stormy sea, where by moonlight, between clouds, we saw a Flanders ship roll clean over and sink. Again, though Hugh laboured

85

with Witta all night, I lay under the deck with the Talking Bird, and cared not whether I lived or died. There is a sickness of the sea which for three days is pure death! When we next saw land Witta said it was Spain, and we stood out to sea. That coast was full of ships busy in the Duke's war against the Moors, and we feared to be hanged by the Duke's men or sold into slavery by the Moors. So we put into a small harbour which Witta knew. At night men came down with loaded mules, and Witta exchanged amber out of the North [11] against little wedges of iron and packets of beads in earthen pots. The pots he put under the decks, and the wedges of iron he laid on the bottom of the ship after he had cast out the stones and shingle which till then had been our ballast. Wine, too, he bought for lumps of sweet-smelling grey amber [12] – a little morsel no bigger than a thumbnail purchased a cask of wine. But I speak like a merchant.'

'No, no. Tell us what you had to eat,' cried Dan.

'Meat dried in the sun, and dried fish and ground beans, Witta took in; and corded frails of a certain sweet, soft fruit, which the Moors use, which is like paste of figs, but with thin, long stones. Aha! Dates is the name.

'"Now," said Witta, when the ship was loaded, "I counsel you strangers to pray to your gods, for from here on our road is No Man's road." He and his men killed a black goat for sacrifice on the bows; and the Yellow Man brought out a small, smiling image of dull-green stone and burned incense before it. Hugh and I commended ourselves to God, and Saint Barnabas,[13] and Our Lady of the Assumption, who was specially dear to my Lady. We were not young, but I think no shame to say whenas we drove out of that secret harbour at sunrise over a still sea, we two rejoiced and sang as did the knights of old when they followed our great Duke to England. Yet was our leader an heathen pirate; all our proud fleet but one galley perilously overloaded; for guidance we leaned on a pagan sorcerer; and our port was beyond the world's end. Witta told us that his father Guthrum had once in his life rowed along the shores of Africa to a land where naked men sold gold for iron and beads. There had he bought much gold, and no few elephants' teeth, and thither by help of the Wise Iron would Witta go. Witta feared nothing – except to be poor.

'"My father told me," said Witta, "that a great Shoal runs three days' sail out from that land, and south of the shoal lies a Forest which grows in the sea. South and east of the Forest my father came to a place where the men hid gold in their hair; but all that country, he said, was full of Devils who lived in trees, and tore folk limb from limb. How think ye?"

'"Gold or no gold," said Hugh, fingering his sword, "it is a joyous venture. Have at these devils of thine, Witta!"

'"Venture!" said Witta, sourly. "I am only a poor sea-thief. I do not set my life adrift on a plank for joy, or the venture. Once I beach ship again at Stavanger, and feel the wife's arms round my neck, I'll seek no more ventures. A ship is heavier care than a wife or cattle."

'He leaped down among the rowers, chiding them for their little strength and their great stomachs. Yet Witta was a wolf in fight, and a very fox in cunning.

'We were driven South by a storm, and for three days and three nights he took the stern-oar, and threddled the longship through the sea. When it rose beyond measure he brake a pot of whale's oil upon the water, which wonderfully smoothed it, and in that anointed patch he turned her head to the wind and threw out oars at the end of a rope, to make, he said, an anchor at which we lay rolling sorely, but dry. This craft his father Guthrum had shown him. He knew, too, all the Leech-Book of Bald,[14] who was a wise doctor, and he knew the Ship-Book of Hlaf the Woman,[15] who robbed Egypt. He knew all the care of a ship.

'After the storm we saw a mountain whose top was covered with snow and pierced the clouds.[16] The grasses under this mountain, boiled and eaten, are a good cure for soreness of the gums and swelled ankles. We lay there eight days, till men in skins threw stones at us. When the heat increased Witta spread a cloth on bent sticks above the rowers, for the wind failed between the Island of the Mountain and the shore of Africa, which is east of it. That shore is sandy, and we rowed along it within three bowshots. Here we saw whales, and fish in the shape of shields, but longer than our ship. Some slept, some opened their mouths at us, and some danced on the hot waters. The water was hot to the hand, and the sky was hidden by hot, grey mists, out of which blew a fine dust that whitened our hair and beards of a morning. Here, too, were fish that flew in the air like birds. They would fall on the laps of the rowers, and when we went ashore we would roast and eat them.'

The knight paused to see if the children doubted him, but they only nodded and said, 'Go on.'

'The yellow land lay on our left, the grey sea on our right. Knight though I was, I pulled my oar amongst the rowers. I caught seaweed and dried it, and stuffed it between the pots of beads lest they should break. Knighthood is for the land. At sea, look you, a man is but a spurless rider on a bridle-less horse. I learned to make strong knots in ropes – yes, and to join two ropes end to end, so that even Witta could scarcely see where they had been married. But Hugh had tenfold more sea-cunning than I. Witta gave him charge of the rowers of the left side. Thorkild of Borkum, a man with a broken nose, that wore a Norman steel cap, had the rowers of the right, and each side rowed and sang against the other. They saw that no man was idle. Truly, as Hugh said, and Witta would laugh at him, a ship is all more care than a Manor.

'How? Thus. There was water to fetch from the shore when we could find it, as well as wild fruit and grasses, and sand for scrubbing of the decks and benches to keep them sweet. Also we hauled the ship out on low islands and emptied all her gear, even to the iron wedges, and burned off the weed, that had grown on her, with torches of rush, and smoked below the decks with rushes dampened in salt water, as Hlaf the Woman orders in her Ship-Book. Once when we were thus stripped, and the ship lay propped on her keel, the bird cried, "Out swords!" as though she saw an enemy. Witta vowed he would wring her neck.'

'Poor Polly! Did he?' said Una.

'Nay. She was the ship's bird. She could call all the rowers by name . . . Those were good days – for a wifeless man – with Witta and his heathen – beyond the world's end . . . After many weeks we came on the Great Shoal [17] which stretched, as Witta's father had said, far out to sea. We skirted it till we were giddy with the sight and dizzy with the sound of bars and breakers, and when we reached land again we found a naked black people dwelling among woods, who for one wedge of iron loaded us with fruits and grasses and eggs. Witta scratched his head at them in sign he would buy gold. They had no gold, but they understood the sign (all the gold-traders hide their gold in their thick hair), for they pointed along the coast. They beat, too, on their chests with their clenched hands, and that, if we had known it, was an evil sign.'

'What did it mean?' said Dan.

'Patience. Ye shall hear. We followed the coast eastward sixteen days (counting time by sword-cuts on the helm-rail) till we came to the Forest in the Sea.[18] Trees grew there out of mud, arched upon lean and high roots, and many muddy waterways ran all whither into darkness under the trees. Here we lost the sun. We followed the winding channels between the trees, and where we could not row we laid hold of the crusted roots and hauled ourselves along. The water was foul, and great glittering flies tormented us. Morning and evening a blue mist covered the mud, which bred fevers. Four of our rowers sickened, and were bound to their benches, lest they should leap overboard and be eaten by the monsters of the mud. The Yellow Man lay sick beside the Wise Iron, rolling his head and talking in his own tongue. Only the Bird throve. She sat on Witta's shoulder and screamed in that noisome, silent darkness. Yes; I think it was the silence we feared.'

He paused to listen to the comfortable home noises of the brook.

'When we had lost count of time among those black gullies and swashes we heard, as it were, a drum beat far off, and following it we broke into a broad, brown river by a hut in a clearing among fields of pumpkins. We thanked God to see the sun again. The people of the village gave the good welcome, and Witta scratched his head at them (for gold), and showed them our iron and beads. They ran to the bank – we were still in the ship – and pointed to our swords and bows, for always when near shore we lay armed. Soon they fetched store of gold in bars and in dust from their huts, and some great blackened elephant teeth. These they piled on the bank, as though to tempt us, and made signs of dealing blows in battle, and pointed up to the tree tops, and to the forest behind. Their captain or chief sorcerer then beat on his chest with his fists, and gnashed his teeth.

'Said Thorkild of Borkum: "Do they mean we must fight for all this gear?" and he half drew sword.

'"Nay," said Hugh. "I think they ask us to league against some enemy."

'"I like this not," said Witta, of a sudden. "Back into mid-stream."

'So we did, and sat still all, watching the black folk and the gold they piled on the bank. Again we heard drums beat in the forest, and the people fled to their huts, leaving the gold un-guarded.

'Then Hugh, at the bows, pointed without speech, and we saw a great Devil come out of the forest. He shaded his brows with his hand, and moistened his pink tongue between his lips – thus.'

'A Devil!' said Dan, delightfully horrified.

'Yea. Taller than a man; covered with reddish hair. When he had well regarded our ship, he beat on his chest with his fists till it sounded like rolling drums, and came to the bank swinging all his body between his long arms, and gnashed his teeth at us. Hugh loosed arrow, and pierced him through the throat. He fell roaring, and three other Devils ran out of the forest and hauled him into a tall tree out of sight. Anon they cast down the blood-stained arrow, and lamented together among the leaves. Witta saw the gold on the bank; he was loath to leave it. "Sirs," said he (no man had spoken till then), "yonder is what we have come so far and so painfully to find, laid out to our very hand. Let us row in while these Devils bewail themselves, and at least bear off what we may."

'Bold as a wolf, cunning as a fox was Witta! He set four archers on the foredeck to shoot the Devils if they should leap from the tree, which was close to the bank. He manned ten oars a-side, and bade them watch his hand to row in or back out, and so coaxed he them toward the bank. But none would set foot ashore, though the gold was within ten paces. No man is hasty to his hanging! They whimpered at their oars like beaten hounds, and Witta bit his fingers for rage.

'Said Hugh of a sudden, "Hark!" At first we thought it was the buzzing of the glittering flies on the water; but it grew loud and fierce, so that all men heard.'

'What?' said Dan and Una.

'It was the Sword.' Sir Richard patted the smooth hilt. 'It sang as a Dane sings before battle. "I go," said Hugh, and he leaped from the bows and fell among the gold. I was afraid to my four bones' marrow, but for shame's sake I followed, and Thorkild of Borkum leaped after me. None other came. "Blame me not," cried Witta behind us, "I must abide by my ship." We three had no time to blame or praise. We stooped to the gold and threw it back over our shoulders, one hand on our swords and one eye on the tree, which nigh overhung us.

'I know not how the Devils leaped down, or how the fight began. I heard Hugh cry: "Out! out!" as though he were at Santlache again; I saw Thorkild's steel cap smitten off his head by a great hairy hand, and I felt an arrow from the ship whistle past my ear. They say that till Witta took his sword to the rowers he could not bring his ship inshore; and each one of the four archers said afterwards that he alone had pierced the Devil that fought me. I do not know. I went to it in my mail-shirt, which saved my skin. With long-sword and belt-dagger I fought for the life against a Devil whose very feet were hands, and who whirled me back and forth like a dead branch. He had me by the waist, my arms to my side, when an arrow from the ship pierced him between the shoulders, and he loosened grip. I passed my sword twice through him, and he crutched himself away between his long arms, coughing and moaning. Next, as I remember, I saw Thorkild of Borkum bare-headed and smiling, leaping up and down before a Devil that leaped and gnashed his teeth. Then Hugh passed, his sword shifted to his left hand, and I wondered why I had not known that Hugh was a left-handed man; and thereafter I remembered nothing till I felt spray on my face, and we were in sunshine on the open sea. That was twenty days after.'

'What had happened? Did Hugh die?' the children asked.

'Never was such a fight fought by christened man,' said Sir Richard. 'An arrow from the ship had saved me from my Devil, and Thorkild of Borkum had given back before his Devil, till the bowmen on the ship could shoot it all full of arrows from near by; but Hugh's Devil was cunning, and had kept behind trees, where no arrow could reach. Body to body there, by stark strength of sword and hand, had Hugh slain him, and, dying, the Thing had clenched his teeth on the sword. Judge what teeth they were!'

Sir Richard turned the sword again that the children might see the two great chiselled gouges on either side of the blade.

'Those same teeth met in Hugh's right arm and side,' Sir Richard went on. 'I? Oh, I had no more than a broken foot and a fever. Thorkild's ear was bitten, but Hugh's arm and side clean withered away. I saw him where he lay along, sucking a fruit in his left hand. His flesh was wasted off his bones, his hair was patched with white, and his hand was blue-veined like a woman's. He put his left hand round my neck and whispered, "Take my sword. It has been thine since Hastings, O my brother, but I can never hold hilt again." We lay there on the high deck talking of Santlache, and, I think, of every day since Santlache, and it came so that we both wept. I was weak, and he little more than a shadow.

'"Nay – nay," said Witta, at the helm-rail. "Gold is a good right arm to any man. Look – look at the gold!" He bade Thorkild show us the gold and the elephants' teeth, as though we had been children. He had brought away all the gold on the bank, and twice as much more, that the people of the village gave him for slaying the Devils. They worshipped us as gods, Thorkild told me: it was one of their old women healed up Hugh's poor arm.'

'How much gold did you get?' asked Dan.

'How can I say? Where we came out with wedges of iron under the rowers' feet we returned with wedges of gold hidden beneath planks. There was dust of gold in packages where we slept and along the side, and crosswise under the benches we lashes the blackened elephants' teeth.

'"I had sooner have my right arm," said Hugh, when he had seen all.

'"Ahai! That was my fault," said Witta. "I should have taken ransom and landed you in France when first you came aboard, ten months ago."

'"It is over-late now," said Hugh, laughing.

'Witta plucked at his long shoulder-lock. "But think!" said he. "If I had let ye go – which I swear I would never have done, for I love ye more than brothers – if I had let ye go, by now ye might have been horribly slain by some mere Moor in the Duke of Burgundy's war, or ye might have been murdered by land-thieves, or ye might have died of the plague at an inn. Think of this and do not blame me overmuch, Hugh. See! I will only take a half of the gold.'

'"I blame thee not at all, Witta," said Hugh. "It was a joyous venture, and we thirty-five here have done what never men have done. If I live till England, I will build me a stout keep over Dallington out of my share."

'"I will buy cattle and amber and warm red cloth for the wife," said Witta, "and I will hold all the land at the head of Stavanger Fiord.[19] Many will fight for me now. But first we must turn North, and with this honest treasure aboard I pray we meet no pirate ships."

'We did not laugh. We were careful. We were afraid lest we should lose one grain of our gold, for which we had fought Devils.

'"Where is the Sorcerer?" said I, for Witta was looking at the Wise Iron in the box, and I could not see the Yellow Man.

'"He has gone to his own country," said he. "He rose up in the night while we were beating out of that forest in the mud, and said that he could see it behind the trees. He leaped out on

93

to the mud, and did not answer when we called; so we called no more. He left the Wise Iron, which is all that I care for – and see, the Spirit still points to the South."

'We were troubled for fear that the Wise Iron should fail us now that its Yellow Man had gone, and when we saw the Spirit still served us we grew afraid of too strong winds, and of shoals, and of careless leaping fish, and of all the people on all the shores where we landed.'

'Why?' said Dan.

'Because of the gold – because of our gold. Gold changes men altogether. Thorkild of Borkum did not change. He laughed at Witta for his fears, and at us for our counselling Witta to furl sail when the ship pitched at all.

'"Better be drowned out of hand," said Thorkild of Borkum, "than go tied to a deck-load of yellow dust."

'He was a landless man, and had been slave to some King in the East. He would have beaten out the gold into deep bands to put round the oars, and round the prow.

'Yet, though he vexed himself for the gold, Witta waited upon Hugh like a woman, lending him his shoulder when the ship rolled, and tying of ropes from side to side that Hugh might hold by them. But for Hugh, he said – and so did all his men – they would never have won the gold. I remember Witta made a little, thin gold ring for our Bird to swing in.

'Three months we rowed and sailed and went ashore for fruits or to clean the ship. When we saw wild horsemen, riding among sand-dunes, flourishing spears, we knew we were on the Moors' coast, and stood over north to Spain; and a strong south-west wind bore us in ten days to a coast of high red rocks, where we heard a hunting-horn blow among the yellow gorse and knew it was England.

'"Now find ye Pevensey yourselves," said Witta. "I love not these narrow ship-filled seas."

'He set the dried, salted head of the Devil, which Hugh had killed, high on our prow, and all boats fled from us. Yet, for our gold's sake, we were more afraid than they. We crept along the coast by night till we came to the chalk cliffs, and so east to Pevensey. Witta would not come ashore with us, though Hugh promised him wine at Dallington enough to swim in. He was on fire to see his wife, and ran into the Marsh after sunset, and there he left us and our share of gold, and backed out on the same tide. He made no promise; he swore no oath; he looked for no thanks; but to Hugh, an armless man, and to me, an old cripple whom he could have flung into the sea, he passed over wedge upon wedge, packet upon packet of gold and dust of gold, and only ceased when we would take no more. As he stooped from the rail to bid us farewell he stripped off his right-arm bracelets and put them all on Hugh's left, and he kissed Hugh on the cheek. I think when Thorkild of Borkum bade the rowers give way we were near weeping. It is true that Witta was an heathen and a pirate; true it is he held us by force many months in his ship, but I loved that bow-legged, blue-eyed man for his great boldness, his cunning, his skill, and, beyond all, for his simplicity.'

'Did he get home all right?' said Dan.

'I never knew. We saw him hoist sail under the moon-track and stand away. I have prayed that he found his wife and the children.'

'And what did you do?'

'We waited on the Marsh till the day. Then I sat by the gold, all tied in an old sail, while Hugh went to Pevensey, and De Aquila sent us horses.'

Sir Richard crossed hands on his sword-hilt, and stared down stream through the soft warm shadows.

'A whole shipload of gold!' said Una, looking at the little *Golden Hind*. 'But I'm glad I didn't see the Devils.'

'I don't believe they were Devils,' Dan whispered back.

'Eh?' said Sir Richard. 'Witta's father warned him they were unquestionable Devils. One must believe one's father, and not one's children. What were my Devils, then?'

Dan flushed all over. 'I – I only thought,' he stammered; 'I've got a book called *The Gorilla Hunters* – it's a continuation of *Coral Island*,[20] sir – and it says there that the gorillas (they're big monkeys, you know) were always chewing iron up.'

'Not always,' said Una. 'Only twice.' They had been reading *The Gorilla Hunters* in the orchard.

'Well, anyhow, they always drummed on their chests, like Sir Richard's did, before they went for people. And they built houses in trees, too.'

'Ha!' Sir Richard opened his eyes. 'Houses like flat nests did our Devils make, where their imps lay and looked at us. I did not see them (I was sick after the fight), but Witta told me, and, lo, ye know it also? Wonderful! Were our Devils only nest-building apes? Is there no sorcery left in the world?'

'I don't know,' answered Dan, uncomfortable. 'I've seen a man take rabbits out of a hat, and he told us we could see how he did it, if we watched hard. And we did.'

'But we didn't,' said Una, sighing. 'Oh! there's Puck!'

The little fellow, brown and smiling, peered between two stems of an ash, nodded, and slid down the bank into the cool beside them.

'No sorcery, Sir Richard?' he laughed, and blew on a full dandelion head he had picked.

'They tell me that Witta's Wise Iron was a toy. The boy carries such an iron with him. They tell me our Devils were apes, called gorillas!' said Sir Richard, indignantly.

'That is the sorcery of books,' said Puck. 'I warned thee they were wise children. All people can be wise by reading of books.'

'But are the books true?' Sir Richard frowned. 'I like not all this reading and writing.'

'Ye-es,' said Puck, holding the naked dandelion head at arm's length. 'But if we hang all fellows who write falsely, why did De Aquila not begin with Gilbert, the Clerk? *He* was false enough.'

'Poor false Gilbert. Yet, in his fashion, he was bold,' said Sir Richard.

'What did he do?' said Dan.

'He wrote,' said Sir Richard. 'Is the tale meet for children, think you?' He looked at Puck; but 'Tell us! Tell us!' cried Dan and Una together.

Thorkild's Song [1]

There's no wind along these seas,
  Out oars for Stavanger!
  Forward all for Stavanger!
So we must wake the white-ash breeze,
  Let fall for Stavanger!
  A long pull for Stavanger!

Oh, hear the benches creak and strain!
  (*A long pull for Stavanger!*)
She thinks she smells the Northland rain!
  (*A long pull for Stavanger!*)

She thinks she smells the Northland snow,
And she's as glad as we to go.

She thinks the smells the Northland rime,
And the dear dark nights of winter-time.

Her very bolts are sick for shore,
And we – we want it ten times more!

So all you Gods that love brave men,
Send us a three-reef gale again!

Send us a gale, and watch us come,
With close-cropped canvas slashing home!

But – there's no wind in all these seas,
  A long pull for Stavanger!
So we must wake the white-ash breeze,
  A long pull for Stavanger!

Old Men at Pevensey

'It has nought to do with apes or devils,' Sir Richard went on, in an undertone. 'It concerns De Aquila, than whom there was never bolder nor craftier, nor more hardy knight born. And remember he was an old, old man at that time.'

'When?' said Dan.

'When we came back from sailing with Witta.'

'What did you do with your gold?' said Dan.

'Have patience. Link by link is chain-mail made. I will tell all in its place. We bore the gold to Pevensey on horseback – three loads of it – and then up to the north chamber, above the Great Hall of Pevensey Castle, where De Aquila lay in winter. He sat on his bed like a little white falcon, turning his head swiftly from one to the other as we told our tale. Jehan the Crab, an old sour man-at-arms, guarded the stairway, but De Aquila bade him wait at the stair-foot, and let down both leather curtains over the door. It was Jehan whom De Aquila had sent to us with the horses, and only Jehan had loaded the gold. When our story was told, De Aquila gave us the news of England, for we were as men waked from a year-long sleep. The Red King was dead – slain (ye remember?) the day we set sail – and Henry, his younger brother, had made himself King of England over the head of Robert of Normandy. This was the very thing that the Red King had done to Robert when our Great William died. Then Robert of Normandy, mad, as De Aquila said, at twice missing of this kingdom, had sent an army against England, which army had been well beaten back to their ships at Portsmouth. A little earlier, and Witta's ship would have rowed through them.

'"And now," said De Aquila, "half the great Barons of the north and west are out against the King between Salisbury and Shrewsbury, and half the other half wait to see which way the game shall go. They say Henry is overly English for their stomachs, because he hath married an English wife and she hath coaxed him to give back their old laws to our Saxons.[1] (Better ride a horse on the bit he knows, *I* say.) But that is only a cloak to their falsehood." He cracked his finger on the table where the wine was spilt, and thus he spoke:

'"William crammed us Norman barons full of good English acres after Santlache. *I* had my share too," he said, and clapped Hugh on the shoulder; "but I warned him – I warned him before Odo rebelled [2] – that he should have bidden the Barons give up their lands and lordships in Normandy if they would be English lords. Now they are all but princes both in England and Normandy – trencher-fed hounds, with a foot in one trough and both eyes on the other! Robert of Normandy [3] has sent them word that if they do not fight for him in England he will sack and harry out their lands in Normandy. Therefore Clare has risen, FitzOsborne has risen, Montgomery has risen – whom our First William made an English earl. Even D'Arcy is out with his men, whose father I remember a little hedge-sparrow knight nearby Caen. If Henry wins, the Barons can still flee to Normandy, where Robert will welcome them. If Henry loses, Robert, he says, will give them more lands in England. Oh, a pest – a pest on Normandy, for she will be our England's curse this many a long year!"

'"Amen," said Hugh. "But will the war come our ways, think you?"

'"Not from the north," said De Aquila. "But the sea is always open. If the Barons gain the upper hand Robert will send another army into England for sure, and this time I think he will land here – where his father, the Conqueror, landed. Ye have brought your pigs to a pretty market! Half England alight, and gold enough on the ground" – he stamped on the bars beneath the table – "to set every sword in Christendom fighting."

'"What is to do?" said Hugh. "I have no keep at Dallington; and if we buried it, whom could we trust?"

'"Me," said De Aquila. "Pevensey walls are strong. No man but Jehan, who is my dog, knows what is between them." He drew a curtain by the shot-window and showed us the shaft of a well in the thickness of the wall.

'"I made it for a drinking-well," he said, "but we found salt water, and it rises and falls with the tide. Hark!" We heard the water whistle and blow at the bottom. "Will it serve?" said he.

'"Needs must," said Hugh. "Our lives are in thy hands." So we lowered all the gold down except one small chest of it by De Aquila's bed, which we kept as much for his delight in its weight and colour as for any of our needs.

'In the morning, ere we rode to our Manors, he said: "I do not say farewell; because ye will return and bide here. Not for love nor for sorrow, but to be with the gold. Have a care," he said, laughing, "lest I use it to make myself Pope. Trust me not, but return!"'

Sir Richard paused and smiled sadly.

'In seven days, then, we returned from our Manors – from the Manors which had been ours.'

'And were the children quite well?' said Una.

'My sons were young. Land and governance belong by right to young men.' Sir Richard was talking to himself. 'It would have broken their hearts if we had taken back our Manors. They made us great welcome, but we could see – Hugh and I could see – that our day was done. I was a cripple and he a one-armed man. No!' He shook his head. 'And therefore' – he raised his voice – 'we rode back to Pevensey.'

'I'm sorry,' said Una, for the knight seemed very sorrowful.

'Little maid, it all passed long ago. They were young; we were old. We let them rule the Manors. "Aha!" cried De Aquila from his shot-window, when we dismounted. "Back again to earth, old foxes?" but when we were in his chamber above the Hall he puts his arms about us and says, "Welcome, ghosts! Welcome, poor ghosts!" . . . Thus it fell out that we were rich beyond belief, and lonely. And lonely!'

'What did you do?' said Dan.

'We watched for Robert of Normandy,' said the knight. 'De Aquila was like Witta. He suffered no idleness. In fair weather we would ride along between Bexlei on the one side, to

Cuckmere on the other – sometimes with hawk, sometimes with hound (there are stout hares both on the Marsh and the Down-land), but always with an eye to the sea, for fear of fleets from Normandy. In foul weather he would walk on the top of his tower, frowning against the rain – peering here and pointing there. It always vexed him to think how Witta's ship had come and gone without his knowledge. When the wind ceased and ships anchored, to the wharf's edge he would go and, leaning on his sword among the stinking fish, would call to the mariners for their news from France. His other eye he kept landward for word of Henry's war against the Barons.

'Many brought him news – jongleurs, harpers, pedlars, sut-lers, priests, and the like; and, though he was secret enough in small things, yet, if their news misliked him, then, regarding neither time nor place nor people, would he curse our King Henry for a fool or a babe. I have heard him cry aloud by the fishing-boats: "If I were King of England I would do thus and thus"; and when I rode out to see that the warning-beacons were laid and dry, he hath often called to me from the shot-window: "Look to it, Richard, do not copy our blind King, but see with thine own eyes and feel with thine own hands." I do not think he knew any sort of fear. And so we lived at Pevensey, in the little chamber above the Hall.

'One foul night came word that a messenger of the King waited below. We were chilled after a long riding in the fog towards Bexlei, which is an easy place for ships to land. De Aquila sent word the man might either eat with us or wait till we had fed. Anon Jehan, at the stair-head, cried that he had called for horse, and was gone. "Pest on him!" said De Aquila. "I have more to do than to shiver in the Great Hall for every gadling the King sends. Left he no word?"

'"None," said Jehan, "except" – he had been with De Aquila at Santlache – "except he said that if an old dog could not learn new tricks it was time to sweep out the kennel."

'"Oho!" said De Aquila, rubbing his nose, "to whom did he say that?"

'"To his beard, chiefly, but some to his horse's flank as he was girthing up. I followed him out," said Jehan the Crab.

'"What was his shield-mark?"'

'"Gold horseshoes on black," said the Crab.'

'"That is one of Fulke's men," said De Aquila.'

Puck broke in very gently, 'Gold horseshoes on black is *not* the Fulkes' shield. The Fulkes' arms are —'

The knight waved one hand statelily.

'Thou knowest that evil man's true name,' he replied, 'but I have chosen to call him Fulke because I promised him I would not tell the story of his wickedness so that any man might guess it. I have changed *all* the names in my tale. His children's children may be still alive.'

'True — true,' said Puck, smiling softly. 'It is knightly to keep faith — even after a thousand years.'

Sir Richard bowed a little and went on:

'"Gold horseshoes on black?" said De Aquila. "I had heard Fulke had joined the Barons, but if this is true our King must be of the upper hand. No matter, all Fulkes are faithless. Still, I would not have sent the man away empty."

'"He fed," said Jehan. "Gilbert the Clerk fetched him meat and wine from the kitchens. He ate at Gilbert's table."

'This Gilbert was a clerk from Battle Abbey, who kept the accounts of the Manor of Pevensey. He was tall and pale-coloured, and carried those new-fashioned beads for counting of prayers.[4] They were large brown nuts or seeds, and hanging from his girdle with his penner and inkhorn they clashed when he walked. His place was in the great fireplace. There was his table of accounts, and there he lay o' nights. He feared the hounds in the Hall that came nosing after bones or to sleep on the warm ashes, and would slash at them with his beads — like a woman. When De Aquila sat in Hall to do justice, take fines, or grant lands, Gilbert would so write it in the Manor-roll. But it was none of his work to feed our guests, or to let them depart without his lord's knowledge.

'Said De Aquila, after Jehan was gone down the stair: "Hugh, hast thou ever told my Gilbert thou canst read Latin hand-of-write?"

'"No," said Hugh. "He is no friend to me, or to Odo my hound either." "No matter," said De Aquila. "Let him never know thou canst tell one letter from its fellow, and" – here he jerked us in the ribs with his scabbard – "watch him both of ye. There be devils in Africa, as I have heard, but by the Saints there be greater devils in Pevensey!" And that was all he would say.

'It chanced, some small while afterwards, a Norman man-at-arms would wed a Saxon wench of the Manor, and Gilbert (we had watched him well since De Aquila spoke) doubted whether her folk were free or slave. Since De Aquila would give them a field of good land, if she were free, the matter came up at the justice in Great Hall before De Aquila. First the wench's father spoke; then her mother; then all together, till the hall rang and the hounds bayed. De Aquila held up his hands. "Write her free," he called to Gilbert by the fireplace. "A' God's Name write her free, before she deafens me! Yes, yes," he said to the wench that was on her knees at him; "thou art Cerdic's sister, and own cousin to the Lady of Mercia,[5] if thou wilt be silent. In fifty years there will be neither Norman or Saxon, but all English," said he, "and *these* are the men that do our work!" He clapped the man-at-arms, that was Jehan's nephew, on the shoulder, and kissed the wench, and fretted with his feet among the rushes to show it was finished. (The Great Hall is always bitter cold.) I stood at his side; Hugh was behind Gilbert in the fireplace making to play with wise rough Odo. He signed to De Aquila, who bade Gilbert measure the new field for the new couple. Out then runs our Gilbert between man and maid, his beads clashing at his waist, and the Hall being empty, we three sit by the fire.

'Said Hugh, leaning down to the hearth-stones, "I saw this stone move under Gilbert's foot when Odo snuffed at it. Look!" De Aquila digged in the ashes with his sword; the stone tilted; beneath it lay a parchment folden, and the writing atop was: "Words spoken against the King by our Lord of Pevensey – the second part".

'Here was set out (Hugh read it us whispering) every jest De Aquila had made to us touching the King; every time he had called out to me from the shot-window, and every time he had said what he would do if he were King of England.

Yes, day by day had his daily speech, which he never stinted, been set down by Gilbert, tricked out and twisted from its true meaning, yet withal so cunningly that none could deny who knew him that De Aquila had in some sort spoken those words. Ye see?'

Dan and Una nodded.

'Yes,' said Una, gravely. 'It isn't what you say so much. It's what you mean when you say it. Like calling Dan a beast in fun. Only grown-ups don't always understand.'

'"He hath done this day by day before our very face?" said De Aquila.

'"Nay, hour by hour," said Hugh. "When De Aquila spoke even now, in the hall, of Saxons and Normans, I saw Gilbert write on a parchment, which he kept beside the Manor-roll, that De Aquila said soon there would be no Normans left in England if his men-at-arms did their work aright."

'"Bones of the Saints!" said De Aquila. "What avail is honour or a sword against a pen? Where did Gilbert hide that writing? He shall eat it."

'"In his breast when he ran out," said Hugh. "Which made me look to see where he kept his finished stuff. When Odo scratched at this stone here, I saw his face change. So I was sure."

'"He is bold," said De Aquila. "Do him justice. In his own fashion, my Gilbert is bold."

'"Overbold," said Hugh. "Hearken here," and he read: "Upon the Feast of St Agatha, our Lord of Pevensey, lying in his upper chamber, being clothed in his second fur gown reversed with rabbit –"

'"Pest on him! He is not my tire-woman!" said De Aquila, and Hugh and I laughed.

'"Reversed with rabbit, seeing a fog over the marshes, did wake Sir Richard Dalyngridge, his drunken cup-mate" (here they laughed at me) "and said, 'Peer out, old fox, for God is on the Duke of Normandy's side.'"

'"So did I. It was a black fog. Robert could have landed ten thousand men, and we none the wiser. Does he tell how we were out all day riding the marsh, and how I near perished in a

quicksand, and coughed like a sick ewe for ten days after?"
cried De Aquila.

'"No," said Hugh. "But here is the prayer of Gilbert himself
to his master Fulke."

'"Ah," said De Aquila. "Well I knew it was Fulke. What is
the price of my blood?"

'"Gilbert prayeth that when our Lord of Pevensey is stripped
of his lands on this evidence which Gilbert hath, with fear and
pains, collected –"

'"Fear and pains is a true word," said De Aquila, and sucked
in his cheeks. "But how excellent a weapon is a pen! I must
learn it."

'"He prays that Fulke will advance him from his present
service to that honour in the Church which Fulke promised
him. And lest Fulke should forget, he has written below, 'To be
Sacristan of Battle'."

'At this De Aquila whistled. "A man who can plot against
one lord can plot against another. When I am stripped of my
lands Fulke will whip off my Gilbert's foolish head. None the
less Battle needs a new Sacristan. They tell me the Abbot
Henry keeps no sort of rule there."

'"Let the Abbot wait," said Hugh. "It is our heads and our
lands that are in danger. This parchment is the second part of
the tale. The first has gone to Fulke, and so to the King, who
will hold us traitors."

'"Assuredly," said De Aquila. "Fulke's man took the first
part that evening when Gilbert fed him, and our King is so
beset by his brother and his Barons (small blame, too!) that he
is mad with mistrust. Fulke has his ear, and pours poison into
it. Presently the King gives him my land and yours. This is
old," and he leaned back and yawned.

'"And thou wilt surrender Pevensey without word or blow?"
said Hugh. "We Saxons will fight your King then. I will go
warn my nephew at Dallington. Give me a horse!"

'"Give thee a toy and a rattle," said De Aquila. "Put back the
parchment, and rake over the ashes. If Fulke is given my
Pevensey, which is England's gate, what will he do with it? He
is Norman at heart, and his heart is in Normandy, where he can

kill peasants at his pleasure. He will open England's gate to our sleepy Robert, as Odo and Mortain tried to do,[6] and then there will be another landing and another Santlache. Therefore I cannot give up Pevensey."

'"Good," said we two.

'"Ah, but wait! If my King be made, on Gilbert's evidence, to mistrust me, he will send his men against me here, and, while we fight, England's gate is left unguarded. Who will be the first to come through thereby? Even Robert of Normandy. Therefore I cannot fight my King." He nursed his sword – thus.

'"This is saying and unsaying like a Norman," said Hugh. "What of our Manors?"

'"I do not think for myself," said De Aquila, "nor for our King, nor for your lands. I think for England, for whom neither King nor Baron thinks. I am not Norman, Sir Richard, nor Saxon, Sir Hugh. English am I."

'"Saxon, Norman, or English," said Hugh, "our lives are thine, however the game goes. When do we hang Gilbert?"

'"Never," said De Aquila. "Who knows he may yet be Sacristan of Battle, for, to do him justice, he is a good writer. Dead men make dumb witnesses. Wait."

'"But the King may give Pevensey to Fulke. And our Manors go with it," said I. "Shall we tell our sons?"

'"No. The King will not wake up a hornets' nest in the south till he has smoked out the bees in the north. He may hold me a traitor; but at least he sees I am not fighting against him, and every day that I lie still is so much gain to him while he fights the Barons. If he were wise he would wait till that war were over before he made new enemies. But I think Fulke will play upon him to send for me, and if I do not obey the summons that will, to Henry's mind, be proof of my treason. But mere talk, such as Gilbert sends, is no proof nowadays. We Barons follow the Church, and, like Anselm,[7] we speak what we please. Let us go about our day's dealings, and say naught to Gilbert."

'"Then we do nothing?" said Hugh.

'"We wait," said De Aquila. "I am old, but still I find that the most grievous work I know."

'And so we found it, but in the end De Aquila was right.

'A little later in the year, armed men rode over the hill, the Golden Horseshoes flying behind the King's banner. Said De Aquila, at the window of our chamber: "How did I tell you? Here comes Fulke himself to spy out his new lands which our King hath promised him if he can bring proof of my treason."

'"How dost thou know?" said Hugh.

'"Because that is what I would do if I were Fulke, but *I* should have brought more men. My roan horse to your old shoes," said he, "Fulke brings me the King's Summons to leave Pevensey and join the war." He sucked in his cheeks and drummed on the edge of the shaft, where the water sounded all hollow.

'"Shall we go?" said I.

'"Go! At this time of year? Stark madness," said he. "Take *me* from Pevensey to fisk and flyte [8] through fern and forest, and in three days Robert's keels would be lying on Pevensey mud with ten thousand men! Who would stop them – Fulke?"

'The horns blew without, and anon Fulke cried the King's Summons at the great door that De Aquila with all men and horse should join the King's camp at Salisbury.

'"How did I tell you?" said De Aquila. "There are twenty Barons 'twixt here and Salisbury could give King Henry good land service, but he has been worked upon by Fulke to send south and call me – *me*! – off the Gate of England, when his enemies stand about to batter it in. See that Fulke's men lie in the big south barn," said he. "Give them drink, and when Fulke has eaten we will drink in my chamber. The Great Hall is too cold for old bones."

'As soon as he was off-horse Fulke went to the chapel with Gilbert to give thanks for his safe coming, and when he had eaten – he was a fat man, and rolled his eyes greedily at our good roast Sussex wheatears – we led him to the little upper chamber, whither Gilbert had already gone with the Manor-roll. I remember when Fulke heard the tide blow and whistle in the shaft he leaped back, and his long down-turned stirrup-shoes caught in the rushes and he stumbled, so that Jehan behind him found it easy to knock his head against the wall.'

'Did you know it was going to happen?' said Dan.

'Assuredly,' said Sir Richard, with a sweet smile. 'I put my foot on his sword and plucked away his dagger, but he knew not whether it was day or night for awhile. He lay rolling his eyes and bubbling with his mouth, and Jehan roped him like a calf. He was cased all in that new-fangled armour which we call lizard-mail. Not rings like my hauberk [9] here' – Sir Richard tapped his chest – 'but little pieces of dagger-proof steel overlapping on stout leather. We stripped it off (no need to spoil good harness by wetting it), and in the neck-piece De Aquila found the same folden piece of parchment which we had put back under the hearthstone.

'At this Gilbert would have run out. I laid my hand on his shoulder. It sufficed. He fell to trembling and praying on his beads.

'"Gilbert," said De Aquila, "here be more notable sayings and doings of our Lord of Pevensey for thee to write down. Take penner and inkhorn, Gilbert. We cannot all be Sacristans of Battle."

'Said Fulke from the floor, "Ye have bound a King's messenger. Pevensey shall burn for this."

'"Maybe. I have seen it besieged once," said De Aquila, "but heart up, Fulke. I promise thee that thou shalt be hanged in the middle of the flames at the end of that siege, if I have to share my last loaf with thee; and that is more than Odo would have done when we starved out him and Mortain."

'Then Fulke sat up and looked long and cunningly at De Aquila.

'"By the Saints," said he, "why didst thou not say thou wast on the Duke's side at the first?"

'"Am I?" said De Aquila.

'Fulke laughed and said, "No man who serves King Henry dare do this much to his messenger. When didst thou come over to the Duke? Let me up and we can smooth it out together." And he smiled and becked and winked.

'"Yes, we will smooth it out," said De Aquila. He nodded to

me, and Jehan and I heaved up Fulke – he was a heavy man – and lowered him into the shaft by a rope, not so as to stand on our gold, but dangling by his shoulders a little above. It was turn of ebb, and the water came to his knees. He said nothing, but shivered somewhat.

'Then Jehan of a sudden beat down Gilbert's wrist with his sheathed dagger. "Stop!" he said. "He swallows his beads."

'"Poison, belike," said De Aquila. "It is good for men who know too much. I have carried it these thirty years. Give me!"

'Then Gilbert wept and howled. De Aquila ran the beads through his fingers. The last one – I have said they were large nuts – opened in two halves on a pin, and there was a small folded parchment within. On it was written: "*The Old Dog goes to Salisbury to be beaten. I have his Kennel. Come quickly.*"

'"This is worse than poison," said De Aquila, very softly, and sucked in his cheeks. Then Gilbert grovelled in the rushes, and told us all he knew. The letter, as we guessed, was from Fulke to the Duke (and not the first that had passed between them); Fulke had given it to Gilbert in the chapel, and Gilbert thought to have taken it by morning to a certain fishing-boat at the wharf, which trafficked between Pevensey and the French shore. Gilbert was a false fellow, but he found time between his quakings and shakings to swear that the master of the boat knew nothing of the matter.

'"He hath called me shaved head," said Gilbert, "and he hath thrown haddock-guts at me; but for all that, he is no traitor."

'"I will have no clerk of mine mishandled or miscalled," said De Aquila. "That seaman shall be whipped at his own mast. Write me first a letter, and thou shalt bear it, with the order for the whipping, tomorrow to the boat."

'At this Gilbert would have kissed De Aquila's hand – he had not hoped to live until the morning – and when he trembled less he wrote a letter as from Fulke to the Duke, saying that the Kennel, which signified Pevensey, was shut, and that the Old Dog (which was De Aquila) sat outside it, and, moreover, that all had been betrayed.

'"Write to any man that all is betrayed," said De Aquila, "and even the Pope himself would sleep uneasily. Eh, Jehan? If one told thee all was betrayed, what wouldst thou do?"

'"I would run away," said Jehan. "It might be true."

'"Well said," quoth De Aquila. "Write, Gilbert, that Montgomery, the great Earl, hath made his peace with the King, and that little D'Arcy, whom I hate, hath been hanged by the heels. We will give Robert full measure to chew upon. Write also that Fulke himself is sick to death of a dropsy."

'"Nay?" cried Fulke, hanging in the well-shaft. "Drown me out of hand, but do not make a jest of me."

'"Jest? I?" said De Aquila. "I am but fighting for life and lands with a pen, as thou hast shown me, Fulke."

'Then Fulke groaned, for he was cold, and, "Let me confess," said he.

'"Now, this is right neighbourly," said De Aquila, leaning over the shaft. "Thou hast read my sayings and doings – or at least the first part of them – and thou art minded to repay me with thy own doings and sayings. Take penner and inkhorn, Gilbert. Here is work that will not irk thee."

'"Let my men go without hurt, and I will confess my treason against the King," said Fulke.

'"Now, why has he grown so tender of his men of a sudden?" said Hugh to me; for Fulke had no name for mercy to his men. Plunder he gave them, but pity, none.

'"Té! Té!" said Aquila. "Thy treason was all confessed long ago by Gilbert. It would be enough to hang Montgomery himself."

'"Nay; but spare my men," said Fulke; and we heard him splash like a fish in a pond, for the tide was rising.

'"All in good time," said De Aquila. "The night is young; the wine is old; and we need only the merry tale. Begin the story of thy life since when thou wast a lad at Tours.[10] Tell it nimbly!"

'"Ye shame me to my soul," said Fulke.

'"Then I have done what neither King nor Duke could do," said De Aquila. "But begin, and forget nothing."

'"Send thy man away," said Fulke.

'"That much can I do," said De Aquila. 'But, remember, I am like the Danes' King;[11] I cannot turn the tide."

'"How long will it rise?" said Fulke, and splashed anew.

'"For three hours," said De Aquila. "Time to tell all thy good deed.[12] Begin, and Gilbert — I have heard thou art somewhat careless — do not twist his words from their true meaning."

'So — fear of death in the dark being upon him — Fulke began, and Gilbert not knowing what his fate might be, wrote it word by word. I have heard many tales, but never heard I aught to match the tale of Fulke, his black life, as Fulke told it hollowly, hanging in the shaft.'

'Was it bad?' said Dan, awestruck.

'Beyond belief,' Sir Richard answered. 'None the less, there was that in it which forced even Gilbert to laugh. We three laughed till we ached. At one place his teeth so chattered that we could not well hear, and we reached him down a cup of wine. Then he warmed to it, and smoothly set out all his shifts, malices, and treacheries, his extreme boldness (he was desperately bold); his retreats, shufflings, and counterfeitings (he was also inconveniently a coward); his lack of gear and honour; his despair at their loss; his remedies, and well-coloured contrivances. Yes, he waved the filthy rags of his life before us, and though they had been some proud banner. When he ceased, we saw by torches that the tide stood at the corners of his mouth, and he breathed strongly through his nose.

'We had him out, and rubbed him; we wrapped him in a cloak, and gave him wine, and we leaned and looked upon him, the while he drank. He was shivering, but shameless.

'Of a sudden we heard Jehan at the stairway wake, but a boy pushed past him, and stood before us, the hall rushes in his hair, all slubbered with sleep. "My father! My father! I dreamed of treachery," he cried, and babbled thickly.

'"There is no treachery here," said Fulke. "Go," and the boy turned, even then not fully awake, and Jehan led him by the hand to the Great Hall.

'"Thy only son!" said De Aquila. "Why didst thou bring the child here?"

'"He is my heir. I dared not trust him to my brother," said

Fulke, and he was ashamed. De Aquila said nothing, but sat weighing a wine cup in his two hands – thus. Anon, Fulke touched him on the knee.

'"Let the boy escape to Normandy," said he, "and do with me at thy pleasure. Yea, hang me tomorrow, with my letter to Robert round my neck, but let the boy go."

' "Be still," said De Aquila. "I think for England."

'So we waited what our Lord of Pevensey should devise; and the sweat ran down Fulke's forehead.

'At last said De Aquila: "I am too old to judge, or to trust any man. I do not covet thy lands, as thou hast coveted mine; and whether thou art any better or any worse than any other black Angevin[13] thief, it is for thy King to find out. Therefore, go back to thy King, Fulke."

'"And thou wilt say nothing of what has passed?" said Fulke.

' "Why should I? Thy son will stay with me. If the King calls ne again to leave Pevensey, which I must guard against England's enemies; if the King sends his men against me for a traitor; or if I hear that the King in his bed thinks any evil of me or my two knights, thy son will be hanged from out this window, Fulke."'

'But it hadn't anything to do with his son,' cried Una, startled.

'How could we have hanged Fulke?' said Sir Richard. 'We needed him to make our peace with the King. He would have betrayed half England for the boy's sake. Of that we were sure.'

'I don't understand,' said Una. 'But I think it was simply awful.'

'So did not Fulke. He was well pleased.'

'What? Because his son was going to be killed?'

'Nay. Because De Aquila had shown him how he might save the boy's life and his own lands and honours. "I will do it," he said. "I swear I will do it. I will tell the King thou art no traitor, but the most excellent, valiant, and perfect of us all. Yes, I will save thee."

'De Aquila looked still into the bottom of the cup, rolling the wine-dregs to and fro.

'"Ay," he said. "If I had a son, I would, I think, save him.

But do not by any means tell me how thou wilt go about it."

'"Nay, nay," said Fulke, nodding his bald head wisely. "That is my secret. But rest at ease, De Aquila, no hair of thy head nor rood of thy land shall be forfeited," and he smiled like one planning great good deeds.

'"And henceforward," said De Aquila, "I counsel thee to serve one master — not two."

'"What?" said Fulke. "Can I work no more honest trading between the two sides these troublous times?"

'"Serve Robert or the King — England or Normandy," said De Aquila. "I care not which it is, but make thy choice here and now."

'"The King, then," said Fulke, "for I see he is better served than Robert. Shall I swear it?"

'"No need," said De Aquila, and he laid his hand on the parchments which Gilbert had written. "It shall be some part of my Gilbert's penance to copy out the savoury tale of thy life, till we have made ten, twenty, an hundred, maybe, copies. How many cattle, think you, would the Bishop of Tours give for that tale? Or thy brother? Or the Monks of Blois? Minstrels will turn it into songs which thy own Saxon serfs shall sing behind their plough-stilts, and men-at-arms riding through thy Norman towns. From here to Rome, Fulke, men will make very merry over that tale, and how Fulke told it, hanging in a well, like a drowned puppy. This shall be thy punishment, if ever I find thee double-dealing with thy King any more. Meantime, the parchments stay here with thy son. Him I will return to thee when thou hast made my peace with the King. The parchments never."

'Fulke hid his face and groaned.

'"Bones of the Saints!" said De Aquila, laughing. "The pen cuts deep. I could never have fetched that grunt out of thee with any sword."[14]

'"But so long as I do not anger thee, my tale will be secret?" said Fulke.

'"Just so long. Does that comfort thee, Fulke?" said De Aquila.

'"What other comfort have ye left me?" he said, and of a

sudden he wept hopelessly like a child, dropping his face on his knees.'

'Poor Fulke,' said Una.

'I pitied him also,' said Sir Richard.

'"After the spur, corn," said De Aquila, and he threw Fulke three wedges of gold that he had taken from our little chest by the bedplace.

'"If I had known this," said Fulke, catching his breath, "I would never have lifted hand against Pevensey. Only lack of this yellow stuff has made me so unlucky in my dealings."

'It was dawn then, and they stirred in the Great Hall below. We sent down Fulke's mail to be scoured, and when he rode away at noon under his own and the King's banner very splendid and stately did he show. He smoothed his long beard, and called his son to his stirrup and kissed him. De Aquila rode with him as far as the New Mill landward. We thought the night had been all a dream."'

'But did he make it right with the King?' Dan asked. 'About your not being traitors, I mean?'

Sir Richard smiled. 'The King sent no second summons to Pevensey, nor did he ask why De Aquila had not obeyed the first. Yes, that was Fulke's work. I know not how he did it, but it was well and swiftly done.'

'Then you didn't do anything to his son?' said Una.

'The boy? Oh, he was an imp. He turned the keep doors out of dortoirs [15] while we had him. He sang foul songs, learned in the Barons' camps – poor fool; he set the hounds fighting in hall; he lit the rushes to drive out, as he said, the fleas; he drew his dagger on Jehan, who threw him down the stairway for it; and he rode his horse through crops and among sheep. But when we had beaten him, and showed him wolf and deer, he followed us old men like a young, eager hound, and called us "uncle". His father came the summer's end to take him away, but the boy had no lust to go, because of the otter-hunting, and he stayed on till the fox-hunting. I gave him a bittern's claw to bring him good luck at shooting. An imp, if ever there was!'

'And what happened to Gilbert?' said Dan.

'Not even a whipping. De Aquila said he would sooner a

clerk, however false, that knew the Manor-roll than a fool, however true, that must be taught his work afresh. Moreover, after that night I think Gilbert loved as much as he feared De Aquila. At least he would not leave us – not even when Vivian, the King's Clerk, would have made him Sacristan of Battle Abbey. A false fellow, but, in his fashion, bold.'

'Did Robert ever land in Pevensey after all?' Dan went on.

'We guarded the coast too well while Henry was fighting his Barons; and three or four years later, when England had peace, Henry crossed to Normandy and showed his brother some work at Tenchebrai[16] that cured Robert of fighting. Many of Henry's men sailed from Pevensey to that war. Fulke came, I remember, and we all four lay in the little chamber once again, and drank together. De Aquila was right. One should not judge men. Fulke was merry. Yes, always merry – with a catch in his breath.'

'And what did you do afterwards?' said Una.

'We talked together of times past. That is all men can do when they grow old, little maid.'

The bell for tea rang faintly across the meadows. Dan lay in the bows of the *Golden Hind*; Una in the stern, the book of verses open in her lap, was reading from 'The Slave's Dream':[17]

> 'Again in the mist and shadow of sleep
> He saw his native land.'

'I don't know when you began that,' said Dan, sleepily.

On the middle thwart of the boat, beside Una's sun-bonnet, lay an Oak leaf, an Ash leaf, and a Thorn leaf, that must have dropped down from the trees above; and the brook giggled as though it had just seen some joke.

The Runes on Weland's Sword

A Smith makes me
To betray my Man
In my first fight.

To gather Gold
At the world's end
I am sent.

The Gold I gather
Comes into England
Out of deep Water.

Like a shining Fish
Then it descends
Into deep Water.

It is not given
For goods or gear,
But for The Thing.

The Gold I gather
A King covets
For an ill use.

The Gold I gather
Is drawn up
Out of deep Water.

Like a shining Fish
Then it descends
Into deep Water.

It is not given
For goods or gear
But for The Thing.

A Centurion of the Thirtieth

'Cities and Thrones and Powers'

Cities and Thrones and Powers,
  Stand in Time's eye,
Almost as long as flowers,
  Which daily die:
But, as new buds put forth,
  To glad new men,
Out of the spent and unconsidered Earth,
  The Cities rise again.

This season's Daffodil,
  She never hears,
What change, what chance, what chill,
  Cut down last year's:
But with bold countenance,
  And knowledge small,
Esteems her seven days' continuance
  To be perpetual.

So Time that is o'er-kind,
  To all that be,
Ordains us e'en as blind,
  As bold as she:
That in our very death,
  And burial sure,
Shadow to shadow, well-persuaded, saith,
  'See how our works endure!'

A Centurion of the Thirtieth

Dan had come to grief over his Latin, and was kept in; so Una
went alone to Far Wood. Dan's big catapult and the lead bullets
that Hobden had made for him were hidden in an old hollow
beech-stub on the west of the wood. They had named the place
out of the verse in *Lays of Ancient Rome*.[1]

> From lordly Volaterrae,
>   Where scowls the far-famed hold,
> Piled by the hands of giants
>   For Godlike Kings of old.

They were the 'Godlike Kings', and when old Hobden piled
some comfortable brushwood between the big wooden knees of
Volaterrae, they called him 'Hands of Giants'.

Una slipped through their private gap in the fence, and sat
still awhile, scowling as scowlily and lordlily as she knew how;
for 'Volaterrae' is an important watch-tower that juts out of Far
Wood just as Far Wood juts out of the hillside. Pook's Hill lay
below her, and all the turns of the brook as it wanders out of
the Willingford Woods, between hop-gardens, to old Hobden's
cottage at the Forge. The Sou'-West wind (there is always a
wind by Volaterrae) blew from the bare ridge where Cherry
Clack Windmill stands.

Now wind prowling through woods sounds like exciting
things going to happen, and that is why on blowy days you
stand up in Volaterrae and shout bits of the *Lays* to suit its
noises.

Una took Dan's catapult from its secret place, and made
ready to meet Lars Porsena's army stealing through the wind-
whitened aspens by the brook. A gust boomed up the valley,
and Una chanted sorrowfully:

> 'Verbenna down to Ostia
>   Hath wasted all the plain;

Astur hath stormed Janiculum
And the stout guards are slain.'[2]

But the wind, not charging fair to the wood, started aside and shook a single oak in Gleason's pasture. Here it made itself all small and crouched among the grasses, waving the tips of them as a cat waves the tip of her tail before she springs.

'Now welcome – welcome Sextus,' sang Una, loading the catapult –

'Now welcome to thy home,
Why dost thou stay and turn away?
Here lies the road to Rome.'[3]

She fired into the face of the lull, to wake up the cowardly wind, and heard a grunt from behind a thorn in the pasture.

'Oh, my Winkie!' she said aloud, and that was something she had picked up from Dan. 'I b'lieve I've tickled up a Gleason cow.'

'You little painted beast!' a voice cried. 'I'll teach you to sling your masters!'

She looked down most cautiously, and saw a young man covered with hoopy bronze armour all glowing among the late broom. But what Una admired beyond all was his great bronze helmet with a red horse-tail that flicked in the wind. She could hear the long hairs rasp on his shimmery shoulder-plates.

'What does the Faun mean,' he said, half aloud to himself, 'by telling me the Painted People have changed?' He caught sight of Una's yellow head. 'Have you seen a painted lead-slinger?' he called.

'No-o,' said Una. 'But if you've seen a bullet –'

'Seen?' cried the man. 'It passed within a hair's breadth of my ear.'

'Well, that was me. I'm most awfully sorry.'

'Didn't the Faun tell you I was coming?' He smiled.

'Not if you mean Puck. I thought you were a Gleason cow. I – I didn't know you were a – a – What are you?'

He laughed outright, showing a set of splendid teeth. His face and his eyes were dark, and his eyebrows met above his big nose in one bushy black bar.

'They call me Parnesius. I have been a Centurion of the Seventh Cohort of the Thirtieth Legion – the Ulpia Victrix.[4] Did you sling that bullet?'

'I did. I was using Dan's catapult,'[5] said Una.

'Catapults!' said he. 'I ought to know something about them. Show me!'

He leaped the rough fence with a rattle of spear, shield, and armour, and hoisted himself into Volaterrae as quickly as a shadow.

'A sling on a forked stick. *I* understand!' he cried, and pulled at the elastic. 'But what wonderful beast yields this stretching leather?'

'It's laccy – elastic. You put the bullet into that loop, and then you pull hard.'

The man pulled, and hit himself square on his thumb-nail.

'Each to his own weapon,' he said, gravely, handing it back. 'I am better with the bigger machine, little maiden. But it's a pretty toy. A wolf would laugh at it. Aren't you afraid of wolves?'

'There aren't any,' said Una.

'Never believe it! A wolf's like a Winged Hat. He comes when he isn't expected. Don't they hunt wolves here?'

'We don't hunt,' said Una, remembering what she had heard from grown-ups. 'We preserve – pheasants. Do you know them?'

'I ought to,' said the young man, smiling again, and he imitated the cry of the cock-pheasant so perfectly that a bird answered out of the wood.

'What a big painted clucking fool is a pheasant,' he said. 'Just like some Romans!'

'But you're a Roman yourself, aren't you?' said Una.

'Ye-es and no. I'm one of a good few thousands who have never seen Rome except in a picture. My people have lived at Vectis for generations. Vectis. That island West yonder that you can see from so far in clear weather.'

'Do you mean the Isle of Wight? It lifts up just before rain, and you see it from the Downs.'

'Very likely. Our Villa's[6] on the South edge of the Island, by the Broken Cliffs. Most of it is three hundred years old, but

the cow-stables, where our first ancestor lived, must be a
hundred years older. Oh, quite that, because the founder of our
family had his land given him by Agricola at the Settlement.[7]
It's not a bad little place for its size. In spring-time violets grow
down to the very beach. I've gathered sea-weeds for myself and
violets for my Mother many a time with our old nurse.'

'Was your nurse a – a Romaness too?'

'No, a Numidian.[8] Gods be good to her! A dear, fat, brown
thing with a tongue like a cow-bell. She was a free woman. By
the way, are you free, maiden?'

'Oh, quite,' said Una. 'At least, till tea-time; and in summer
our governess doesn't say much if we're late.'

The young man laughed again – a proper understanding
laugh.

'I see,' said he. 'That accounts for your being in the wood.
We hid among the cliffs.'

'Did *you* have a governess, then?'

'Did we not? A Greek, too. She had a way of clutching her
dress when she hunted us among the gorse-bushes that made us
laugh. Then she'd say she'd get us whipped. She never did,
though, bless her! Aglaia was a thorough sportswoman, for all
her learning.'

'But what lessons did you do – when – when you were little?'

'Ancient history, the Classics, arithmetic, and so on,' he
answered. 'My sister and I were thickheads, but my two
brothers (I'm the middle one) liked those things, and, of
course, Mother was clever enough for any six. She was nearly
as tall as I am, and she looked like the new statue on the
Western Road – the Demeter of the Baskets,[9] you know. And
funny! Roma Dea! How Mother could make us laugh!'

'What at?'

'Little jokes and sayings that every family has. Don't you
know?'

'I know *we* have, but I didn't know other people had them
too,' said Una. 'Tell me about all your family, please.'

'Good families are very much alike. Mother would sit
spinning of evenings while Aglaia read in her corner, and
Father did accounts, and we four romped about the passages.

When our noise grew too loud the Pater would say, "Less tumult! Less tumult! Have you never heard of a Father's right over his children? He can slay them, my loves – slay them dead, and the Gods highly approve of the action!" Then Mother would prim up her dear mouth over the wheel and answer: "H'm! I'm afraid there can't be much of the Roman Father about you!" Then the Pater would roll up his accounts, and say, "I'll show you!" and then – then, he'd be worse than any of us!'

'Fathers can – if they like,' said Una, her eyes dancing.

'Didn't I say all good families are very much the same?'

'What did you do in summer?' said Una. 'Play about, like us?'

'Yes, and we visited our friends. There are no wolves in Vectis. We had many friends, and as many ponies as we wished.'

'It must have been lovely,' said Una. 'I hope it lasted for ever.'

'Not quite, little maid. When I was about sixteen or seventeen, the Father felt gouty, and we all went to the Waters.'

'What waters?'

'At Aquae Sulis.[10] Everyone goes there. You ought to get your Father to take you some day.'

'But where? I don't know,' said Una.

The young man looked astonished for a moment. 'Aquae Sulis,' he repeated. 'The best baths in Britain. Just as good, I'm told, as Rome. All the old gluttons sit in hot water, and talk scandal and politics. And the Generals come through the streets with their guards behind them; and the magistrates come in their chairs with their stiff guards behind them; and you meet fortune-tellers, and goldsmiths, and merchants, and philosophers, and feather-sellers, and ultra-Roman Britons, and ultra-British Romans, and tame tribesmen pretending to be civilized, and Jew lecturers, and – oh, everybody interesting. We young people, of course, took no interest in politics. We had not the gout: there were many of our age like us. We did not find life sad.

'But while we were enjoying ourselves without thinking, my sister met the son of a magistrate in the west[11] – and a year afterwards she was married to him. My young brother, who was always interested in plants and roots, met the First Doctor of a Legion from the City of the Legions,[12] and he decided that he would be an Army doctor. I do not think it is a profession for a well-born man, but then – I'm not my brother. He went to Rome to study medicine, and now he's First Doctor of a Legion in Egypt – at Antinoe,[13] I think, but I have not heard from him for some time.

'My eldest brother came across a Greek philosopher, and told my Father that he intended to settle down on the estate as a farmer and a philosopher. You see' – the young man's eyes twinkled – 'his philosopher was a long-haired one!'

'I thought philosophers were bald,' said Una.

'Not all. She was very pretty. I don't blame him. Nothing could have suited me better than my eldest brother's doing this, for I was only too keen to join the Army. I had always feared I should have to stay at home and look after the estate while my brother took *this*.'

He rapped on his great glistening shield that never seemed to be in his way.

'So we were well contented – we young people – and we rode back to Clausentum[14] along the Wood Road very quietly. But when we reached home, Aglaia, our governess, saw what had come to us. I remember her at the door, the torch over her head, watching us climb the cliff-path from the boat. "Aie! Aie!" she said. "Children you went away. Men and a woman you return!" Then she kissed Mother, and Mother wept. Thus our visit to the Waters settled our fates for each of us, Maiden.'

He rose to his feet and listened, leaning on the shield-rim.

'I think that's Dan – my brother,' said Una.

'Yes; and the Faun is with him,' he replied, as Dan with Puck stumbled through the copse.

'We should have come sooner,' Puck called, 'but the beauties of your native tongue, O Parnesius, have enthralled this young citizen.'

Parnesius looked bewildered, even when Una explained.

'Dan said the plural of "dominus" was "dominoes", and

when Miss Blake said it wasn't he said he supposed it was
"backgammon", and so he had to write it out twice – for cheek,
you know.'

Dan had climbed into Volaterrae, hot and panting.

'I've run nearly all the way,' he gasped, 'and then Puck met
me. How do you do, Sir?'

'I am in good health,' Parnesius answered. 'See! I have tried
to bend the bow of Ulysses,[15] but –' He held up his thumb.

'I'm sorry. You must have pulled off too soon,' said Dan.
'But Puck said you were telling Una a story.'

'Continue, O Parnesius,' said Puck, who had perched himself
on a dead branch above them. 'I will be chorus. Has he puzzled
you much, Una?'

'Not a bit, except – I didn't know where Ak – Ak something
was,' she answered.

'Oh, Aquae Sulis. That's Bath, where the buns come from.
Let the hero tell his own tale.'

Parnesius pretended to thrust his spear at Puck's legs, but
Puck reached down, caught at the horse-tail plume, and pulled
off the tall helmet.

'Thanks, jester,' said Parnesius, shaking his curly dark head.
'That is cooler. Now hang it up for me . . .

'I was telling your sister how I joined the Army,' he said to
Dan.

'Did you have to pass an Exam?' Dan asked, eagerly.

'No. I went to my Father, and said I should like to enter the
Dacian Horse (I had seen some at Aquae Sulis); but he said I
had better begin service in a regular Legion from Rome.[16]
Now, like many of our youngsters, I was not too fond of
anything Roman. The Roman-born officers and magistrates
looked down on us British-born as though we were barbarians.
I told my Father so.'

'"I know they do," he said; "but remember, after all, we are
the people of the Old Stock, and our duty is to the Empire."

'"To which Empire?" I asked. "We split the Eagle[17] before
I was born."

'"What thieves' talk is that?" said my Father. He hated
slang.

'"Well, Sir," I said, "we've one Emperor in Rome, and I don't know how many Emperors the outlying Provinces have set up from time to time. Which am I to follow?"

'"Gratian,"[18] said he. "At least he's a sportsman."

'"He's all that," I said. "Hasn't he turned himself into a raw-beef-eating Scythian?"[19]

'"Where did you hear of it?" said the Pater.

'"At Aquae Sulis," I said. It was perfectly true. This precious Emperor Gratian of ours had a bodyguard of fur-cloaked Scythians, and he was so crazy about them that he dressed like them. In Rome of all places in the world! It was as bad as if my own Father had painted himself blue!

'"No matter for the clothes," said the Pater. "They are only the fringe of the trouble. It began before your time or mine. Rome has forsaken her Gods, and must be punished. The great war with the Painted People broke out in the very year the temples of our Gods were destroyed.[20] We beat the Painted People in the very year our temples were rebuilt. Go back further still . . ." He went back to the time of Diocletian;[21] and to listen to him you would have thought Eternal Rome herself was on the edge of destruction, just because a few people had become a little large-minded.

'*I* knew nothing about it. Aglaia never taught us the history of our own country. She was so full of her ancient Greeks.

'"There is no hope for Rome," said the Pater, at last. "She has forsaken her Gods, but if the Gods forgive *us* here, we may save Britain. To do that, we must keep the Painted People back. Therefore, I tell you, Parnesius, as a Father, that if your heart is set on service, your place is among men on the Wall – and not with women among the cities."'

'What Wall?' asked Dan and Una at once.

'Father meant the one we call Hadrian's Wall.[22] I'll tell you about it later. It was built long ago, across North Britain, to keep out the Painted People – Picts you call them. Father had fought in the great Pict War that lasted more than twenty years, and he knew what fighting meant. Theodosius,[23] one of our great Generals, had chased the little beasts back far into the North before I was born: down at Vectis of course we never troubled our heads about them. But when my Father spoke as he did, I kissed his hand, and waited for orders. We British-born Romans know what is due to our parents.'

'If I kissed my Father's hand, he'd laugh,' said Dan.

'Customs change; but if you do not obey your father, the Gods remember it. You may be quite sure of *that*.

'After our talk, seeing I was in earnest, the Pater sent me over to Clausentum to learn my foot-drill in a barrack full of foreign auxiliaries – as unwashed and unshaved a mob of mixed barbarians as ever scrubbed a breastplate. It was your stick in their stomachs and your shield in their faces to push them into any sort of formation. When I had learned my work the Instructor gave me a handful – and they were a handful! – of Gauls and Iberians to polish up till they were sent to their stations up-country. I did my best, and one night a villa in the suburbs caught fire, and I had my handful out and at work before any of the other troops. I noticed a quiet-looking man on the lawn, leaning on a stick. He watched us passing buckets from the pond, and at last he said to me: "Who are you?"

'"A probationer, waiting for a command," I answered. *I* didn't know who he was from Deucalion![24]

'"Born in Britain?" he said.

'"Yes, if you were born in Spain," I said, for he neighed his words like an Iberian mule.

'"And what might you call yourself when you are at home?" he said, laughing.

'"That depends," I answered; "sometimes one thing and sometimes another. But now I'm busy."

'He said no more till we had saved the family gods (they were respectable householders), and then he grunted across the laurels: "Listen, young sometimes-one-thing-and-sometimes-another. In future call yourself Centurion of the Seventh Cohort of the Thirtieth, the Ulpia Victrix. That will help me to remember you. Your Father and a few other people call me Maximus."

'He tossed me the polished stick he was leaning on, and went away. You might have knocked me down with it!'

'Who was he?' said Dan.

'Maximus himself, our great General![25] *The* General of Britain who had been Theodosius's right hand in the Pict War! Not only had he given me my Centurion's stick direct, but three steps in a good Legion as well! A new man generally begins in the Tenth Cohort of his Legion, and works up.'

'And were you pleased?' said Una.

'Very. I thought Maximus had chosen me for my good looks and fine style in marching, but, when I went home, the Pater told me he had served under Maximus in the great Pict War, and had asked him to befriend me.'

'A child you were!' said Puck, from above.

'I was,' said Parnesius. 'Don't begrudge it me, Faun. Afterwards – the Gods know I put aside the games!' And Puck nodded, brown chin on brown hand, his big eyes still.

'The night before I left we sacrificed to our ancestors – the usual little Home Sacrifice – but I never prayed so earnestly to all the Good Shades, and then I went with my Father by boat to Regnum, and across the chalk eastwards to Anderida yonder.'

'Regnum? Anderida?' The children turned their faces to Puck.

'Regnum's Chichester,' he said, pointing towards Cherry Clack, and – he threw his arm South behind him – 'Anderida's Pevensey.'

'Pevensey again!' said Dan. 'Where Weland landed?'

'Weland and a few others,' said Puck. 'Pevensey isn't young – even compared to me!'

'The headquarters of the Thirtieth lay at Anderida in summer, but my own Cohort, the Seventh, was on the Wall up North. Maximus was inspecting Auxiliaries – the Abulci,[26] I think – at Anderida, and we stayed with him, for he and my Father were very old friends. I was only there ten days when I was ordered to go up with thirty men to my Cohort.' He laughed merrily. 'A man never forgets his first march. I was happier than any Emperor when I led my handful through the North Gate of the Camp, and we saluted the guard and the Altar of Victory there.'

'How? How?' said Dan and Una.

Parnesius smiled, and stood up, flashing in his armour.

'So!' said he; and he moved slowly through the beautiful movements of the Roman Salute, that ends with a hollow clang of the shield coming into its place between the shoulders.

'Hai!' said Puck. 'That sets one thinking!'

'We went out fully armed,' said Parnesius, sitting down; 'but as soon as the road entered the Great Forest, my men expected the pack-horses to hang their shields on. "No!" I said; "you can dress like women in Anderida, but while you're with me you will carry your own weapons and armour."

'"But it's hot," said one of them, "and we haven't a doctor. Suppose we get sunstroke, or a fever?"

'"Then die," I said, "and a good riddance to Rome! Up shield – up spears, and tighten your foot-wear!"

'"Don't think yourself Emperor of Britain already," a fellow shouted. I knocked him over with the butt of my spear, and explained to these Roman-born Romans that, if there were any further trouble, we should go on with one man short. And, by the Light of the Sun, I meant it too! My raw Gauls at Clausentum had never treated me so.

'Then, quietly as a cloud, Maximus rode out of the fern (my Father behind him), and reined up across the road. He wore the Purple,[27] as though he were already Emperor; his leggings were of white buckskin laced with gold.

'My men dropped like – like partridges.

'He said nothing for some time, only looked, with his eyes puckered. Then he crooked his forefinger, and my men walked – crawled, I mean – to one side.

'"Stand in the sun, children," he said, and they formed up on the hard road.

'"What would you have done?" he said to me, "if I had not been here?"

'"I should have killed that man," I answered.

'"Kill him now," he said. "He will not move a limb."

'"No," I said. "You've taken my men out of my command. I should only be your butcher if I killed him now." Do you see what I meant?' Parnesius turned to Dan.

'Yes,' said Dan. 'It wouldn't have been fair, somehow.'

'That was what I thought,' said Parnesius. 'But Maximus frowned. "You'll never be an Emperor," he said. "Not even a General will you be."

'I was silent, but my Father seemed pleased.

'"I came here to see the last of you," he said.

'"You have seen it," said Maximus. "I shall never need your son any more. He will live and he will die an officer of a Legion – and he might have been Prefect of one of my Provinces. Now eat and drink with us," he said. "Your men will wait till you have finished."

'My miserable thirty stood like wine-skins glistening in the hot sun, and Maximus led us to where his people had set a meal. Himself he mixed the wine.

'"A year from now," he said, "you will remember that you have sat with the Emperor of Britain – and Gaul."

'"Yes," said the Pater, "you can drive two mules – Gaul and Britain."

'"Five years hence you will remember that you have drunk," – he passed me the cup and there was blue borage in it – "with the Emperor of Rome!"

'"No; you can't drive three mules; they will tear you in pieces," said my Father.

'"And you on the Wall, among the heather, will weep because your notion of justice was more to you than the favour of the Emperor of Rome."

'I sat quite still. One does not answer a General who wears the Purple.

'"I am not angry with you," he went on; "I owe too much to your Father –"

'"You owe me nothing but advice that you never took," said the Pater.

'"– to be unjust to any of your family. Indeed, I say you may make a good Tribune,[28] but, so far as I am concerned, on the Wall you will live, and on the Wall you will die," said Maximus.

'"Very like," said my Father. "But we shall have the Picts *and* their friends breaking through before long. You cannot move all troops out of Britain to make you Emperor, and expect the North to sit quiet."

'"I follow my destiny," said Maximus.

'"Follow it, then," said my Father, pulling up a fern root; "and die as Theodosius died."[29]

'"Ah!" said Maximus. "My old General was killed because he served the Empire too well. *I* may be killed, but not for that reason," and he smiled a little grey smile that made my blood run cold.

'"Then I had better follow my destiny," I said, "and take my men to the Wall."

'He looked at me a long time, and bowed his head slanting like a Spaniard. "Follow it, boy," he said. That was all. I was only too glad to get away, though I had many messages for home. I found my men standing as they had been put – they had not even shifted their feet in the dust, and off I marched, still feeling that terrific smile like an east wind up my back. I never halted them till sunset, and' – he turned about and looked at Pook's Hill below him – 'then I halted yonder.' He pointed to the broken, bracken-covered shoulder of the Forge Hill behind old Hobden's cottage.

'There? Why, that's only the old Forge – where they made iron once,' said Dan.

'Very good stuff it was too,' said Parnesius, calmly. 'We mended three shoulder-straps here and had a spear-head riveted. The forge was rented from the Government by a one-eyed smith from Carthage. I remember we called him Cyclops.[30] He sold me a beaver-skin rug for my sister's room.'

'But it couldn't have been here,' Dan insisted.

'But it was! From the Altar of Victory at Anderida to the First Forge in the Forest here is twelve miles seven hundred paces. It is all in the Road Book.[31] A man doesn't forget his first march. I think I could tell you every station between this and –' He leaned forward, but his eye was caught by the setting sun.

It had come down to the top of Cherry Clack Hill, and the light poured in between the tree trunks so that you could see red and gold and black deep into the heart of Far Wood;

and Parnesius in his armour shone as though he had been afire.

'Wait,' he said, lifting a hand, and the sunlight jinked on his glass bracelet. 'Wait! I pray to Mithras!' [32]

He rose and stretched his arms westward, with deep, splendid-sounding words.

Then Puck began to sing too, in a voice like bells tolling, and as he sang he slipped from Volaterrae to the ground, and beckoned the children to follow. They obeyed; it seemed as though the voices were pushing them along; and through the goldy-brown light on the beech leaves they walked, while Puck between them chanted something like this:

'Cur mundus militat sub vana gloria
Cujus prosperitas est transitoria?
Tam cito labitur ejus potentia
Quam vasa figuli quae sunt fragilia.'

They found themselves at the little locked gates of the wood.

'Quo Caesar abiit celsus imperio?
Vel Dives splendidus totus in prandio?
Dic ubi Tullius –' [33]

Still singing, he took Dan's hand and wheeled him round to face Una as she came out of the gate. It shut behind her, at the same time as Puck threw the memory-magicking Oak, Ash, and Thorn leaves over their heads.

'Well you *are* jolly late,' said Una. 'Couldn't you get away before?'

'I did,' said Dan. 'I got away in lots of time, but – but I didn't know it was so late. Where've you been?'

'In Volaterrae – waiting for you.'

'Sorry,' said Dan. 'It was all that beastly Latin.'

A British-Roman Song
(A.D. 406) [1]

My father's father saw it not,
   And I, belike, shall never come,
To look on that so-holy spot –
               The very Rome –

Crowned by all Time, all Art, all Might,
   The equal work of Gods and Man,
City beneath whose oldest height –
               The Race began!

Soon to send forth again a brood,
   Unshakeable, we pray, that clings,
To Rome's thrice-hammered hardihood –
               In arduous things.

Strong heart with triple armour bound,
   Beat strongly, for thy life-blood runs,
Age after Age, the Empire round –
               In us thy Sons,

Who, distant from the Seven Hills,
   Loving and serving much, require
Thee – thee to guard 'gainst home-born ills,
               The Imperial Fire!

⊰ On the Great Wall ⊱

'When I left Rome for Lalage's sake
  By the Legions' Road to Rimini,
She vowed her heart was mine to take
  With me and my shield to Rimini –
  (Till the Eagles flew from Rimini!)
      And I've tramped Britain and I've tramped Gaul
      And the Pontic shore where the snow-flakes fall
  As white as the neck of Lalage –
  As cold as the heart of Lalage!
      And I've lost Britain and I've lost Gaul,'

(the voice seemed very cheerful about it),

      'And I've lost Rome, and worst of all,
        I've lost Lalage!' [1]

They were standing by the gate to Far Wood when they heard
this song. Without a word they hurried to their private gap and
wriggled through the hedge almost atop of a jay that was feeding
from Puck's hand.

'Gently!' said Puck. 'What are you looking for?'

'Parnesius, of course,' Dan answered. 'We've only just remembered yesterday. It isn't fair.'

Puck chuckled as he rose. 'I'm sorry, but children who spend
the afternoon with me and a Roman Centurion need a little
settling dose of Magic before they go to tea with their governess.
Ohé, Parnesius!' he called.

'Here, Faun!' came the answer from Volaterrae. They could
see the shimmer of bronze armour in the beech crotch, and the
friendly flash of the great shield uplifted.

'I have driven out the Britons.' Parnesius laughed like a boy.
'I occupy their high forts. But Rome is merciful! You may
come up.' And up the three all scrambled.

'What was the song you were singing just now?' said Una, as
soon as she had settled herself.

'That? Oh, *Rimini*. It's one of the tunes that are always being born somewhere in the Empire. They run like a pestilence for six months or a year, till another one pleases the Legions, and then they march to *that*.'

'Tell them about the marching, Parnesius. Few people nowadays walk from end to end of this country,' said Puck.

'The greater their loss. I know nothing better than the Long March when your feet are hardened. You begin after the mists have risen, and you end, perhaps, an hour after sundown.'

'And what do you have to eat?' Dan asked, promptly.

'Fat bacon, beans, and bread, and whatever wine happens to be in the rest-houses. But soldiers are born grumblers. Their very first day out, my men complained of our water-ground British corn. They said it wasn't so filling as the rough stuff that is ground in the Roman ox-mills. However, they had to fetch and eat it.'

'Fetch it? Where from?' said Una.

'From that newly-invented water-mill below the Forge.'

'That's Forge Mill – *our* Mill!' Una looked at Puck.

'Yes; yours,' Puck put in. 'How old did you think it was?'

'I don't know. Didn't Sir Richard Dalyngridge talk about it?'

'He did, and it was old in his day,' Puck answered. 'Hundreds of years old.'

'It was new in mine,' said Parnesius. 'My men looked at the flour in their helmets as though it had been a nest of adders. They did it to try my patience. But I – addressed them, and we became friends. To tell the truth, they taught me the Roman Step. You see, I'd only served with quick-marching Auxiliaries. A Legion's pace is altogether different. It is a long, slow stride, that never varies from sunrise to sunset. "Rome's Race – Rome's Pace", as the proverb says. Twenty-four miles in eight hours, neither more nor less. Head and spear up, shield on your back, cuirass-collar open one hand's breadth – and that's how you take the Eagles [2] through Britain.'

'And did you meet any adventures?' said Dan.

'There are no adventures South the Wall,' said Parnesius. 'The worst thing that happened me was having to appear before a magistrate up North,[3] where a wandering philosopher had jeered at the Eagles. I was able to show that the old man had deliberately blocked our road; and the magistrate told him, out of his own Book, I believe, that, whatever his Gods might be, he should pay proper respect to Caesar.'[4]

'What did you do?' said Dan.

'Went on. Why should *I* care for such things, my business being to reach my station? It took me twenty days.

'Of course, the farther North you go the emptier are the roads. At last you fetch clear of the forests and climb bare hills, where wolves howl in the ruins of our cities that have been. No more pretty girls; no more jolly magistrates who knew your Father when he was young, and invite you to stay with them; no news at the temples and way-stations except bad news of wild beasts. There's where you meet hunters, and trappers for the Circuses, prodding along chained bears and muzzled wolves. Your pony shies at them, and your men laugh.

'The houses change from gardened villas to shut forts with watch-towers of grey stone, and great stone-walled sheepfolds, guarded by armed Britons of the North Shore. In the naked hills beyond the naked houses, where the shadows of the clouds play like cavalry charging, you see puffs of black smoke from the mines. The hard road goes on and on – and the wind sings through your helmet-plume – past altars to Legions and Generals forgotten, and broken statues of Gods and Heroes, and thousands of graves where the mountain foxes and hares peep at you. Red-hot in summer, freezing in winter, is that big, purple heather country of broken stone.

'Just when you think you are at the world's end, you see a smoke from East to West as far as the eye can turn, and then, under it, also as far as the eye can stretch, houses and temples, shops and theatres, barracks and granaries, trickling along like dice behind – always behind – one long, low, rising and falling, and hiding and showing line of towers. And that is the Wall!'

'Ah!' said the children, taking breath.

'You may well,' said Parnesius. 'Old men who have followed the Eagles since boyhood say nothing in the Empire is more wonderful than first sight of the Wall!'

'Is it just *a* Wall? Like the one round the kitchen-garden?' said Dan.

'No, no! It is *the* Wall. Along the top are towers with guard-houses, small towers, between. Even on the narrowest part of it three men with shields can walk abreast, from guard-house to guard-house. A little curtain wall, no higher than a man's neck, runs along the top of the thick wall, so that from a distance you see the helmets of the sentries sliding back and forth like beads. Thirty feet high is the Wall,[5] and on the Picts' side, the North, is a ditch, strewn with blades of old swords and spear-heads set in wood, and tyres of wheels joined by chains. The Little People come there to steal iron for their arrow-heads.

'But the Wall itself is not more wonderful than the town behind it. Long ago there were great ramparts and ditches on the South side, and no one was allowed to build there. Now the ramparts are partly pulled down and built over, from end to end of the Wall; making a thin town eighty miles long. Think of it! One roaring, rioting, cock-fighting, wolf-baiting, horse-racing town, from Ituna on the West to Segedunum[6] on the cold eastern beach! On one side heather, woods and ruins where Picts hide, and on the other, a vast town – long like a snake, and wicked like a snake. Yes, a snake basking beside a warm wall!

'My Cohort, I was told, lay at Hunno, where the Great North Road runs through the Wall into the Province of Valentia.'[7] Parnesius laughed scornfully. 'The Province of Valentia! We followed the road, therefore, into Hunno town, and stood astonished. The place was a fair – a fair of peoples from every corner of the Empire. Some were racing horses: some sat in wine-shops: some watched dogs baiting bears, and many gathered in a ditch to see cocks fight. A boy not much older than myself, but I could see he was an officer, reined up before me and asked what I wanted.

'"My station," I said, and showed him my shield.' Parnesius held up his broad shield with its three X's like letters on a beer-cask.

'"Lucky omen!" said he. "Your Cohort's the next tower to us, but they're all at the cock-fight. This is a happy place. Come and wet the Eagles." He meant to offer me a drink.

'"When I've handed over my men," I said. I felt angry and ashamed.

'"Oh, you'll soon outgrow that sort of nonsense," he answered. "But don't let me interfere with your hopes. Go on to the Statue of Roma Dea.[8] You can't miss it. The main road into Valentia!" and he laughed and rode off. I could see the statue not a quarter of a mile away, and there I went. At some time or other the Great North Road ran under it into Valentia; but the far end had been blocked up because of the Picts, and on the plaster a man had scratched, "Finish!" It was like marching into a cave. We grounded spears together, my little thirty, and it echoed in the barrel of the arch, but none came. There was a door at one side painted with our number. We prowled in, and I found a cook asleep, and ordered him to give us food. Then I climbed to the top of the Wall, and looked out over the Pict country, and I – thought,' said Parnesius. 'The bricked-up arch with "Finish!" on the plaster was what shook me, for I was not much more than a boy.'

'What a shame!' said Una. 'But did you feel happy after you'd had a good – ' Dan stopped her with a nudge.

'Happy?' said Parnesius. 'When the men of the Cohort I was to command came back unhelmeted from the cock-fight, their birds under their arms, and asked me who I was? No, I was not happy; but I made my new Cohort unhappy too . . . I wrote my Mother I was happy, but, oh, my friends' – he stretched arms over bare knees – 'I would not wish my worst enemy to suffer as I suffered through my first months on the Wall. Remember this: among the officers was scarcely one, except myself (and I thought I had lost the favour of Maximus, my General), scarcely one who had not done something of wrong or folly. Either he had killed a man, or taken money, or insulted the magistrates, or blasphemed the Gods, and so had been sent to the Wall as a hiding-place from shame or fear. And the men were as the officers. Remember, also, that the Wall was manned by every breed and race in the Empire. No two towers spoke the same tongue, or worshipped the same Gods. In one thing only we were all equal. No matter what arms we had used before we came to the Wall, *on* the Wall we were all archers, like the Scythians. The Pict cannot run away from the arrow, or crawl under it. He is a bowman himself. *He* knows!'

'I suppose you were fighting Picts all the time,' said Dan.

'Picts seldom fight. I never saw a fighting Pict for half a year. The tame Picts told us they had all gone North.'

'What is a tame Pict?' said Dan.

'A Pict – there were many such – who speaks a few words of our tongue, and slips across the Wall to sell ponies and wolf-hounds. Without a horse and a dog, *and* a friend, man would perish. The Gods gave me all three, and there is no gift like friendship. Remember this' – Parnesius turned to Dan – 'when you become a young man. For your fate will turn on the first true friend you make.'

'He means,' said Puck, grinning, 'that if you try to make yourself a decent chap when you're young, you'll make rather decent friends when you grow up. If you're a beast, you'll have beastly friends. Listen to the Pious Parnesius on Friendship!'

'I am not pious,' Parnesius answered, 'but I know what goodness means; and my friend, though he was without hope, was ten thousand times better than I. Stop laughing, Faun!'

'Oh Youth Eternal and All-believing,' cried Puck, as he rocked on the branch above. 'Tell them about your Pertinax.'

'He was that friend the Gods sent me – the boy who spoke to me when I first came. Little older than myself, commanding the Augusta Victoria Cohort on the tower next to us and the Numidians. In virtue he was far my superior.'

'Then why was he on the Wall?' Una asked, quickly. 'They'd all done something bad. You said so yourself.'

'He was the nephew, his Father had died, of a great rich man in Gaul who was not always kind to his Mother. When Pertinax grew up, he discovered this, and so his uncle shipped him off, by trickery and force, to the Wall. We came to know each other at a ceremony in our Temple – in the dark. It was the Bull Killing,'[9] Parnesius explained to Puck.

'*I* see,' said Puck, and turned to the children. 'That's something you wouldn't quite understand. Parnesius means he met Pertinax in church.'

'Yes – in the Cave we first met, and we were both raised to

the Degree of Gryphons[10] together.' Parnesius lifted his hand towards his neck for an instant. 'He had been on the Wall two years, and knew the Picts well. He taught me first how to take Heather.'

'What's that?' said Dan.

'Going out hunting in the Pict country with a tame Pict. You are quite safe so long as you are his guest, and wear a sprig of heather where it can be seen. If you went alone you would surely be killed, if you were not smothered first in the bogs. Only the Picts know their way about those black and hidden bogs. Old Allo, the one-eyed, withered little Pict from whom we bought our ponies, was our special friend. At first we went only to escape from the terrible town, and to talk together about our homes. Then he showed us how to hunt wolves and those great red deer with horns like Jewish candlesticks. The Roman-born officers rather looked down on us for doing this, but we preferred the heather to their amusements. Believe me,' Parnesius turned again to Dan, 'a boy is safe from all things that really harm when he is astride a pony or after a deer. Do you remember, O Faun,' he turned to Puck, 'the little altar I built to the Sylvan Pan[11] by the pine-forest beyond the brook?'

'Which? The stone one with the line from Xenophon?'[12] said Puck, in quite a new voice.

'No. What do *I* know of Xenophon? That was Pertinax – after he had shot his first mountain-hare with an arrow – by chance! Mine I made of round pebbles in memory of my first bear. It took me one happy day to build.' Parnesius faced the children quickly.

'And that was how we lived on the Wall for two years – a little scuffling with the Picts, and a great deal of hunting with old Allo in the Pict country. He called us his children sometimes, and we were fond of him and his barbarians, though we never let them paint us Pict fashion. The marks endure till you die.'

'How's it done?' said Dan. 'Anything like tattooing?'

'They prick the skin till the blood runs, and rub in coloured juices. Allo was painted blue, green, and red from his forehead to his ankles. He said it was part of his religion. He told us about his religion (Pertinax was always interested in such things), and as we came to know him well, he told us what was happening in Britain behind the Wall. Many things took place behind us in those days. And by the Light of the Sun,' said Parnesius, earnestly, 'there was not much that those little people did not know! He told me when Maximus crossed over to Gaul, after he had made himself Emperor of Britain, and what troops and emigrants he had taken with him. We did not get the news on the Wall till fifteen days later. He told me what troops Maximus was taking out of Britain every month to help him to conquer Gaul; and I always found the numbers as he said. Wonderful! And I tell another strange thing!'

He jointed his hands across his knees, and leaned his head on the curve of the shield behind him.

'Late in the summer, when the first frosts begin and the Picts kill their bees, we three rode out after wolf with some new hounds. Rutilianus, our General, had given us ten days' leave, and we had pushed beyond the Second Wall[13] – beyond the Province of Valentia – into the higher hills, where there are not even any of Rome's old ruins. We killed a she-wolf before noon, and while Allo was skinning her he looked up and said to me, "When you are Captain of the Wall, my child, you won't be able to do this any more!"

'I might as well have been made Prefect of Lower Gaul, so I laughed and said, "Wait till I am Captain." "No, don't wait," said Allo. "Take my advice and go home – both of you." "We have no homes," said Pertinax. "You know that as well as we do. We're finished men – thumbs down against both of us. Only men without hope would risk their necks on your ponies." The old man laughed one of those short Pict laughs – like a fox barking on a frosty night. "I'm fond of you two," he said. "Besides, I've taught you what little you know about hunting. Take my advice and go home."

'"We can't," I said. "I'm out of favour with my General, for one thing; and for another, Pertinax has an uncle."

'"I don't know about his uncle," said Allo, "but the trouble with you, Parnesius, is that your General thinks well of you."

'"Roma Dea!" said Pertinax, sitting up. "What can you guess what Maximus thinks, you old horse-coper?"

'Just then (you know how near the brutes creep when one is eating?) a great dog-wolf jumped out behind us, and away our rested hounds tore after him, with us at their tails. He ran us far out of any country we'd ever heard of, straight as an arrow till sunset, towards the sunset. We came at last to long capes stretching into winding waters, and on a grey beach below us we saw ships drawn up. Forty-seven we counted – not Roman galleys but the raven-winged ships from the North where Rome does not rule.[14] Men moved in the ships, and the sun flashed on their helmets – winged helmets of the red-haired men from the North where Rome does not rule. We watched, and we counted, and we wondered, for though we had heard rumours concerning these Winged Hats, as the Picts called them, never before had we looked upon them.

'"Come away! come away!" said Allo. "My Heather won't protect you here. We shall all be killed!" His legs trembled like his voice. Back we went – back across the heather under the moon, till it was nearly morning, and our poor beasts stumbled on some ruins.

'When we woke, very stiff and cold, Allo was mixing the meal and water. One does not light fires in the Pict country except near a village. The little men are always signalling to each other with smokes, and a strange smoke brings them out buzzing like bees. They can sting, too!

'"What we saw last night was a trading-station," said Allo. "Nothing but a trading-station."

'"I do not like lies on an empty stomach," said Pertinax. "I suppose" (he had eyes like an eagle's) – "I suppose *that* is a trading-station also?" He pointed to a smoke far off on a hill-top, ascending in what we call the Picts' Call: Puff – double-puff: double-puff – puff! They make it by raising and dropping a wet hide on a fire.

'"No," said Allo, pushing the platter back into the bag. "That is for you and me. Your fate is fixed.[15] Come."

'We came. When one takes Heather, one must obey one's Pict – but that wretched smoke was twenty miles distant, well over on the east coast, and the day was as hot as a bath.

'"Whatever happens," said Allo, while our ponies grunted along, "I want you to remember me."

'"I shall not forget," said Pertinax. "You have cheated me out of my breakfast."

'"What is a handful of crushed oats to a Roman?" he said. Then he laughed his laugh that was not a laugh. "What would *you* do if *you* were a handful of oats being crushed between the upper and lower stones of a mill?"

'"I'm Pertinax, not a riddle-guesser," said Pertinax.

'"You're a fool," said Allo. "Your Gods and my Gods are threatened by strange Gods,[16] and all you can do is to laugh."

'"Threatened men live long," I said.

'"I pray the Gods that may be true," he said. "But I ask you again not to forget me."

'We climbed the last hot hill and looked out on the eastern sea, three or four miles off. There was a small sailing-galley of the North Gaul pattern at anchor, her landing-plank down and her sail half up; and below us, alone in a hollow holding his pony, sat Maximus, Emperor of Britain! He was dressed like a hunter, and he leaned on his little stick; but I knew that back as far as I could see it, and I told Pertinax.

'"You're madder than Allo!" he said. "It must be the sun!"

'Maximus never stirred till we stood before him. Then he looked me up and down, and said: "Hungry again? It seems to be my destiny to feed you whenever we meet. I have food here. Allo shall cook it."

'"No," said Allo. "A Prince in his own land does not wait on wandering Emperors. I feed my two children without asking your leave." He began to blow up the ashes.

'"I was wrong," said Pertinax. "We are all mad. Speak up, O Madman called Emperor!"

'Maximus smiled his terrible tight-lipped smile, but two years on the Wall do not make a man afraid of mere looks. So I was not afraid.

'"I meant you, Parnesius, to live and die a Centurion of the Wall," said Maximus. "But it seems from these," he fumbled in his breast, "you can think as well as draw." He pulled out a roll of letters I had written to my people, full of drawings of

Picts, and bears, and men I had met on the Wall. Mother and my sister always liked my pictures.

'He handed me one that I had called "Maximus's Soldiers". It showed a row of fat wine-skins, and our old Doctor of the Hunno hospital snuffing at them. Each time that Maximus had taken troops out of Britain to help him to conquer Gaul, he used to send the garrisons more wine – to keep them quiet, I suppose. On the Wall, we always called a wine-skin a "Maximus". Oh, yes; and I had drawn them in Imperial helmets.

'"Not long since," he went on, "men's names were sent up to Caesar for smaller jokes than this."

'"True, Caesar," said Pertinax; "but you forget that was before I, your friend's friend, became such a good spear-thrower."

'He did not actually point his hunting spear at Maximus, but balanced it on his palm – so!

'"I was speaking of time past," said Maximus, never fluttering an eyelid. "Nowadays one is only too pleased to find boys who can think for themselves, *and* their friends." He nodded at Pertinax. "Your Father lent me the letters, Parnesius, so you run no risk from me."

'"None whatever," said Pertinax, and rubbed the spear-point on his sleeve.

'"I have been forced to reduce the garrisons in Britain, because I need troops in Gaul. Now I come to take troops from the Wall itself," said he.

'"I wish you joy of us," said Pertinax. "We're the last sweepings of the Empire – the men without hope. Myself, I'd sooner trust condemned criminals."

'"You think so?" he said, quite seriously. "But it will only be till I win Gaul. One must always risk one's life, or one's soul, or one's peace – or some little thing."

'Allo passed round the fire with the sizzling deer's meat. He served us two first.

'"Ah!" said Maximus, waiting his turn. "I perceive you are in your own country. Well, you deserve it. They tell me you have quite a following among the Picts, Parnesius."

'"I have hunted with them," I said. "Maybe I have a few friends among the Heather."

'"He is the only armoured man of you all who understands us," said Allo, and he began a long speech about our virtues, and how we had saved one of his grandchildren from a wolf the year before.'

'Had you?' said Una.

'Yes; but that was neither here nor there. The little green man orated like a – like Cicero.[17] He made us out to be magnificent fellows. Maximus never took his eyes off our faces.

'"Enough," he said. "I have heard Allo on you. I wish to hear you on the Picts."

'I told him as much as I knew, and Pertinax helped me out. There is never harm in a Pict if you but take the trouble to find out what he wants. Their real grievance against us came from our burning their heather. The whole garrison of the Wall moved out twice a year, and solemnly burned the heather for ten miles North. Rutilianus, our General, called it clearing the country. The Picts, of course, scampered away, and all we did was to destroy their bee-bloom in the summer, and ruin their sheep-food in the spring.

'"True, quite true," said Allo. "How can we make our holy heather-wine, if you burn our bee-pasture?"

'We talked long, Maximus asking keen questions that showed he knew much and had thought more about the Picts. He said presently to me: "If I gave you the old Province of Valentia to govern, could you keep the Picts contented till I won Gaul? Stand away, so that you do not see Allo's face; and speak your own thoughts."

'"No," I said. "You cannot remake that Province. The Picts have been free too long."

'"Leave them their village councils, and let them furnish their own soldiers," he said. "You, I am sure, would hold the reins very lightly."

'"Even then, no," I said. "At least not now. They have been too oppressed by us to trust anything with a Roman name for years and years."

'I heard old Allo behind me mutter: "Good child!"

'"Then what do you recommend," said Maximus, "to keep the North quiet till I win Gaul?"

'"Leave the Picts alone," I said. "Stop the heather-burning at once, and – they are improvident little animals – send them a shipload or two of corn now and then."

'"Their own men must distribute it – not some cheating Greek accountant," said Pertinax.

'"Yes, and allow them to come to our hospitals when they are sick," I said.

'"Surely they would die first," said Maximus.

'"Not if Parnesius brought them in," said Allo. "I could show you twenty wolf-bitten, bear-clawed Picts within twenty miles of here. But Parnesius must stay with them in Hospital, else they would go mad with fear."

'"*I* see," said Maximus. "Like everything else in the world, it is one man's work. You, I think, are that one man."

'"Pertinax and I are one," I said.

'"As you please, so long as you work. Now, Allo, you know that I mean your people no harm. Leave us to talk together," said Maximus.

'"No need!" said Allo. "I am the corn between the upper and lower millstones. I must know what the lower millstone means to do. These boys have spoken the truth as far as they know it. I, a Prince, will tell you the rest. I am troubled about the Men of the North." He squatted like a hare in the heather, and looked over his shoulder.

'"I also," said Maximus, "or I should not be here."

'"Listen," said Allo. "Long and long ago the Winged Hats" – he meant the Northmen – "came to our beaches and said, 'Rome falls! Push her down!' We fought you. You sent men. We were beaten. After that we said to the Winged Hats, 'You are liars! Make our men alive that Rome killed, and we will believe you.' They went away ashamed. Now they come back bold, and they tell the old tale, which we begin to believe – that Rome falls!"

'"Give me three years' peace on the Wall," cried Maximus, "and I will show you and all the ravens how they lie!"

'"Ah, I wish it too! I wish to save what is left of the corn from the millstones. But you shoot us Picts when we come to borrow a little iron from the Iron Ditch; you burn our heather,

145

which is all our crop; you trouble us with your great catapults. Then you hide behind the Wall, and scorch us with Greek fire.[18] How can I keep my young men from listening to the Winged Hats – in winter especially, when we are hungry? My young men will say, 'Rome can neither fight nor rule. She is taking her men out of Britain.[19] The Winged Hats will help us to push down the Wall. Let us show them the secret roads across the bogs.' Do *I* want that? No!" He spat like an adder. "*I* would keep the secrets of my people though I were burned alive. My two children here have spoken truth. Leave us Picts alone. Comfort us, and cherish us, and feed us from far off – with the hand behind your back. Parnesius understands us. Let *him* have rule on the Wall, and I will hold my young men quiet for" – he ticked it off on his fingers – "one year easily: the next year not so easily: the third year, perhaps! See, I give you three years. If then you do not show us that Rome is strong in men and terrible in arms, the Winged Hats, I tell you, will sweep down the Wall from either sea till they meet in the middle, and you will go. *I* shall not grieve over that, but well I know tribe never helps tribe except for one price. We Picts will go too. The Winged Hats will grind us to this!" He tossed a handful of dust in the air.

'"Oh, Roma Dea!" said Maximus, half aloud. "It is always one man's work – always and everywhere!"

'"And one man's life," said Allo. "You are Emperor, but not a God. You may die."

'"I have thought of that too," said he. "Very good. If this wind holds, I shall be at the East end of the Wall by morning. Tomorrow, then, I shall see you two when I inspect, and I will make you Captains of the Wall for this work."

'"One instant, Caesar," said Pertinax. "All men have their price. I am not bought yet."

'"Do *you* also begin to bargain so early!" said Maximus. "Well?"

'"Give me justice against my uncle Icenus, the Duumvir of Divio[20] in Gaul," he said.

'"Only a life? I thought it would be money or an office. Certainly you shall have him. Write his name on these tablets –

on the red side; the other is for the living!" And Maximus held out his tablets.

'"He is of no use to me dead," said Pertinax. "My mother is a widow. I am far off. I am not sure he pays her all her dowry."

'"No matter. My arm is reasonably long. We will look through your uncle's accounts in due time. Now, farewell till tomorrow, O Captains of the Wall!"

'We saw him grow small across the heather as he walked to the galley. There were Picts, scores, each side of him, hidden behind stones. He never looked left or right. He sailed away Southerly, full spread before the evening breeze, and when we had watched him out to sea, we were silent. We understood Earth bred few men like this man.

'Presently Allo brought the ponies and held them for us to mount – a thing he had never done before.

'"Wait awhile," said Pertinax, and he made a little altar of cut turf, and strewed heather-bloom atop, and laid upon it a letter from a girl in Gaul.

'"What do you do, O my friend?" I said.

'"I sacrifice to my dead youth," he answered, and, when the flames had consumed the letter, he ground them out with his heel. Then we rode back to that Wall of which we were to be Captains.'

Parnesius stopped. The children sat still, not even asking if that were all the tale. Puck beckoned, and pointed the way out of the wood. 'Sorry,' he whispered, 'but you must go now.'

'We haven't made him angry, have we?' said Una. 'He looks so far off, and – and – thinky.'

'Bless your heart, no. Wait till tomorrow. It won't be long. Remember, you've been playing *Lays of Ancient Rome*.'

And as soon as they had scrambled through their gap where Oak, Ash, and Thorn grew, that was all they remembered.

A Song to Mithras [1]

Mithras, God of the Morning, our trumpets waken the Wall!
'Rome is above the Nations, but Thou art over all!'
Now as the names are answered, and the guards are marched
away,
Mithras, also a soldier, give us strength for the day!

Mithras, God of the Noontide, the heather swims in the heat,
Our helmets scorch our foreheads; our sandals burn our feet.
Now in the ungirt hour; now ere we blink and drowse,
Mithras, also a soldier, keep us true to our vows!

Mithras, God of the Sunset, low on the Western main,
Thou descending immortal, immortal to rise again!
Now when the watch is ended, now when the wine is drawn,
Mithras, also a soldier, keep us pure till the dawn!

Mithras, God of the Midnight, here where the great bull dies,
Look on thy children in darkness. Oh take our sacrifice!
Many roads Thou has fashioned: all of them lead to the Light,
Mithras, also a soldier, teach us to die aright!

❧ The Winged Hats ❧

The next day happened to be what they called a Wild After-noon. Father and Mother went out to pay calls; Miss Blake went for a ride on her bicycle, and they were left all alone till eight o'clock.

When they had seen their dear parents and their dear pre-ceptress politely off the premises they got a cabbage-leaf full of raspberries from the gardener, and a Wild Tea from Ellen. They ate the raspberries to prevent their squashing, and they meant to divide the cabbage-leaf with Three Cows down at the Theatre, but they came across a dead hedgehog which they simply *had* to bury, and the leaf was too useful to waste.

Then they went on to the Forge and found old Hobden the hedger at home with his son, the Bee Boy who is not quite right in his head, but who can pick up swarms of bees in his naked hands; and the Bee Boy told them the rhyme about the slow-worm:

> 'If I had eyes *as* I could see,
> No mortal man would trouble me.'

They all had tea together by the hives, and Hobden said the loaf-cake which Ellen had given them was almost as good as what his wife used to make, and he showed them how to set a wire at the right height for hares. They knew about rabbits already.

Then they climbed up Long Ditch into the lower end of Far Wood. This is sadder and darker than the Volaterrae end be-cause of an old marlpit full of black water, where weepy, hairy moss hangs round the stumps of the willows and alders. But the birds come to perch on the dead branches, and Hobden says that the bitter willow-water is a sort of medicine for sick animals.

They sat down on a felled oak-trunk in the shadows of the

beech undergrowth, and were looping the wires Hobden had given them, when they saw Parnesius.

'How quietly you came!' said Una, moving up to make room. 'Where's Puck?'

'The Faun and I have disputed whether it is better that I should tell you all my tale, or leave it untold,' he replied.

'I only said that if he told it as it happened you wouldn't understand it,' said Puck, jumping up like a squirrel from behind the log.

'I don't understand all of it,' said Una, 'but I like hearing about the little Picts.'

'What *I* can't understand,' said Dan, 'is how Maximus knew all about the Picts when he was over in Gaul.'

'He who makes himself Emperor anywhere must know everything, everywhere,' said Parnesius. 'We had this much from Maximus's mouth after the Games.'

'Games? What games?' said Dan.

Parnesius stretched his arm out stiffly, thumb pointed to the ground. 'Gladiators! *That* sort of game,' he said. 'There were two days' Games in his honour when he landed all un-expected at Segedunum on the East end of the Wall. Yes, the day after we had met him we held two days' games; but I think the greatest risk was run, not by the poor wretches on the sand, but by Maximus. In the old days the Legions kept silence before their Emperor. So did not we! You could hear the solid roar run West along the Wall as his chair was carried rocking through the crowds. The garrison beat round him – clamouring, clowning, asking for pay, for change of quarters, for anything that came into their wild heads. That chair was like a little boat among waves, dipping and falling, but always rising again after one had shut the eyes.' Parnesius shivered.

'Were they angry with him?' said Dan.

'No more angry than wolves in a cage when their trainer walks among them. If he had turned his back an instant, or for an instant had ceased to hold their eyes, there would have been another Emperor made on the Wall that hour. Was it not so, Faun?'

'So it was. So it always will be,' said Puck.

'Late in the evening his messenger came for us, and we followed to the Temple of Victory, where he lodged with Rutilianus, the General of the Wall. I had hardly seen the General before, but he always gave me leave when I wished to take Heather. He was a great glutton, and kept five Asian cooks, and he came of a family that believed in oracles. We could smell his good dinner when we entered, but the tables were empty. He lay snorting on a couch. Maximus sat apart among long rolls of accounts. Then the doors were shut.

'"These are your men," said Maximus to the General, who propped his eye-corners open with his gouty fingers, and stared at us like a fish.

'"I shall know them again, Caesar," said Rutilianus.

'"Very good," said Maximus. "Now hear! You are not to move man or shield on the Wall except as these boys shall tell you. You will do nothing, except eat, without their permission. They are the head and arms. You are the belly!" [1]

'"As Caesar pleases," the old man grunted. "If my pay and profits are not cut, you may make my Ancestors' Oracle my master. Rome has been! Rome has been!" Then he turned on his side to sleep.

'"He has it," said Maximus. "We will get to what *I* need."

'He unrolled full copies of the number of men and supplies on the Wall – down to the sick that very day in Hunno Hospital. Oh, but I groaned when his pen marked off detachment after detachment of our best – of our least worthless men! He took two towers of our Scythians, two of our North British auxiliaries, two Numidian cohorts, the Dacians all, and half the Belgians. It was like an eagle pecking a carcass.

'"And now, how many catapults have you?" He turned up a new list, but Pertinax laid his open hand there.

'"No, Caesar," he said. "Do not tempt the Gods too far. Take men, or engines, but not both; else we refuse."'

'Engines?' said Una.

'The catapults of the Wall – huge things forty feet high to the head – firing nets of raw stone or forged bolts. Nothing can stand against them. He left us our catapults at last, but he took a Caesar's half of our men without pity. We were a shell when he rolled up the lists!

'"Hail, Caesar! We, about to die, salute you!" [2] said Pertinax, laughing. "If any enemy even leans against the Wall now, it will tumble."

'"Give me the three years Allo spoke of," he answered, "and you shall have twenty thousand men of your own choosing up here. But now it is a gamble – a game played against the Gods, and the stakes are Britain, Gaul, and perhaps, Rome. You play on my side?"

'"We will play, Caesar," I said, for I had never met a man like this man.

'"Good. Tomorrow," said he, "I proclaim you Captains of the Wall before the troops."

'So we went into the moonlight, where they were cleaning the ground after the Games. We saw great Roma Dea atop of the Wall, the frost on her helmet, and her spear pointed towards the North Star. We saw the twinkle of night-fires all along the guard towers, and the line of the black catapults growing smaller and smaller in the distance. All these things we knew till we were weary; but that night they seemed very strange to us, because the next day we knew we were to be their masters.

'The men took the news well; but when Maximus went away with half our strength, and we had to spread ourselves into the emptied towers, and the townspeople complained that trade would be ruined, and the Autumn gales blew – it was dark days for us two. Here Pertinax was more than my right hand. Being born and bred among the great country-houses in Gaul, he knew the proper words to address to all – from Roman-born Centurions to those dogs of the Third – the Libyans. And he spoke to each as though that man were as high-minded as himself. Now *I* saw so strongly what things were needed to be done, that I forgot things are only accomplished by means of men. That was a mistake.

'I feared nothing from the Picts, at least for that year, but Allo warned me that the Winged Hats would soon come in from the sea at each end of the Wall to prove to the Picts how weak we were. So I made ready in haste, and none too soon. I shifted our best men to the ends of the Wall, and set up screened catapults by the beach. The Winged Hats would drive in before the snow-squalls – ten or twenty boats at a time – on Segedunum or Ituna, according as the wind blew.

'Now a ship coming in to land men must furl her sail. If you wait till you see her men gather up the sail's foot, your catapults can jerk a net of loose stones (bolts only cut through the cloth) into the bag of it. Then she turns over, and the sea makes everything clean again. A few men may come ashore, but very few . . . It was not hard work, except the waiting on the beach in blowing sand and snow. And that was how we dealt with the Winged Hats that winter.

'Early in the Spring, when the East winds blow like skinning-knives, they gathered again off Segedunum with many ships. Allo told me they would never rest till they had taken a tower in open fight. Certainly they fought in the open. We dealt with them thoroughly through a long day: and when all was finished, one man dived clear of the wreckage of his ship, and swam towards shore. I waited, and a wave tumbled him at my feet.

'As I stooped, I saw he wore such a medal as I wear.' Parnesius raised his hand to his neck. 'Therefore, when he could speak, I addressed him a certain Question which can only be answered in a certain manner. He answered with the necessary Word – the Word that belongs to the Degree of Gryphons in the science of Mithras my God. I put my shield over him till he could stand up. You see I am not short, but he was a head taller than I. He said: "What now?" I said: "At your pleasure, my brother, to stay or go."

'He looked out across the surf. There remained one ship unhurt, beyond range of our catapults. I checked the catapults and he waved her in. She came as a hound comes to a master. When she was yet a hundred paces from the beach, he flung back his hair, and swam out. They hauled him in, and went away. I knew that those who worship Mithras are many and of all races, so I did not think much more upon the matter.

'A month later I saw Allo with his horses – by the Temple of Pan, O Faun – and he gave me a great necklace of gold studded with coral.

'At first I thought it was a bribe from some tradesman in the town – meant for old Rutilianus. "Nay," said Allo. "This is a gift from Amal, that Winged Hat whom you saved on the beach. He says you are a Man."

'"He is a Man, too. Tell him I can wear his gift," I answered.

'"Oh, Amal is a young fool; but, speaking as sensible men, your Emperor is doing such great things in Gaul that the Winged Hats are anxious to be his friends, or, better still, the friends of his servants. They think you and Pertinax could lead them to victories." Allo looked at me like a one-eyed raven.

'"Allo," I said, "you are the corn between the two millstones. Be content if they grind evenly, and don't thrust your hand between them."

'"I?" said Allo. "I hate Rome and the Winged Hats equally; but if the Winged Hats thought that some day you and Pertinax might join them against Maximus, they would leave you in peace while you considered. Time is what we need – you and I and Maximus. Let me carry a pleasant message back to the Winged Hats – something for them to make a council over. We barbarians are all alike. We sit up half the night to discuss anything a Roman says. Eh?"

'"We have no men. We must fight with words," said Pertinax. "Leave it to Allo and me."

'So Allo carried word back to the Winged Hats that we would not fight them if they did not fight us; and they (I think they were a little tired of losing men in the sea) agreed to a sort of truce. I believe Allo, who being a horse-dealer loved lies, also told them we might some day rise against Maximus as Maximus had risen against Rome.

'Indeed, they permitted the corn-ships which I sent to the Picts to pass North that season without harm. Therefore the Picts were well fed that winter, and since they were in some sort my children, I was glad of it. We had only two thousand men on the Wall, and I wrote many times to Maximus and begged – prayed – him to send me only one cohort of my old North British troops. He could not spare them. He needed them to win more victories in Gaul.

'Then came news that he had defeated and slain the Emperor Gratian, and thinking he must now be secure, I wrote again for men. He answered: "You will learn that I have at last settled accounts with the pup Gratian. There was no need that he should have died, but he became confused and lost his head, which is a bad thing to befall any Emperor. Tell your Father I am content to drive two mules only; for unless my old General's son thinks himself destined to destroy me, I shall rest Emperor of Gaul and Britain, and then you, my two children, will presently get all the men you need. Just now I can spare none."'

'What did he mean by his General's son?' said Dan.

'He meant Theodosius Emperor of Rome, who was the son of Theodosius the General under whom Maximus had fought in the old Pict War. The two men never loved each other, and when Gratian made the younger Theodosius Emperor of the East (at least, so I've heard), Maximus carried on the war to the second generation. It was his fate, and it was his fall. But Theodosius the Emperor is a good man. As I know.' Parnesius was silent for a moment and then continued.

'I wrote back to Maximus that, though we had peace on the Wall, I should be happier with a few more men and some new catapults. He answered: "You must live a little longer under the shadow of my victories, till I can see what young Theodosius intends. He may welcome me as a brother-Emperor, or he may be preparing an army. In either case I cannot spare men just now."'

'But he was always saying that,' cried Una.

'It was true. He did not make excuses; but thanks, as he said, to the news of his victories, we had no trouble on the Wall for a long, long time. The Picts grew fat as their own sheep among the heather, and as many of my men as lived were well exercised in their weapons. Yes, the Wall looked strong. For myself, I knew how weak we were. I knew that if even a false rumour of any defeat to Maximus broke loose among the Winged Hats, they might come down in earnest, and then – the Wall must go! For the Picts I never cared, but in those years I learned something of the strength of the Winged Hats. They increased their strength every day, but I could not increase my men. Maximus had emptied Britain behind us, and I felt myself to be a man with a rotten stick standing before a broken fence to turn bulls.

'Thus, my friends, we lived on the Wall, waiting – waiting – waiting for the men that Maximus never sent.

'Presently he wrote that he was preparing an army against Theodosius. He wrote – and Pertinax read it over my shoulder in our quarters: "*Tell your Father that my destiny orders me to drive three mules or be torn to pieces by them. I hope within a year to finish with Theodosius, son of Theodosius, once and for all. Then you shall have Britain to rule, and Pertinax, if he chooses, Gaul. Today I wish strongly you were with me to beat my Auxiliaries into shape. Do not, I pray you, believe any rumour of my sickness. I have a little evil in my old body which I shall cure by riding swiftly into Rome.*"

'Said Pertinax: "It is finished with Maximus. He writes as a man without hope. I, a man without hope, can see this. What does he add at the bottom of the roll? '*Tell Pertinax I have met his late Uncle, the Duumvir of Divio, and that he accounted to me quite truthfully for all his Mother's monies. I have sent her with a fitting escort, for she is the mother of a hero, to Nicaea,*[3] *where the climate is warm.*'

'"That is proof," said Pertinax. "Nicaea is not far by sea from Rome. A woman there could take ship and fly to Rome in time of war. Yes, Maximus foresees his death, and is fulfilling his promises one by one. But I am glad my Uncle met him."

'"You think blackly today?" I asked.

'"I think truth. The Gods weary of the play we have played against them. Theodosius will destroy Maximus. It is finished!"

'"Will you write him that?" I said.

'"See what I shall write," he answered, and he took pen and wrote a letter cheerful as the light of day, tender as a woman's and full of jests. Even I, reading over his shoulder, took comfort from it till – I saw his face!

'"And now," he said, sealing it, "we be two dead men, my brother. Let us go to the Temple."

'We prayed awhile to Mithras, where we had many times

prayed before. After that, we lived day by day among evil rumours till winter came again.

'It happened one morning that we rode to the East shore, and found on the beach a fair-haired man, half frozen, bound to some broken planks. Turning him over, we saw by his belt-buckle that he was a Goth of an Eastern Legion. Suddenly he opened his eyes and cried loudly, "He is dead! The letters were with me, but the Winged Hats sank the ship." So saying, he died between our hands.

'We asked not who was dead. We knew! We raced before the driving snow to Hunno, thinking perhaps Allo might be there. We found him already at our stables, and he saw by our faces what we had heard.

'"It was in a tent by the sea,"[4] he stammered. "He was beheaded by Theodosius. He sent a letter to you, written while he waited to be slain. The Winged Hats met the ship and took it. The news is running through the heather like fire. Blame me not! I cannot hold back my young men any more."

'"I would we could say as much for our men," said Pertinax, laughing. "But, Gods be praised, they cannot run away."

'"What do you do?" said Allo. "I bring an order – a message – from the Winged Hats that you join them with your men, and march South to plunder Britain."

'"It grieves me," said Pertinax, "but we are stationed here to stop that thing."

'"If I carry back such an answer they will kill me," said Allo. "I always promised the Winged Hats that you would rise when Maximus fell. I – I did not think he could fall."

'"Alas! my poor barbarian," said Pertinax, still laughing. "Well, you have sold us too many good ponies to be thrown back to your friends. We will make you a prisoner, although you are an ambassador."

'"Yes, that will be best," said Allo, holding out a halter. We bound him lightly, for he was an old man.

'"Presently the Winged Hats may come to look for you, and that will give us more time. See how the habit of playing for time sticks to a man!" said Pertinax, as he tied the rope.

'"No," I said. "Time may help. If Maximus wrote us a

letter while he was a prisoner, Theodosius must have sent the ship that brought it. If he can send ships, he can send men."

'"How will that profit us?" said Pertinax. "We serve Maximus, not Theodosius. Even if by some miracle of the Gods Theodosius down South sent and saved the Wall, we could not expect more than the death Maximus died."

'"It concerns us to defend the Wall, no matter what Emperor dies, or makes die," I said.

'"That is worthy of your brother the philosopher," said Pertinax. "Myself I am without hope, so I do not say solemn and stupid things! Rouse the Wall!"

'We armed the Wall from end to end; we told the officers that there was a rumour of Maximus's death which might bring down the Winged Hats, but we were sure, even if it were true, that Theodosius, for the sake of Britain, would send us help. Therefore, we must stand fast . . . My friends, it is above all things strange to see how men bear ill news! Often the strongest till then become the weakest, while the weakest, as it were, reach up and steal strength from the Gods. So it was with us. Yet my Pertinax by his jests and his courtesy and his labours had put heart and training into our poor numbers during the past years – more than I should have thought possible. Even our Libyan cohort – the Thirds – stood up in their padded cuirasses and did not whimper.

'In three days came seven chiefs and elders of the Winged Hats. Among them was that tall young man, Amal, whom I had met on the beach, and he smiled when he saw my necklace. We made them welcome, for they were ambassadors. We showed them Allo, alive but bound. They thought we had killed him, and I saw it would not have vexed them if we had. Allo saw it too, and it vexed him. Then in our quarters at Hunno we came to Council.

'They said that Rome was falling, and that we must join them. They offered me all South Britain to govern after they had taken a tribute out of it.

'I answered, "Patience. This Wall is not weighed off like plunder. Give me proof that my General is dead."

'"Nay," said one elder, "prove to us that he lives"; and

another said, cunningly, "What will you give us if we read you his last words?"

'"We are not merchants to bargain," cried Amal. "Moreover, I owe this man my life. He shall have his proof." He threw across to me a letter (well I knew the seal) from Maximus.

'"We took this out of the ship we sank," he cried. "I cannot read, but I know one sign, at least, which makes me believe." He showed me a dark stain on the outer roll that my heavy heart perceived was the valiant blood of Maximus.

'"Read!" said Amal. "Read, and then let us hear whose servants you are!"

'Said Pertinax, very softly, after he had looked through it: "I will read it all. Listen, barbarians!" He read that which I have carried next my heart ever since.'

Parnesius drew from his neck a folded and spotted piece of parchment, and began in a hushed voice:

'"*To Parnesius and Pertinax, the not unworthy Captains of the Wall, from Maximus, once Emperor of Gaul and Britain, now prisoner waiting death by the sea in the camp of Theodosius – Greeting and Goodbye!*"

'"Enough," said young Amal; "there is your proof! You must join us now!"

'Pertinax looked long and silently at him, till that fair man blushed like a girl. Then read Pertinax:

'"*I have joyfully done much evil in my life to those who have wished me evil, but if ever I did any evil to you two I repent, and I ask your forgiveness. The three mules which I strove to drive have torn me in pieces as your Father prophesied. The naked swords wait at the tent door to give me the death I gave to Gratian. Therefore I, your General and your Emperor, send you free and honourable dismissal from my service, which you entered, not for money or office, but, as it makes me warm to believe, because you loved me!*"

'"By the Light of the Sun," Amal broke in. "This was in some sort a Man! We may have been mistaken in his servants!"

'And Pertinax read on: "*You gave me the time for which I asked. If I have failed to use it, do not lament. We have gambled very splendidly against the Gods, but they hold weighted dice, and*

*I must pay the forfeit. Remember, I have been; but Rome is; and
Rome will be. Tell Pertinax his Mother is in safety at Nicaea, and
her monies are in charge of the Prefect at Antipolis.*[5] *Make my
remembrances to your Father and to your Mother, whose friendship
was great gain to me. Give also to my little Picts and to the Winged
Hats such messages as their thick heads can understand. I would
have sent you three Legions this very day if all had gone aright. Do
not forget me. We have worked together. Farewell! Farewell!
Farewell!"*

'Now, that was my Emperor's last letter.' (The children heard
the parchment crackle as Parnesius returned it to its place.)

'"I was mistaken," said Amal. "The servants of such a man
will sell nothing except over the sword. I am glad of it." He
held out his hand to me.

'"But Maximus has given you your dismissal," said an elder.
"You are certainly free to serve – or to rule – whom you please.
Join – do not follow – join us!"

'"We thank you," said Pertinax. "But Maximus tells us to
give you such messages as – pardon me, but I use his words –
your thick heads can understand." He pointed through the door
to the foot of a catapult wound up.

'"We understand," said an elder. "The Wall must be won at
a price?"

'"It grieves me," said Pertinax, laughing, "but so it must be
won," and he gave them of our best Southern wine.

'They drank, and wiped their yellow beards in silence till
they rose to go.

'Said Amal, stretching himself (for they were barbarians),
"We be a goodly company; I wonder what the ravens and the
dogfish will make of some of us before this snow melts."

'"Think rather what Theodosius may send," I answered;
and though they laughed, I saw that my chance shot troubled
them.

'Only old Allo lingered behind a little.

'"You see," he said, winking and blinking, "I am no more
than their dog. When I have shown their men the secret short
ways across our bogs, they will kick me like one."

'"Then I should not be in haste to show them those ways,"

said Pertinax, "till I was sure that Rome could not save the Wall."

'"You think so? Woe is me!" said the old man. "I only wanted peace for my people," and he went out stumbling through the snow behind the tall Winged Hats.

'In this fashion then, slowly, a day at a time, which is very bad for doubting troops, the War came upon us. At first the Winged Hats swept in from the sea as they had done before, and there we met them as before – with the catapults; and they sickened of it. Yet for a long time they would not trust their duck-legs on land, and I think when it came to revealing the secrets of the tribe, the little Picts were afraid or ashamed to show them all the roads across the heather. I had this from a Pict prisoner. They were as much our spies as our enemies, for the Winged Hats oppressed them, and took their winter stores. Ah, foolish Little People!

'Then the Winged Hats began to roll us up from each end of the Wall. I sent runners Southward to see what the news might be in Britain, but the wolves were very bold that winter, among the deserted stations where the troops had once been, and none came back. We had trouble too with the forage for the ponies along the Wall. I kept ten, and so did Pertinax. We lived and slept in the saddle, riding east or west, and we ate our worn-out ponies. The people of the town also made us some trouble till I gathered them all in one quarter behind Hunno. We broke down the Wall on either side of it to make as it were a citadel. Our men fought better in close order.

'By the end of the second month we were deep in the War as a man is deep in a snowdrift or in a dream. I think we fought in our sleep. At least I know I have gone on the Wall and come off again, remembering nothing between, though my throat was harsh with giving orders, and my sword, I could see, had been used.

'The Winged Hats fought like wolves – all in a pack. Where they had suffered most, there they charged in most hotly. This was hard for the defender, but it held them from sweeping on into Britain.

'In those days Pertinax and I wrote on the plaster of the

bricked archway into Valentia the names of the towers, and the days on which they fell one by one. We wished for some record.

'And the fighting? The fight was always hottest to left and right of the great statue of Roma Dea, near to Rutilianus's house. By the Light of the Sun, that old fat man, whom we had not considered at all, grew young again among the trumpets! I remember he said his sword was an oracle! "Let us consult the Oracle," he would say, and put the handle against his ear, and shake his head wisely. "And *this* day is allowed Rutilianus to live," he would say, and, tucking up his cloak, he would puff and pant and fight well. Oh, there were jests in plenty on the Wall to take the place of food!

'We endured for two months and seventeen days – always being pressed from three sides into a smaller space. Several times Allo sent in word that help was at hand. We did not believe it, but it cheered our men.

'The end came not with shoutings of joy, but, like the rest, as in a dream. The Winged Hats suddenly left us in peace for one night, and the next day; which is too long for spent men. We slept at first lightly, expecting to be roused, and then like logs, each where he lay. May you never need such sleep! When I waked our towers were full of strange, armed men, who watched us snoring. I roused Pertinax, and we leaped up together.

'"What?" said a young man in clean armour. "Do you fight against Theodosius? Look!"

'North we looked over the red snow. No Winged Hats were there. South we looked over the white snow, and behold there were the Eagles of two strong Legions encamped. East and west we saw flame and fighting, but by Hunno all was still.

'"Trouble no more," said the young man. "Rome's arm is long. Where are the Captains of the Wall?"

'We said we were those men.

'"But you are old and grey-haired," he cried. "Maximus said that they were boys."

'"Yes, that was true some years ago," said Pertinax. "What is our fate to be, you fine and well-fed child?"

'"I am called Ambrosius, a secretary of the Emperor," he

answered. "Show me a certain letter which Maximus wrote from a tent at Aquileia,[6] and perhaps I will believe."

'I took it from my breast, and when he had read it he saluted us, saying: "Your fate is in your own hands. If you choose to serve Theodosius, he will give you a Legion. If it suits you to go to your homes, we will give you a Triumph."

'"I would like better a bath, wine, food, razors, soaps, oils, and scents," said Pertinax, laughing.

'"Oh, I see you are a boy," said Ambrosius. "And you?" turning to me.

'"We bear no ill-will against Theodosius, but in War –" I began.

'"In War it is as it is in Love," said Pertinax. "Whether she be good or bad, one gives one's best once, to one only. That given, there remains no second worth giving or taking."

'"That is true," said Ambrosius. "I was with Maximus before he died. He warned Theodosius that you would never serve him, and frankly I say I am sorry for my Emperor."

'"He has Rome to console him," said Pertinax. "I ask you of your kindness to let us go to our homes and get this smell out of our nostrils."

'None the less they gave us a Triumph!'

'It was well earned,' said Puck, throwing some leaves into the still water of the marlpit. The black, oily circles spread dizzily as the children watched them.

'I want to know, oh, ever so many things,' said Dan. 'What happened to old Allo? Did the Winged Hats ever come back? And what did Amal do?'

'And what happened to the fat old General with the five cooks?' said Una. 'And what did your Mother say when you came home? . . .'

'She'd say you're settin' too long over this old pit, so late as 'tis already,' said old Hobden's voice behind them. 'Hst!' he whispered.

He stood still, for not twenty paces away a magnificent dog-fox sat on his haunches and looked at the children as though he were an old friend of theirs.

'Oh, Mus' Reynolds, Mus' Reynolds!' said Hobden, under his breath. 'If I knowed all was inside your head, I'd know something wuth knowin'. Mus' Dan an' Miss Una, come along o' me while I lock up my liddle hen-house.'

A Pict Song

Rome never looks where she treads,
    Always her heavy hooves fall,
On our stomachs, our hearts or our heads;
    And Rome never heeds when we bawl.
Her sentries pass on – that is all,
    And we gather behind them in hordes,
And plot to reconquer the Wall,
    With only our tongues for our swords.

We are the Little Folk – we!
    Too little to love or to hate.
Leave us alone and you'll see
    How we can drag down the Great! [1]
We are the worm in the wood!
    We are the rot at the root!
We are the germ in the blood!
    We are the thorn in the foot!

Mistletoe killing an oak –
    Rats gnawing cables in two –
Moths making holes in a cloak –
    How they must love what they do!
Yes – and we Little Folk too,
    We are as busy as they –
Working our works out of view –
    Watch, and you'll see it some day!

No indeed! We are not strong,
    But we know Peoples that are.
Yes, and we'll guide them along,
    To smash and destroy you in War!
We shall be slaves just the same?
    Yes, we have always been slaves,
But you – you will die of the shame,
    And then we shall dance on your graves!

We are the Little Folk, we, etc.

⨎ Hal o' the Draft ⨎

'Prophets have honour all over the Earth'

Prophets have honour all over the Earth,
   Except in the village where they were born;
Where such as knew them boys from birth,
   Nature-ally hold 'em in scorn.

When Prophets are naughty and young and vain,
   They make a won'erful grievance of it;
(You can see by their writings how they complain),
   But O, 'tis won'erful good for the Prophet!

There's nothing Nineveh Town [1] can give
   (Nor being swallowed by whales between),
Makes up for the place where a man's folk live,
   That don't care nothing what he has been.
He might ha' been that, or he might ha' been this,
But they love and they hate him for what he is.

Hal o' the Draft

A rainy afternoon drove Dan and Una over to play pirates in the Little Mill. If you don't mind rats on the rafters and oats in your shoes, the mill-attic, with its trap-doors and inscriptions on beams about floods and sweethearts, is a splendid place. It is lighted by a foot-square window, called Duck Window, that looks across to Little Lindens Farm, and the spot where Jack Cade [1] was killed.

When they had climbed the attic ladder (they called it the mainmast tree, out of the ballad of Sir Andrew Barton,[2] and Dan 'swarved [3] it with might and main', as the ballad says) they saw a man sitting on Duck Window-sill. He was dressed in a plum-coloured doublet and tight plum-coloured hose, and he drew busily in a red-edged book.

'Sit ye! Sit ye!' Puck cried from a rafter overhead. 'See what it is to be beautiful! Sir Harry Dawe – pardon, Hal – says I am the very image of a head for a gargoyle.'

The man laughed and raised his dark velvet cap to the children, and his grizzled hair bristled out in a stormy fringe. He was old – forty at least – but his eyes were young, with funny little wrinkles all round them. A satchel of embroidered leather hung from his broad belt, which looked interesting.

'May we see?' said Una, coming forward.

'Surely – sure-ly!' he said, moving up on the window-seat, and returned to his work with a silver-pointed pencil. Puck sat as though the grin were fixed for ever on his broad face, while they watched the quick, certain fingers that copied it. Presently the man took a reed pen from his satchel, and trimmed it with a little ivory knife, carved in the semblance of a fish.

'Oh, what a beauty!' cried Dan.

''Ware fingers! That blade is perilous sharp. I made it myself of the best Low Country cross-bow steel. And so, too, this fish. When his back-fin travels to his tail – so – he swallows up the

167

blade, even as the whale swallowed Gaffer Jonah . . . Yes, and that's my ink-horn. I made the four silver saints round it. Press Barnabas's head.[4] It opens, and then –' He dipped the trimmed pen, and with careful boldness began to put in the essential lines of Puck's rugged face, that had been but faintly revealed by the silver-point.

The children gasped, for it fairly leaped from the page.

As he worked, and the rain fell on the tiles, he talked – now clearly, now muttering, now breaking off to frown or smile at his work. He told them he was born at Little Lindens Farm, and his father used to beat him for drawing things instead of doing things, till an old priest called Father Roger, who drew illuminated letters in rich people's books, coaxed the parents to let him take the boy as a sort of painter's apprentice. Then he went with Father Roger to Oxford, where he cleaned plates and carried cloaks and shoes for the scholars of a College called Merton.

'Didn't you hate that?' said Dan after a great many other questions.

'I never thought on 't. Half Oxford was building new colleges or beautifying the old, and she had called to her aid the master-craftsmen of all Christendie – kings in their trade and honoured of Kings. I knew them. I worked for them: that was enough. No wonder –' He stopped and laughed.

'You became a great man, Hal,' said Puck.

'They said so, Robin. Even Bramante[5] said so.'

'Why? What did you do?' Dan asked.

The artist looked at him queerly. 'Things in stone and such, up and down England. You would not have heard of 'em. To come nearer home, I re-built this little St Barnabas' church[6] of ours. It cost me more trouble and sorrow than aught I've touched in my life. But 'twas a sound lesson.'

'Um,' said Dan. 'We had lessons this morning.'

'I'll not afflict ye, lad,' said Hal, while Puck roared. 'Only 'tis strange to think how that little church was re-built, re-roofed, and made glorious, thanks to some few godly Sussex ironmasters, a Bristow[7] sailor lad, a proud ass called Hal o' the Draft because, d'you see, he was always drawing and drafting; and' – he dragged the words slowly – '*and* a Scotch pirate.'

'Pirate?' said Dan. He wriggled like a hooked fish.

'Even that Andrew Barton you were singing of on the stair just now.' He dipped again in the ink-well, and held his breath over a sweeping line, as though he had forgotten everything else.

'Pirates don't build churches, do they?' said Dan. 'Or *do* they?'

'They help mightily,' Hal laughed. 'But you were at your lessons this morn, Jack Scholar.'

'Oh, pirates aren't lessons. It was only Bruce and his silly old spider,'[8] said Una. 'Why did Sir Andrew Barton help you?'

'I question if he ever knew it,' said Hal, twinkling. 'Robin, how a' mischief's name am I to tell these innocents what comes of sinful pride?'

'Oh, we know all about *that*,' said Una pertly. 'If you get too beany – that's cheeky – you get sat upon, of course.'

Hal considered a moment, pen in air, and Puck said some long words.

'Aha! That was my case too,' he cried. 'Beany – you say – but certainly I did not conduct myself well. I was proud of – of such things as porches – a Galilee porch at Lincoln[9] for choice – proud of one Torrigiano's[10] arm on my shoulder, proud of my knighthood when I made the gilt scroll-work for the *Sovereign* – our King's ship.[11] But Father Roger sitting in Merton Library, he did not forget me. At the top of my pride, when I and no other should have builded the porch at Lincoln, he laid it on me with a terrible forefinger to go back to my Sussex clays and re-build, at my own charges, my own church, where us Dawes[12] have been buried for six generations. "Out! Son of my Art!" said he. "Fight the Devil at home ere you call yourself a man and a craftsman." And I quaked, and I went . . . How's yon, Robin?' He flourished the finished sketch before Puck.

'Me! Me past peradventure,' said Puck, smirking like a man at a mirror. 'Ah, see! The rain has took off! I hate housen in daylight.'

'Whoop! Holiday!' cried Hal, leaping up. 'Who's for my Little Lindens? We can talk there.'

They tumbled downstairs, and turned past the dripping willows by the sunny mill-dam.

'Body o' me,' said Hal, staring at the hop-garden, where the hops were just ready to blossom. 'What, are these vines? No, not vines, and they twine the wrong way to beans.' He began to draw in his ready book.

'Hops. New since your day,' said Puck. 'They're an herb of Mars, and their flowers dried flavour ale. We say –

> 'Turkeys, Heresy, Hops and Beer
> Came into England all in one year.'

'Heresy I know. I've seen Hops – God be praised for their beauty! What is your Turkis?'

The children laughed. They knew the Lindens turkeys, and as soon as they reached Lindens orchard on the hill the full flock charged at them.

Out came Hal's book at once. 'Hoity-toity!' he cried. 'Here's Pride in purple feathers! Here's wrathy contempt and the Pomps of the Flesh! How d'you call *them*?'

'Turkeys! Turkeys!' the children shouted, as the old gobbler raved and flamed against Hal's plum-coloured hose.

''Save Your Magnificence!' he said. 'I've drafted two good new things today.' And he doffed his cap to the bubbling bird.

Then they walked through the grass to the knoll where Little Lindens stands. The old farmhouse, weather-tiled to the ground, took almost the colour of a blood-ruby in the afternoon light. The pigeons pecked at the mortar in the chimney-stacks; the bees that had lived under the tiles since it was built filled the hot August air with their booming; and the smell of the box-tree by the dairy-window mixed with the smell of earth after rain, bread after baking, and a tickle of wood-smoke.

The farmer's wife came to the door, baby on arm, shaded her brows against the sun, stooped to pluck a sprig of rosemary, and turned down the orchard. The old spaniel in his barrel barked once or twice to show he was in charge of the empty house. Puck clicked back the garden-gate.

'D'you marvel that I love it?' said Hal, in a whisper. 'What can town folk know of the nature of housen – or land?'

They perched themselves arow on the old hacked oak bench in Lindens garden, looking across the valley of the brook at the fern-covered dimples and hollows of the Forge behind Hobden's cottage. The old man was cutting a faggot in his garden by the hives. It was quite a second after his chopper fell that the chump of the blow reached their lazy ears.

'Eh – yeh!' said Hal. 'I mind when where that old gaffer stands was Nether Forge – Master John Collins's foundry.[13] Many a night has his big trip-hammer shook me in my bed here. *Boom-bitty! Boom-bitty!* If the wind was east, I could hear Master Tom Collins's forge at Stockens answering his brother, *Boom-oop! Boom-oop!* and midway between, Sir John Pelham's[14] sledge-hammers at Brightling would strike in like a pack o' scholars, and "*Hic-haec-hoc*" they'd say, "*Hic-haec-hoc*", till I fell asleep. Yes. The valley was as full o' forges and fineries as a May shaw[15] o' cuckoos. All gone to grass now!'

'What did they make?' said Dan.

'Guns for the King's ships – and for others. Serpentines and cannon mostly. When the guns were cast, down would come the King's Officers, and take our plough-oxen to haul them to the coast. Look! Here's one of the first and finest craftsmen of the Sea!'

He fluttered back a page of his book, and showed them a young man's head. Underneath was written: 'Sebastianus'.

'He came down with a King's Order on Master John Collins for twenty serpentines (wicked little cannon they be!) to furnish a venture of ships. I drafted him thus sitting by our fire telling Mother of the new lands he'd find the far side the world. And he found them, too! There's a nose to cleave through unknown seas! Cabot[16] was his name – a Bristol lad – half a foreigner. I set a heap by him. He helped me to my church-building.'

'I thought that was Sir Andrew Barton,' said Dan.

'Ay, but foundations before roofs,' Hal answered. 'Sebastian first put me in the way of it. I had come down here, not to serve God as a craftsman should, but to show my people how great a craftsman I was. They cared not; and it served me right; one split straw for my craft or my greatness. What a murrain call had I, they said, to mell[17] with old St Barnabas'? Ruinous the church had been since the Black Death, and ruinous she should remain; and I could hang myself in my new scaffold-ropes! Gentle and simple, high and low – the Hayes, the Fowles, the Fanners, the Collinses – they were all in a tale against me. Only Sir John Pelham up yonder at Brightling bade me heart-up and go on. Yet how could I? Did I ask Master Collins for his timber-tug to haul beams? The oxen had gone to Lewes after lime. Did he promise me a set of iron cramps or ties for the roof? They never came to hand, or else they were spaulty [18] or cracked. So with everything. Nothing said, but naught done except I stood by them, and then done amiss. I thought the countryside was fair bewitched.'

'It was, sure-ly,' said Puck, knees under chin. 'Did you never suspect ary one?' [19]

'Not till Sebastian came for his guns, and John Collins played him the same dog's tricks as he'd played me with my ironwork. Week in, week out, two of three serpentines would be flawed in the casting, and only fit, they said, to be re-melted. Then John Collins would shake his head, and vow he could pass no can-non for the King's service that were not perfect. Saints! How Sebastian stormed! *I* know, for we sat on this bench sharing our sorrows inter-common.

'When Sebastian had fumed away six weeks at Lindens and gotten just six serpentines, Dirk Brenzett, Master of the *Cygnet* hoy,[20] sends me word that the block of stone he was fetching me from France for our new font he'd hove overboard to lighten his ship, chased by Andrew Barton up to Rye Port.'

'Ah! The pirate!' said Dan.

'Yes. And while I am tearing my hair over this, Ticehurst Will, my best mason, comes to me shaking, and vowing that the Devil, horned, tailed, and chained, has run out on him from the church-tower, and the men would work there no more. So I took 'em off the foundations, which we were strengthening, and went into the Bell Tavern [21] for a cup of ale. Says Master John Collins: "Have it your own way, lad; but if I was you, I'd take the sinnification o' the sign, and leave old Barnabas' Church alone!" And they all wagged their sinful heads, and agreed. Less afraid of the Devil than of me – as I saw later.

'When I brought my sweet news to Lindens, Sebastian was

limewashing the kitchen-beams for Mother. He loved her like a son.

'"Cheer up, lad," he says. "God's where He was. Only you and I chance to be pure pute [22] asses. We've been tricked, Hal, and more shame to me, a sailor, that I did not guess it before! You must leave your belfry alone, forsooth, because the Devil is adrift there; and I cannot get my serpentines because John Collins cannot cast them aright. Meantime Andrew Barton hawks off the Port of Rye. And why? To take those very serpentines which poor Cabot must whistle for; the said serpentines, I'll wager my share of new Continents, being now hid away in St Barnabas' church tower. Clear as the Irish coast at noonday!"

'"They'd sure never dare to do it," I said; "and for another thing, selling cannon to the King's enemies is black treason – hanging and fine."

'"It is sure, large profit. Men'll dare any gallows for that. I have been a trader myself," says he. "We must be upsides with 'em for the honour of Bristol."

'Then he hatched a plot, sitting on the limewash bucket. We gave out to ride o' Tuesday to London and made a show of taking farewells of our friends – especially of Master John Collins. But at Wadhurst Woods we turned; rode home to the watermeadows; hid our horses in a willow-tot [23] at the foot of the glebe, and, come night, stole a-tiptoe up hill to Barnabas' church again. A thick mist, and a moon striking through.

'I had no sooner locked the tower-door behind us than over goes Sebastian full length in the dark.

'"Pest!" he says. "Step high and feel low, Hal. I've stumbled over guns before."

'I groped, and one by one – the tower was pitchy dark – I counted the lither [24] barrels of twenty serpentines laid out on pease straw. No conceal at all!

'"There's two demi-cannon my end," says Sebastian, slapping metal. "They'll be for Andrew Barton's lower deck. Honest – honest John Collins! So this is his warehouse, his arsenal, his armoury! Now, see you why your pokings and pryings have raised the Devil in Sussex? You've hindered John's lawful trade for months," and he laughed where he lay.

'A clay-cold tower is no fireside at midnight, so we climbed the belfry stairs, and there Sebastian trips over a cow-hide with its horns and tail.

'"Aha! Your Devil has left his doublet! Does it become me, Hal?" He draws it on and capers in the slits of window-moonlight – won'erful devilish-like. Then he sits on the stairs, rapping with his tail on a board, and his back-aspect was dreader than his front, and a howlet lit in, and screeched at the horns of him.

'"If you'd keep out the Devil, shut the door," he whispered. "And that's another false proverb, Hal, for I can hear your tower-door opening."

'"I locked it. Who a-plague has another key, then?" I said.

'"All the congregation to judge by their feet," he says, and peers into the blackness. "Still! Still, Hal! Hear 'em grunt! That's more o' my serpentines, I'll be bound. One – two – three – four they bear in! Faith, Andrew equips himself like an admiral! Twenty-four serpentines in all!"

'As if it had been an echo, we heard John Collins's voice come up all hollow: "Twenty-four serpentines and two demi-cannon. That's the full tally for Sir Andrew Barton."

'"Courtesy costs naught," whispers Sebastian. "Shall I drop my dagger on his head?"

'"They go over to Rye o' Thursday in the wool-wains, hid under the wool packs. Dirk Brenzett meets them at Udimore, as before," says John.

'"Lord! What a worn, handsmooth trade it is!" says Sebastian. "I lay we are the sole two babes in the village that have not our lawful share in the venture."

'There was a full score folk below, talking like all Roberts-bridge Market. We counted them by voice.

'Master John Collins pipes: "The guns for the French carrack[25] must lie here next month. Will, when does your young fool (me, so please you!) come back from Lunnon?"

'"No odds," I heard Ticehurst Will answer. "Lay 'em just where you've a mind, Mus' Collins. We're all too afraid o' the Devil to mell with the tower now." And the long knave laughed.

'"Ah! 'tis easy enow for you to raise the Devil, Will," says another – Ralph Hobden of the Forge.

'"Aaa-men!" roars Sebastian, and ere I could hold him, he leaps down the stairs – won'erful devilish-like – howling no bounds. He had scarce time to lay out for the nearest than they ran. Saints, how they ran! We heard them pound on the door of the Bell Tavern, and then we ran too.

'"What's next?" says Sebastian, looping up his cow-tail as he leaped the briars. "I've broke honest John's face."

'"Ride to Sir John Pelham's," I said. "He is the only one that ever stood by me."

'We rode to Brightling, and past Sir John's lodges, where the keepers would have shot at us for deer-stealers, and we had Sir John down into his Justice's chair,[26] and when we had told him our tale and showed him the cow-hide which Sebastian wore still girt about him, he laughed till the tears ran.

'"Wel-a-well!" he says. "I'll see justice done before daylight. What's your complaint? Master Collins is my old friend."

'"He's none of mine," I cried. "When I think how he and his likes have baulked and dozened and cozened me at every turn over the church" – and I choked at the thought.

'"Ah, but ye see now they needed it for another use," says he, smoothly.

'"So they did my serpentines," Sebastian cries. "I should be half across the Western Ocean by now if my guns had been ready. But they're sold to a Scotch pirate by your old friend."

'"Where's your proof?" says Sir John, stroking his beard.

'"I broke my shins over them not an hour since, and I heard John give order where they were to be taken," says Sebastian.

'"Words! Words only," says Sir John. "Master Collins is somewhat of a liar at best."

'He carried it so gravely, that for the moment, I thought he was dipped in this secret traffick too, and that there was not an honest ironmaster in Sussex.

'"Name o' Reason!" says Sebastian, and raps with his cow-tail on the table, "whose guns are they, then?"

'"Yours, manifestly," says Sir John. "You come with the King's Order for 'em, and Master Collins casts them in his foundry. If he chooses to bring them up from Nether Forge and lay 'em out in the church tower, why they are e'en so much the nearer to the main road and you are saved a day's hauling. What a coil to make of a mere act of neighbourly kindness, lad!"

' "I fear I have requited him very scurvily," says Sebastian, looking at his knuckles. "But what of the demi-cannon? I could do with 'em well, but *they* are not in the King's Order."

' "Kindness – loving-kindness," says Sir John. "Questionless, in his zeal for the King and his love for you, John adds those two cannon as a gift. 'Tis plain as this coming daylight, ye stockfish!" [27]

' "So it is," says Sebastian. "Oh, Sir John, Sir John, why did you never use the sea? You are lost ashore." And he looked on him with great love.

' "I do my best in my station." Sir John strokes his beard again and rolls forth his deep drumming Justice's voice thus: "But – suffer me! – you two lads, on some midnight frolic into which I probe not, roystering around the taverns, surprise Master Collins at his" – he thinks a moment – "at his good deeds done by stealth. Ye surprise him, I say, cruelly."

' "Truth, Sir John. If you had seen him run!" says Sebastian.

' "On this you ride breakneck to me with a tale of pirates, and wool-wains, and cow-hides, which, though it hath moved my mirth as a man, offendeth my reason as a magistrate. So I will e'en accompany you back to the tower with, perhaps, some few of my own people, and three–four wagons, and I'll be your warrant that Master John Collins will freely give you your guns and your demi-cannon, Master Sebastian." He breaks into his proper voice – "I warned the old tod [28] and his neighbours long ago that they'd come to trouble with their side-sellings and bye-dealings; but we cannot have half Sussex hanged for a little gun-running. Are ye content, lads?"

' "I'd commit any treason for two demi-cannon," said Sebastian, and rubs his hands.

' "Ye have just compounded with rank treason-felony for the same bribe," says Sir John. "Wherefore to horse, and get the guns." '

'But Master Collins meant the guns for Sir Andrew Barton all along, didn't he?' said Dan.

'Questionless, that he did,' said Hal. 'But he lost them. We poured into the village on the red edge of dawn, Sir John horsed, in half-armour, his pennon flying; behind him thirty stout Brightling knaves, five abreast; behind them four wool-wains, and behind them four trumpets to triumph over the jest, blowing: *Our King went forth to Normandie*.[29] When we halted and rolled the ringing guns out of the tower, 'twas for all the world like Friar Roger's picture of the French siege in the Queen's Missal-book.'

'And what did we – I mean, what did our village do?' said Dan.

'Oh! Bore it nobly – nobly,' cried Hal. 'Though they had tricked me, I was proud of them. They came out of their housen, looked at that little army as though it had been a post, and went their shut-mouthed way. Never a sign! Never a word! They'd ha' perished sooner than let Brightling overcrow us. Even that villain, Ticehurst Will, coming out of the Bell for his morning ale, he all but runs under Sir John's horse.

'"'Ware, Sirrah Devil!" cries Sir John, reining back.

'"Oh!" says Will. "Market day, is it? And all the bullocks from Brightling here?"

'I spared him his belting for that – the brazen knave!

'But John Collins was our masterpiece! He happened along-street (his jaw tied up where Sebastian had clouted him) when we were trundling the first demi-cannon through the lych-gate.

'"I reckon you'll find her middlin' heavy," he says. "If you've a mind to pay, I'll loan ye my timber-tug.[30] She won't lie easy on ary wool-wain."[31]

'That was the one time I ever saw Sebastian taken flat aback. He opened and shut his mouth, fishy-like.

'"No offence," says Master John. "You've got her reasonable good cheap. I thought ye might not grudge me a groat if I help move her." Ah, he was a masterpiece! They say that morning's work cost our John two hundred pounds, and he never winked an eyelid, not even when he saw the guns all carted off to Lewes.'

'Neither then nor later?' said Puck.

'Once. 'Twas after he gave St Barnabas' the new chime of bells. (Oh, there was nothing the Collinses, or the Hayes, or the

Fowles, or the Fanners would not do for the church then! "Ask and have" was their song.) We had rung 'em in, and he was in the tower with Black Nick Fowle, that gave us our rood-screen. The old man pinches the bell-rope one hand and scratches his neck with t'other. "Sooner she was pulling yon clapper than my neck," he says. That was all! That was Sussex – seely [32] Sussex for everlastin'!'

'And what happened after?' said Una.

'I went back into England,' said Hal, slowly. 'I'd had my lesson against pride. But they tell me I left St Barnabas' a jewel – justabout a jewel! Wel-a-well! 'Twas done for and among my own people, and – Father Roger was right – I never knew such trouble or such triumph since. That's the nature o' things. A dear – dear land.' He dropped his chin on his chest.

'There's your Father at the Forge. What's he talking to old Hobden about?' said Puck, opening his hand with three leaves in it.

Dan looked towards the cottage.

'Oh, I know. It's that old oak lying across the brook. Pater always wants it grubbed.'

In the still valley they could hear old Hobden's deep tones.

'Have it *as* you've a mind to,' he was saying. 'But the vivers [33] of her roots they hold the bank together. If you grub her out, the bank she'll all come tearin' down, an' next floods the brook'll swarve up. But have it *as* you've a mind. The mistuss she sets a heap by the ferns on her trunk.'

'Oh! I'll think it over,' said the Pater.

Una laughed a little bubbling chuckle.

'What Devil's in *that* belfry?' said Hal, with a lazy laugh. 'That should be a Hobden by his voice.' [34]

'Why, the oak is the regular bridge for all the rabbits between the Three Acre and our meadow. The best place for wires on the farm, Hobden says. He's got two there now,' Una answered. '*He* won't ever let it be grubbed!'

'Ah, Sussex! Silly Sussex for everlastin',' murmured Hal; and the next moment their Father's voice calling across to Little Lindens broke the spell as little St Barnabas' clock struck five.

A Smugglers' Song [1]

If you wake at midnight, and hear a horse's feet,
Don't go drawing back the blind, or looking in the street,
Them that asks no questions isn't told a lie.
Watch the wall, my darling, while the Gentlemen go by!
        Five and twenty ponies,
        Trotting through the dark –
        Brandy for the Parson,
        'Baccy for the Clerk;
        Laces for a lady; letters for a spy,
And watch the wall, my darling, while the Gentlemen go by!

Running round the woodlump if you chance to find
Little barrels, roped and tarred, all full of brandy-wine;
Don't you shout to come and look, nor take 'em for your play;
Put the brishwood back again – and they'll be gone next day!

If you see the stableyard setting open wide;
If you see a tired horse lying down inside;
If your mother mends a coat cut about and tore;
If the lining's wet and warm – don't you ask no more!

If you meet King George's men, dresssed in blue and red,
You be careful what you say, and mindful what is said.
If they call you 'pretty maid', and chuck you 'neath the chin,
Don't you tell where no one is, nor yet where no one's been!

Knocks and footsteps round the house – whistles after dark –
You've no call for running out till the house-dogs bark.
Trusty's here, and *Pincher's* here, and see how dumb they lie –
They don't fret to follow when the Gentlemen go by!

If you do as you've been told, 'likely there's a chance,
You'll be give a dainty doll, all the way from France,
With a cap of Valenciennes,[2] and a velvet hood –
A present from the Gentlemen, along o' being good!
        Five and twenty ponies,
        Trotting through the dark –

Puck of Pook's Hill

Brandy for the Parson,
    'Baccy for the Clerk.
Them that asks no questions isn't told a lie—
Watch the wall, my darling, while the Gentlemen go by!

❴ 'Dymchurch Flit' ❵

The Bee Boy's Song

Bees! Bees! Hark to your bees!
'Hide from your neighbours as much as you please,
But all that has happened, to us you must tell.[1]
Or else we will give you no honey to sell!'

A maiden in her glory,
  Upon her wedding-day,
Must tell her Bees the story,
  Or else they'll fly away.
      Fly away — die away —
        Dwindle down and leave you!
      But if you don't deceive your Bees,
        Your Bees will not deceive you.

Marriage, birth or buryin',
  News across the seas,
All you're sad or merry in,
  You must tell the Bees.
      Tell 'em coming in an' out,
        Where the Fanners[2] fan,
      'Cause the Bees are justabout
        As curious as a man!

Don't you wait where trees are,
  When the lightnings play;
Nor don't you hate where Bees are,
  Or else they'll pine away.
      Pine away — dwine[3] away —
        Anything to leave you!
      But if you never grieve your Bees,
        Your Bees 'll never grieve you.

181

'Dymchurch Flit'

Just at dusk, a soft September rain began to fall on the hop-pickers. The mothers wheeled the bouncing perambulators out of the gardens; bins were put away, and tally-books made up. The young couples strolled home, two to each umbrella, and the single men walked behind them laughing. Dan and Una, who had been picking after their lessons, marched off to roast potatoes at the oast-house, where old Hobden, with Blue-eyed Bess, his lurcher dog, lived all the month through, drying the hops.

They settled themselves, as usual, on the sack-strewn cot in front of the fires, and, when Hobden drew up the shutter, stared, as usual, at the flameless bed of coals spouting its heat up the dark well of the old-fashioned roundel. Slowly he cracked off a few fresh pieces of coal, packed them, with fingers that never flinched, exactly where they would do most good; slowly he reached behind him till Dan tilted the potatoes into his iron scoop of a hand; carefully he arranged them round the fire, and then stood for a moment, black against the glare. As he closed the shutter, the oast-house seemed dark before the day's end, and he lit the candle in the lanthorn. The children liked all these things because they knew them so well.

The Bee Boy, Hobden's son, who is not quite right in his head, though he can do anything with bees, slipped in like a shadow. They only guessed it when Bess's stump-tail wagged against them.

A big voice began singing outside in the drizzle:

'Old Mother Laidinwool [1] had nigh twelve months been dead,
She heard the hops were doing well, and then popped up her head.'

'There can't be two people made to holler like that!' cried old Hobden, wheeling round.

'For, says she, "The boys I've picked with when I was young and
                                      fair,
They're bound to be at hoppin', and I'm –" '

A man showed at the doorway.

'Well, well! They do say hoppin'll draw the very deadest,
and now I belieft 'em. You, Tom? Tom Shoesmith!' Hobden
lowered his lanthorn.

'You're a hem [2] of a time makin' your mind to it, Ralph!'
The stranger strode in – three full inches taller than Hobden, a
grey-whiskered, brown-faced giant with clear blue eyes. They
shook hands, and the children could hear the hard palms rasp
together.

'You ain't lost none o' your grip,' said Hobden. 'Was it thirty
or forty year back you broke my head at Peasmarsh Fair?'

'Only thirty an' no odds 'tween us regardin' heads, neither.
You had it back at me with a hop-pole. How did we get home
that night? Swimmin'?'

'Same way the pheasant come into Gubbs's pocket – by a
little luck an' a deal o' conjurin'.' Old Hobden laughed in his
deep chest.

'I see you've not forgot your way about the woods. D'ye do
any o' *this* still?' The stranger pretended to look along a gun.

Hobden answered with a quick movement of the hand as
though he were pegging down a rabbit-wire.

'No. *That's* all that's left me now. Age she must as Age she
can. An' what's your news since all these years?'

'Oh I've bin to Plymouth, I've bin to Dover –
    I've bin ramblin', boys, the wide world over,' [3]

the man answered cheerily. 'I reckon I know as much of Old
England as most.' He turned towards the children and winked
boldly.

'I lay they told you a sight o' lies, then. I've been into
England fur as Wiltsheer once. I was cheated proper over a pair
of hedging-gloves,' said Hobden.

'There's fancy-talkin' everywhere. *You*'ve cleaved to your
own parts pretty middlin' close, Ralph.'

'Can't shift an old tree 'thout it dyin',' Hobden chuckled. 'An' I be no more anxious to die than you look to be to help me with my hops tonight.'

The great man leaned against the brick-work of the roundel, and swung his arms abroad. 'Hire me!' was all he said, and they stumped upstairs laughing.

The children heard their shovels rasp on the cloth where the yellow hops lie drying above the fires, and all the oast-house filled with the sweet, sleepy smell as they were turned.

'Who is it?' Una whispered to the Bee Boy.

'Dunno, no more'n you – if *you* dunno,' said he, and smiled.

The voices on the drying-floor talked and chuckled together, and the heavy footsteps moved back and forth. Presently a hop-pocket dropped through the press-hole overhead, and stiffened and fattened as they shovelled it full. 'Clank!' went the press, and rammed the loose stuff into tight cake.

'Gently!' they heard Hobden cry. 'You'll bust her crop if you lay on so. You be as careless as Gleason's bull, Tom. Come an' sit by the fires. She'll do now.'

They came down, and as Hobden opened the shutter to see if the potatoes were done Tom Shoesmith said to the children, 'Put a plenty salt on 'em. That'll show you the sort o' man *I* be.' Again he winked and again the Bee Boy laughed and Una stared at Dan.

'*I* know what sort o' man you be,' Old Hobden grunted, groping for the potatoes round the fire.

'Do ye?' Tom went on behind his back. 'Some of us can't abide Horseshoes, or Church Bells, or Running Water; an', talkin' o' runnin' water' – he turned to Hobden, who was backing out of the roundel – 'd'you mind the great floods at Robertsbridge, when the miller's man was drowned in the street?'

'Middlin' well.' Old Hobden let himself down on the coals by the fire door. 'I was courtin' my woman on the Marsh that year. Carter to Mus' Plum I was, gettin' ten shillin's week. Mine was a Marsh woman.'

'Won'erful odd-gates[4] place – Romney Marsh,' said Tom

Shoesmith. 'I've heard say the world's divided like into Europe,
Ashy, Afriky, Ameriky, Australy, an' Romney Marsh.'[5]

'The Marsh folk think so,' said Hobden. 'I had a hem o'
trouble to get my woman to leave it.'

'Where did she come out of? I've forgot, Ralph.'

'Dymchurch under the Wall,' Hobden answered, a potato in
his hand.

'Then she'd be a Pett – or a Whitgift, would she?'

'Whitgift.' Hobden broke open the potato and ate it with the
curious neatness of men who make most of their meals in the
blowy open. 'She growed to be quite reasonable-like after livin'
in the Weald awhile, but our first twenty year or two she was
odd-fashioned, no bounds. And she was a won'erful hand with
bees.' He cut away a little piece of potato and threw it out to the
door.

'Ah! I've heard say the Whitgifts could see further through a
millstone than most,'[6] said Shoesmith. 'Did she, now?'

'She was honest-innocent of any nigromancin','[7] said
Hobden. 'Only she'd read signs and sinnifications out o' birds
flyin', stars fallin', bees hivin', and such. An' she'd lie awake –
listenin' for calls, she said.'

'That don't prove naught,' said Tom. 'All Marsh folk have
been smugglers since time everlastin'. 'Twould be in her blood
to listen out o' nights.'

'Nature-ally,' old Hobden replied, smiling. 'I mind when
there was smugglin' a sight nearer us than the Marsh be. But
that wasn't my woman's trouble. 'Twas a passel[8] o' no-sense
talk,' he dropped his voice, 'about Pharisees.'[9]

'Yes. I've heard Marsh men belief in 'em.' Tom looked
straight at the wide-eyed children beside Bess.

'Pharisees,' cried Una. 'Fairies? Oh, *I* see!'

'People o' the Hills,' said the Bee Boy, throwing half of his
potato towards the door.

'There you be!' said Hobden, pointing at him. 'My boy, he
has her eyes and her out-gate[10] senses. That's what *she* called
'em!'

'And what did you think of it all?'

'Um – um,' Hobden rumbled. 'A man that uses fields an'

shaws after dark as much as I've done, he don't go out of his road excep' for keepers.'

'But settin' that aside?' said Tom, coaxingly. 'I saw ye throw the Good Piece out-at-doors just now. Do ye believe or – *do* ye?'

'There was a great black eye to that tater,' said Hobden, indignantly.

'My liddle eye didn't see un, then. It looked as if you meant it for – for Any One that might need it. But settin' that aside. D'ye believe or – *do* ye?'

'I ain't sayin' nothin', because I've heard naught, an' I've seen naught. But if you was to say there was more things after dark in the shaws than men, or fur, or feather, or fin, I dunno as I'd go far about to call you a liar. Now turnagain, Tom. What's your say?'

'I'm like you. I say nothin'. But I'll tell you a tale, an' you can fit it *as* how you please.'

'Passel o' no-sense stuff,' growled Hobden, but he filled his pipe.

'The Marsh men they call it Dymchurch Flit,' Tom went on slowly. 'Hap you have heard it?'

'My woman she've told it me scores o' times. Dunno as I didn't end by belieftin' it – sometimes.'

Hobden crossed over as he spoke, and sucked with his pipe at the yellow lanthorn flame. Tom rested one great elbow on one great knee, where he sat among the coal.

'Have you ever bin in the Marsh?' he said to Dan.

'Only as far as Rye, once,' Dan answered.

'Ah, that's but the edge. Back behind of her there's steeples settin' beside churches,[11] an' wise women settin' beside their doors, an' the sea settin' above the land, an' ducks herdin' wild in the diks' (he meant ditches). 'The Marsh is justabout riddled with diks an' sluices, an' tide-gates an' water-lets. You can hear 'em bubblin' an' grummelin'[12] when the tide works in 'em, an' then you hear the sea rangin' left and right-handed all up along the Wall. You've seen how flat she is – the Marsh? You'd think nothin' easier than to walk eend-on acrost her? Ah, but the diks an' the water-lets, they twists the roads about as ravelly as witch-yarn[13] on the spindles. So ye get all turned round in broad daylight.'

'That's because they've dreened the waters into the diks,' said Hobden. 'When I courted my woman the rushes was green – Eh me! the rushes was green – an' the Bailiff o' the Marshes, he rode up and down as free as the fog.'

'Who was he?' said Dan.

'Why, the Marsh fever an' ague. He've clapped me on the shoulder once or twice till I shook proper. But now the dreenin' off of the waters have done away with the fevers; so they make a joke, like, that the Bailiff o' the Marshes broke his neck in a dik. A won'erful place for bees an' ducks 'tis too.'

'An' old,' Tom went on. 'Flesh an' Blood have been there since Time Everlastin' Beyond. Well, now, speakin' among themselves, the Marshmen say that from Time Everlastin' Beyond, the Pharisees favoured the Marsh above the rest of Old England. I lay the Marsh men ought to know. They've been out after dark, father an' son, smugglin' some one thing or t'other, since ever wool grew to sheep's backs. They say there was always a middlin' few Pharisees to be seen on the Marsh. Impident as rabbits, they was. They'd dance on the nakid roads in the nakid daytime; they'd flash their liddle green lights along the diks, comin' an' goin', like honest smugglers. Yes, an' times they'd lock the church doors against parson an' clerk of Sundays.'

'That 'ud be smugglers layin' in the lace or the brandy till they could run it out o' the Marsh. I've told my woman so,' said Hobden.

'I'll lay she didn't belieft it, then – not if she was a Whitgift. A won'erful choice place for Pharisees, the Marsh, by all accounts, till Queen Bess's father he come in with his Reformatories.'[14]

'Would that be a Act o' Parliament like?' Hobden asked.

'Sure-ly. Can't do nothing in Old England without Act, Warrant, an' Summons. He got his Act allowed him, an,' they say, Queen Bess's father he used the parish churches something shameful. Justabout tore the gizzards out of I dunnamany.[15] Some folk in England they held with 'en; but some they saw it

different, an' it eended in 'em takin' sides an' burnin' each
other no bounds, accordin' which side was top, time bein'. That
tarrified the Pharisees: for Good-will among Flesh an' Blood is
meat an' drink to 'em, an' ill-will is poison.'

'Same as bees,' said the Bee Boy. 'Bees won't stay by a house
where there's hating.'

'True,' said Tom. 'This Reformations tarrified the Pharisees
same as the reaper goin' round a last stand o' wheat tarrifies
rabbits. They packed into the Marsh from all parts, and they
says, "Fair or foul, we must flit out o' this, for Merry England's
done with, an' we're reckoned among the Images." ' [16]

'Did they *all* see it that way?' said Hobden.

'All but one that was called Robin — if you've heard of
him. What are you laughing at?' Tom turned to Dan. 'The
Pharisees's trouble didn't tech Robin, because he'd cleaved
middlin' close to people like. No more he never meant to go
out of Old England — not he; so he was sent messagin' for
help among Flesh an' Blood. But Flesh an' Blood must always
think of their own concerns, an' Robin couldn't get *through*
at 'em, ye see. They thought it was tide-echoes off the
Marsh.'

'What did you — what did the fai– Pharisees want?' Una
asked.

'A boat, to be sure. Their liddle wings could no more cross
Channel than so many tired butterflies. A boat an' a crew
they desired to sail 'em over to France, where yet awhile folks
hadn't tore down the Images. They couldn't abide cruel Canterbury Bells ringin' to Bulverhithe [17] for more pore men an'
women to be burnded, nor the King's proud messenger ridin'
through the land givin' orders to tear down the Images. They
couldn't abide it no shape. Nor yet they couldn't get their
boat an' crew to flit by without Leave an' Good-will from
Flesh an' Blood; an' Flesh an' Blood came an' went about its
own business the while the Marsh was swarvin' up, an' swarvin'
up with Pharisees from all England over, striving all means to
get *through* at Flesh an' Blood to tell 'em their sore need . . . I
don't know as you've ever heard say Pharisees are like
chickens?'

'My woman used to say that too,' said Hobden, folding his brown arms.

'They be. You run too many chickens together, an' the ground sickens like, an' you get a squat,[18] an' your chickens die. 'Same way, you crowd Pharisees all in one place – *they* don't die, but Flesh an' Blood walkin' among 'em is apt to sick up an' pine off. *They* don't mean it, an' Flesh an' Blood don't know it, but that's the truth – as I've heard. The Pharisees through bein' all stenched up [19] an' frighted, an' tryin' to come *through* with their supplications, they nature-ally changed the thin airs and humours in Flesh an' Blood. It lay on the Marsh like thunder. Men saw their churches ablaze with the wildfire in the windows after dark; they saw their cattle scatterin' and no man scarin'; their sheep flockin' and no man drivin'; their horses latherin' an' no man leadin'; they saw the liddle low green lights more than ever in the dik-sides; they heard the liddle feet patterin' more than ever round the houses; an' night an' day, day an' night, 'twas all as though they were bein' creeped up on, and hinted at by Some One or other that couldn't rightly shape their trouble. Oh, I lay they sweated! Man an' maid, woman an' child, their Nature done 'em no service all the weeks while the Marsh was swarvin' up with Pharisees. But they was Flesh an' Blood, an' Marsh men before all. They reckoned the signs sinnified trouble for the Marsh. Or that the sea 'ud rear up against Dymchurch Wall an' they'd be drownded like Old Winchelsea;[20] or that the Plague was comin'. So they looked for the meanin' in the sea or in the clouds – far an' high up. They never thought to look near an' knee-high, where they could see naught.

'Now there was a poor widow at Dymchurch under the Wall, which, lacking man or property, she had the more time for feeling; and she come to feel there was a Trouble outside her doorstep bigger an' heavier than aught she'd ever carried over it. She had two sons – one born blind, and t'other struck dumb through fallin' off the Wall when he was liddle. They was men grown, but not wage-earnin', an' she worked for 'em, keepin' bees and answerin' Questions.'

'What sort of questions?' said Dan.

'Like where lost things might be found, an' what to put about a crooked baby's neck, an' how to join parted sweethearts. She felt the Trouble on the Marsh same as eels feel thunder. She was a wise woman.'

'My woman was won'erful weather-tender, too,' said Hobden. 'I've seen her brish sparks like off an anvil out of her hair in thunderstorms. But she never laid out to answer Questions.'

'This woman was a Seeker [21] like, an' Seekers they sometimes find. One night, while she lay abed, hot an' aching, there come a Dream an' tapped at her window, and "Widow Whitgift," it said, "Widow Whitgift!"

'First, by the wings an' the whistling, she thought it was peewits, but last she arose an' dressed herself, an' opened her door to the Marsh, an' she felt the Trouble an' the Groaning all about her, strong as fever an' ague, an' she calls: "What is it? Oh, what is it?"

'Then 'twas all like the frogs in the diks peeping: then 'twas all like the reeds in the diks clip-clapping; an' then the great Tide-wave rummelled [22] along the Wall, an' she couldn't hear proper.

'Three times she called, an' three times the Tide-wave did her down. But she catched the quiet between, an' she cries out, "What is the Trouble on the Marsh that's been lying down with my heart an' arising with my body this month gone?" She felt a liddle hand lay hold on her gown-hem, an' she stooped to the pull o' that liddle hand.'

Tom Shoesmith spread his huge fist before the fire and smiled at it.

'"Will the sea drown the Marsh?" she says. She was a Marsh-woman first an' foremost.

'"No," says the liddle voice. "Sleep sound for all o' that."

'"Is the Plague comin' to the Marsh?" she says. Them was all the ills she knowed.

'"No. Sleep sound for all o' that," says Robin.

'She turned about, half mindful to go in, but the liddle voices grieved that shrill an' sorrowful she turns back, an' she cries: "If it is not a Trouble of Flesh an' Blood, what can I do?"

'The Pharisees cried out upon her from all round to fetch them a boat to sail to France, an' come back no more.

'"There's a boat on the Wall," she says, "but I can't push it down to the sea, nor sail it when 'tis there."

'"Lend us your sons," says all the Pharisees. "Give 'em Leave an' Good-will to sail it for us, Mother – O Mother!"

'"One's dumb, an' t'other's blind," she says. "But all the dearer me for that; and you'll lose them in the big sea." The voices justabout pierced through her; an' there was children's voices too. She stood out all she could, but she couldn't rightly stand against *that*. So she says: "If you can draw my sons for your job, I'll not hinder 'em. You can't ask no more of a Mother."

'She saw them liddle green lights dance an' cross till she was dizzy; she heard them liddle feet patterin' by the thousand; she heard cruel Canterbury Bells ringing to Bulverhithe, an' she heard the great Tide-wave ranging along the Wall. That was while the Pharisees was workin' a Dream to wake her two sons asleep: an' while she bit on her fingers she saw them two she'd bore come out an' pass her with never a word. She followed 'em, cryin' pitiful, to the old boat on the Wall, an' that they took an' runned down to the Sea.

'When they'd stepped mast an' sail the blind son speaks: "Mother, we're waitin' your Leave an' Good-will to take Them over."'

Tom Shoesmith threw back his head and half shut his eyes.

'Eh, me!' he said. 'She was a fine, valiant woman, the Widow Whitgift. She stood twistin' the ends of her long hair over her fingers, an' she shook like a poplar, makin' up her mind. The Pharisees all about they hushed their children from cryin' an' they waited dumb-still. She was all their dependence. 'Thout her Leave an' Good-will they could not pass; for she was the Mother. So she shook like a aps-tree[23] makin' up her mind. 'Last she drives the word past her teeth, an' "Go!" she says. "Go with my Leave an' Good-will."

'Then I saw – then, they say, she had to brace back same as if she was wadin' in tide-water; for the Pharisees just about flowed past her – down the beach to the boat, *I* dunnamany of 'em – with their wives an' children an' valooables, all escapin' out of cruel Old England. Silver you could hear clinkin', an' liddle bundles hove down dunt[24] on the bottom-boards, an' passels o' liddle swords an' shields raklin',[25] an' liddle fingers an' toes scratchin' on the boatside to board her when the two sons pushed her off. That boat she sunk lower an' lower, but all the Widow could see in it was her boys movin' hampered-like to get at the tackle. Up sail they did, an' away they went, deep as a Rye barge, away into the off-shore mistes, an' the Widow Whitgift she sat down and eased her grief till mornin' light.'

'I never heard she was *all* alone,' said Hobden.

'I remember now. The one called Robin he stayed with her, they tell. She was all too grievious to listen to his promises.'

'Ah! She should ha' made her bargain beforehand. I allus told my woman so!' Hobden cried.

'No. She loaned her sons for a pure love-loan, bein' as she sensed the Trouble on the Marshes, an' was simple good-willing to ease it.' Tom laughed softly. 'She done that. Yes, she done that! From Hithe to Bulverhithe, fretty[26] man an' petty maid, ailin' woman an' wailin' child, they took the advantage of the change in the thin airs just about *as* soon as the Pharisees flitted. Folks come out fresh an' shining all over the Marsh like snails after wet. An' that while the Widow Whitgift sat grievin' on the Wall. She might have belief us – she might have trusted her sons would be sent back! She fussed, no bounds, when their boat come in after three days.'

'And, of course, the sons were both quite cured?' said Una.

'No-o. That would have been out o' Nature. She got 'em back *as* she sent 'em. The blind man he hadn't seen naught of anything, an' the dumb man nature-ally, he couldn't say aught of what he'd seen. I reckon that was why the Pharisees pitched on 'em for the ferrying job.'

'But what did you – what did Robin promise the Widow?' said Dan.

'What *did* he promise, now?' Tom pretended to think. 'Wasn't your woman a Whitgift, Ralph? Didn't she ever say?'

'She told me a passel o' no-sense stuff when he was born.' Hobden pointed at his son. 'There was always to be one of 'em that could see further into a millstone than most.'

'Me! That's me!' said the Bee Boy so suddenly that they all laughed.

'I've got it now!' cried Tom, slapping his knee. 'So long as Whitgift blood lasted, Robin promised there would allers be one o' her stock that – that no Trouble 'ud lie on, no Maid 'ud sigh on, no Night could frighten, no Fright could harm, no Harm could make sin, an' no Woman could make a fool of.'

'Well, ain't that just me?' said the Bee Boy, where he sat in the silver square of the great September moon that was staring into the oast-house door.

'They was the exact words she told me when we first found he wasn't like others. But it beats me how you known 'em,' said Hobden.

'Aha! There's more under my hat besides hair!' Tom laughed and stretched himself. 'When I've seen these two young folk home, we'll make a night of old days, Ralph, with passin' old tales – eh? An' where might you live?' he said, gravely, to Dan. 'An' do you think your Pa 'ud give me a drink for takin' you there, Missy?'

They giggled so at this that they had to run out. Tom picked them both up, set one on each broad shoulder, and tramped across the ferny pasture where the cows puffed milky puffs at them in the moonlight.

'Oh, Puck! Puck! I guessed you right from when you talked about the salt. How could you ever do it?' Una cried, swinging along delighted.

'Do what?' he said, and climbed the stile by the pollard oak.

'Pretend to be Tom Shoesmith,' said Dan, and they ducked to avoid the two little ashes that grow by the bridge over the brook. Tom was almost running.

'Yes. That's my name, Mus' Dan,' he said, hurrying over the silent shining lawn, where a rabbit sat by the big white-thorn near the croquet ground. 'Here you be.' He strode into the old kitchen yard, and slid them down as Ellen came to ask questions.

'I'm helping in Mus' Spray's oast-house,' he said to her. 'No, I'm no foreigner. I knowed this country 'fore your Mother was born; an' – yes, it's dry work oasting, Miss. Thank you.'

Ellen went to get a jug, and the children went in – magicked once more by Oak, Ash, and Thorn!

A Three-Part Song

I'm just in love with all these three,
The Weald and the Marsh and the Down countrie;
Nor I don't know which I love the most,
The Weald or the Marsh or the white chalk coast!

I've buried my heart in a ferny hill,
Twix' a liddle low shaw [1] an' a great high gill. [2]
Oh hop-bine yaller and woodsmoke blue,
I reckon you'll keep her middling true!

I've loosed my mind for to out and run,
On a Marsh that was old when Kings begun;
Oh Romney level and Brenzett reeds,
I reckon you know what my mind needs!

I've given my soul to the Southdown grass,
And sheep-bells tinkled where you pass.
Oh Firle an' Ditchling an' sails at sea,
I reckon you keep my soul for me!

The Treasure and the Law

Song of the Fifth River

When first by Eden Tree,
The Four Great Rivers ran,[1]
To each was appointed a Man
Her Prince and Ruler to be.

But after this was ordained,
(The ancient legends tell),
There came dark Israel,
For whom no River remained.

Then He That is Wholly Just,[2]
Said to him: 'Fling on the ground
A handful of yellow dust,
And a Fifth Great River shall run,
Mightier than these Four,
In secret the Earth around;
And Her secret evermore,
Shall be shown to thee and thy Race.'

So it was said and done.
And, deep in the veins of Earth,
And, fed by a thousand springs
That comfort the market-place,
Or sap the power of Kings,
The Fifth Great River had birth,
Even as it was foretold –
The Secret River of Gold!

And Israel laid down
His sceptre and his crown,
To brood on that River bank,
Where the waters flashed and sank,

And burrowed in earth and fell,
And bided a season below;
For reason that none might know,
Save only Israel.

He is Lord of the Last –
The Fifth, most wonderful, Flood.
He hears Her thunder past
And Her Song is in his blood.
He can foresay: 'She will fall,'
For he knows which fountain dries,
Behind which desert-belt
A thousand leagues to the South.
He can foresay: 'She will rise.'
He knows what far snows melt;
Along what mountain-wall
A thousand leagues to the North.
He snuffs the coming drought
As he snuffs the coming rain,
He knows what each will bring forth,
And turns it to his gain.

A Prince without a Sword,
A Ruler without a Throne;
Israel follows his quest.
In every land a guest,
Of many lands a lord,
In no land King is he,
But the Fifth Great River keeps
The secret of Her deeps
For Israel alone,
As it was ordered to be.

The Treasure and the Law

Now it was the third week in November, and the woods rang
with the noise of pheasant-shooting. No one hunted that steep,
cramped country except the village beagles, who, as often as
not, escaped from their kennels and made a day of their own.
Dan and Una found a couple of them towling[1] round the
kitchen-garden after the laundry cat. The little brutes were
only too pleased to go rabbiting, so the children ran them all
along the brook pastures and into Little Lindens farm-yard,
where the old sow vanquished them – and up to the quarry-
hole, where they started a fox. He headed for Far Wood, and
there they frightened out all the pheasants, who were sheltering
from a big beat across the valley. Then the cruel guns began
again, and they grabbed the beagles lest they should stray and
get hurt.

'I wouldn't be a pheasant – in November – for a lot,' Dan
panted, as he caught *Folly* by the neck. 'Why did you laugh that
horrid way?'

'I didn't,' said Una, sitting on *Flora*, the fat lady-dog. 'Oh,
look! The silly birds are going back to their own woods instead
of ours, where they would be safe.'

'Safe till it pleased you to kill them.' An old man, so tall he
was almost a giant, stepped from behind the clump of hollies
by Volaterrae. The children jumped, and the dogs dropped like
setters. He wore a sweeping gown of dark thick stuff, lined and
edged with yellowish fur, and he bowed a bent-down bow that
made them feel both proud and ashamed. Then he looked at
them steadily, and they stared back without doubt or fear.

'You are not afraid?' he said, running his hands through his
splendid grey beard. 'Not afraid that those men yonder' – he
jerked his head towards the incessant pop-pop of the guns from
the lower woods – 'will do you hurt?'

'We-ell' – Dan liked to be accurate, especially when he was

197

shy – 'old Hobd– a friend of mine told me that one of the beaters got peppered last week – hit in the leg, I mean. You see, Mr Meyer *will* fire at rabbits. But he gave Wasy Garnett a quid – sovereign, I mean – and Waxy told Hobden he'd have stood both barrels for half the money.'

'He doesn't understand,' Una cried, watching the pale, troubled face. 'Oh, I wish –'

She had scarcely said it when Puck rustled out of the hollies and spoke to the man quickly in foreign words. Puck wore a long cloak too – the afternoon was just frosting down – and it changed his appearance altogether.

'Nay, nay!' he said at last. 'You did not understand the boy. A freeman was a little hurt, by pure mischance, at the hunting.'

'I know that mischance! What did his Lord do? Laugh and ride over him?' the old man sneered.

'It was one of your own people did the hurt, Kadmiel.' Puck's eyes twinkled maliciously. 'So he gave the freeman a piece of gold, and no more was said.'

'A Jew drew blood from a Christian and no more was said?' Kadmiel cried. 'Never! When did they torture him?'

'No man may be bound, or fined, or slain till he has been judged by his peers,' Puck insisted. 'There is but one Law in Old England for Jew or Christian – the Law that was signed at Runnymede.'

'Why, that's Magna Charta!' Dan whispered. It was one of the few history dates that he could remember. Kadmiel turned on him with a sweep and a whirr of his spicy-scented gown.

'Dost *thou* know of that, babe?' he cried, and lifted his hands in wonder.

'Yes,' said Dan, firmly.

'Magna Charta was signed by John,
That Henry the Third put his heel upon.

And old Hobden says that if it hadn't been for *her* (he calls everything "her", you know), the keepers would have him clapped in Lewes Gaol all the year round.'

Again Puck translated to Kadmiel in the strange, solemn-sounding language, and at last Kadmiel laughed.

'Out of the mouths of babes do we learn,' said he. 'But tell me now, and I will not call you a babe but a Rabbi, *why* did the King sign the roll of the New Law at Runnymede? For he was a King.'

Dan looked sideways at his sister. It was her turn.

'Because he jolly well had to,' said Una, softly. 'The Barons made him.'

'Nay,' Kadmiel answered, shaking his head. 'You Christians always forget that gold does more than the sword. Our good King signed because he could not borrow more money from us bad Jews.' He curved his shoulders as he spoke. 'A King without gold is a snake with a broken back, and' – his nose sneered up [2] and his eyebrows frowned down – 'it is a good deed to break a snake's back. That was my work,' he cried, triumphantly, to Puck. 'Spirit of Earth, bear witness that that was *my* work!' He shot up to his full towering height, and his words rang like a trumpet. He had a voice that changed its tone almost as an opal changes colour – sometimes deep and thundery, sometimes thin and waily [3] but always it made you listen.

'Many people can bear witness to that,' Puck answered. 'Tell these babes how it was done. Remember, Master, they do not know Doubt or Fear.'

'So I saw in their faces when we met,' said Kadmiel. 'Yet surely, surely they are taught to spit upon Jews?'

'Are they?' said Dan, much interested. 'Where at?'

Puck fell back a pace, laughing. 'Kadmiel is thinking of King John's reign,' he explained. 'His people were badly treated then.'

'Oh, we know *that*,' they answered, and (it was very rude of them, but they could not help it) they stared straight at Kadmiel's mouth to see if his teeth were all there. It stuck in their lesson-memory that King John used to pull out Jews' teeth [4] to make them lend him money.

Kadmiel understood the look and smiled bitterly.

'No. Your King never drew my teeth: I think, perhaps, I drew his. Listen! I was not born among Christians, but among Moors – in Spain – in a little white town under the mountains. Yes, the Moors are cruel, but at least their learned men dare to

think. It was prophesied of me at my birth that I should be a
Lawgiver to a People of a strange speech and a hard language.
We Jews are always looking for the Prince and the Lawgiver to
come. Why not? My people in the town (we were very few) set
me apart as a child of the prophecy – the Chosen of the Chosen.
We Jews dream so many dreams. You would never guess it to
see us slink about the rubbish-heaps in our quarter; but at the
day's end – doors shut, candles lit – aha! *then* we become the
Chosen again.'

He paced back and forth through the wood as he talked. The
rattle of the shot-guns never ceased, and the dogs whimpered a
little and lay flat on the leaves.

'I was a Prince. Yes! Think of a little Prince who had never
known rough words in his own house handed over to shouting, bearded Rabbis, who pulled his ears and filliped his nose,
all that he might learn – learn – learn to be King when his
time came. Hé! Such a little Prince it was! One eye he kept
on the stone-throwing Moorish boys, and the other it roved
about the streets looking for his Kingdom. Yes, and he learned to cry softly when he was hunted up and down those
streets. He learned to do all things without noise. He played
beneath his father's table when the Great Candle was lit, and
he listened as children listen to the talk of his father's friends
above the table. They came across the mountains, from out
of all the world, for my Prince's father was their councillor.
They came from behind the armies of Sala-ud-Din:[5] from
Rome: from Venice: from England. They stole down our
alley, they tapped secretly at our door, they took off their
rags, they arrayed themselves, and they talked to my father
at the wine. All over the world the heathen fought each other.
They brought news of these wars, and while he played beneath the table, my Prince heard these meanly-dressed ones
decide between themselves how, and when, and for how long
King should draw sword against King, and People rise up
against People. Why not? There can be no war without gold,
and we Jews know how the earth's gold moves with the sea-
sons, and the crops and the winds; circling and looping and
rising and sinking away like a river – a wonderful under-

ground river. How should the foolish Kings know *that* while they fight and steal and kill?'

The children's faces showed that they knew nothing at all as, with open eyes, they trotted and turned beside the long-striding old man. He twitched his gown over his shoulders, and a square plate of gold, studded with jewels, gleamed for an instant through the fur, like a star through flying snow.

'No matter,' he said. 'But, credit me, my Prince saw peace or war decided not once, but many times, by the fall of a coin spun between a Jew from Bury [6] and a Jewess from Alexandria, in his father's house, when the Great Candle was lit. Such power had we Jews among the Gentiles. Ah, my little Prince! Do you wonder that he learned quickly? Why not?' He muttered to himself and went on:

'My trade was that of a physician. When I had learned it in Spain I went to the East to find my Kingdom. Why not? A Jew is as free as a sparrow – or a dog. He goes where he is hunted. In the East I found libraries where men dared to think – schools of medicine where they dared to learn. [7] I was diligent in my business. Therefore I stood before Kings. I have been a brother to Princes and a companion to beggars, [8] and I have walked between the living and the dead. There was no profit in it. I did not find my Kingdom. So, in the tenth year of my travels, when I had reached the Uttermost Eastern Sea, I returned to my father's house. God had wonderfully preserved my people. None had been slain, none even wounded, and only a few scourged. I became once more a son in my father's house. Again the Great Candle was lit; again the meanly-apparelled ones tapped on our door after dusk; and again I heard them weigh out peace and war, as they weighed out the gold on the table. But I was not rich – not very rich. Therefore, when those that had power and knowledge and wealth talked together, I sat in the shadow. Why not?

'Yet all my wanderings had shown me one sure thing, which is, that a King without money is like a spear without a head. He cannot do much harm. I said, therefore, to Elias of Bury, a great one among our people: "Why do our people lend any more to the Kings that oppress us?" "Because," said Elias, "if we refuse they stir up their people against us, and the People are tenfold more cruel than Kings. If thou doubtest, come with me to Bury in England and live as I live."

'I saw my mother's face across the candle flame, and I said, "I will come with thee to Bury. Maybe my Kingdom shall be there."

'So I sailed with Elias to the darkness and the cruelty of Bury in England, where there are no learned men. How can a man be wise if he hate? At Bury I kept his accounts for Elias, and I saw men kill Jews there by the tower. No – none laid hands on Elias. He lent money to the King, and the King's favour was about him. A King will not take the life so long as there is any gold. This King – yes, John – oppressed his people bitterly because they would not give him money. Yet his land was a good land. If he had only given it rest he might have cropped it as a Christian crops his beard. But even *that* little he did not know, for God had deprived him of all understanding, and had multiplied pestilence, and famine, and despair upon the people. Therefore his people turned against us Jews, who are all people's dogs. Why not? Lastly the Barons and the people rose together against the King because of his cruelties. Nay – nay – the Barons did not love the people, but they saw that if the King cut up and destroyed the common people, he would presently destroy the Barons. They joined then, as cats and pigs will join to slay a snake. I kept the accounts, and I watched all these things, for I remembered the Prophecy.

'A great gathering of Barons [9] (to most of whom we had lent money) came to Bury, and there, after much talk and a thousand runnings-about, they made a roll of the New Laws that they would force on the King. If he swore to keep those Laws, they would allow him a little money. That was the King's God – Money – to waste. They showed us the roll of the New Laws. Why not? We had lent them money. We knew all their counsels – we Jews shivering behind our doors in Bury.' He threw out his hands suddenly. 'We did not seek to be paid *all* in money. We sought Power – Power – Power! That is *our* God in our captivity. Power to use!

'I said to Elias: "These New Laws are good. Lend no more

money to the King: so long as he has money he will lie and slay the people."

'"Nay," said Elias. "I know this people. They are madly cruel. Better one King than a thousand butchers. I have lent a little money to the Barons, or they would torture us, but my most I will lend to the King. He hath promised me a place near him at Court, where my wife and I shall be safe."

'"But if the King be made to keep these New Laws," I said, "the land will have peace, and our trade will grow. If we lend he will fight again."

'"Who made thee a Lawgiver in England?" said Elias. "*I* know this people. Let the dogs tear one another! I will lend the King ten thousand pieces of gold, and he can fight the Barons at his pleasure."

'"There are not two thousand pieces of gold in all England this summer," I said, for I kept the accounts, and I knew how the earth's gold moved – that wonderful underground river. Elias barred home the windows, and, his hands about his mouth, he told me how, when he was trading with small wares in a French ship, he had come to the Castle of Pevensey.'

'Oh!' said Dan. 'Pevensey again!' and looked at Una, who nodded and skipped.

'There, after they had scattered his pack up and down the Great Hall, some young knights carried him to an upper room, and dropped him into a well in a wall, that rose and fell with the tide. They called him Joseph, and threw torches at his wet head. Why not?'

'Why, of course,' cried Dan. 'Didn't you know it was –' Puck held up his hand to stop him, and Kadmiel, who never noticed, went on.[10]

'When the tide dropped he thought he stood on old armour, but feeling with his toes, he raked up bar on bar of soft gold. Some wicked treasure of the old days put away, and the secret cut off by the sword. I have heard the like before.'

'So have we,' Una whispered. 'But it wasn't wicked a bit.'

'Elias took a little of the stuff with him, and thrice yearly he would return to Pevensey as a chapman,[11] selling at no price or profit, till they suffered him to sleep in the empty room, where he would plumb and grope, and steal away a few bars. The great store of it still remained, and by long brooding he had come to look on it as his own. Yet when we thought how we should lift and convey it, we saw no way. This was before the Word of the Lord had come to me. A walled fortress possessed by Normans; in the midst a forty-foot tide-well out of which to remove secretly many horse-loads of gold! Hopeless! So Elias wept. Adah, his wife, wept too. She had hoped to stand beside the Queen's Christian tiring-maids at Court, when the King should give them that place at Court which he had promised. Why not? She was born in England – an odious woman.

'The present evil to us was that Elias, out of his strong folly, had, as it were, promised the King that he would arm him with more gold. Wherefore the King in his camp stopped his ears against the Barons and the people. Wherefore men died daily. Adah so desired her place at Court, she besought Elias to tell the King where the treasure lay, that the King might take it by force, and – they would trust in his gratitude. Why not? This Elias refused to do, for he looked on the gold as his own. They quarrelled, and they wept at the evening meal, and late in the night came one Langton [12] – a priest, almost learned – to borrow more money for the Barons. Elias and Adah went to their chamber.'

Kadmiel laughed scornfully in his beard. The shots across the valley stopped as the shooting party changed their ground for the last beat.

'So it was I, not Elias,' he went on, quietly, 'that made terms with Langton touching the fortieth of the New Laws.'

'What terms?' said Puck, quickly. 'The Fortieth of the Great Charter says: "To none will we sell, refuse, or deny right or justice."'

'True, but the Barons had written first : *To no free man*. It cost me two hundred broad pieces of gold to change those narrow words. Langton, the priest, understood. "Jew though thou art," said he, "the change is just, and if ever Christian and Jew come to be equal in England thy people may thank thee." Then he went out stealthily, as men do who deal with Israel by night. I think he spent my gift upon his altar. Why not? I have spoken with Langton. He was such a man as I might have been if – if we Jews had been a people. But yet, in many things, a child.

'I heard Elias and Adah abovestairs quarrel, and, knowing the woman was the stronger, I saw that Elias would tell the King of the gold and that the King would continue in his stubbornness. Therefore I saw that the gold must be put away from the reach of any man. Of a sudden, the Word of the Lord came to me saying, "The Morning is come, O thou that dwellest in the land."'[13]

Kadmiel halted, all black against the pale green sky beyond the wood – a huge robed figure, like a Moses in the picture-Bible.

'I rose. I went out, and as I shut the door on that House of Foolishness, the woman looked from the window and whispered, "I have prevailed on my husband to tell the King!" I answered, "There is no need. The Lord is with me."

'In that hour the Lord gave me full understanding of all that I must do; and His Hand covered me in my ways. First I went to London, to a physician of our people, who sold me certain drugs that I needed. You shall see why. Thence I went swiftly to Pevensey. Men fought all around me, for there were neither rulers nor judges in the abominable land. Yet when I walked by them they cried out that I was one Ahasuerus,[14] a Jew, condemned, as they believe, to live for ever, and they fled from me everyways. Thus the Lord saved me for my work, and at Pevensey I bought me a little boat and moored it on the mud beneath the Marsh-gate of the Castle. That also God showed me.'

He was as calm as though he were speaking of some stranger, and his voice filled the little bare wood with rolling music.

'I cast' – his hand went to his breast, and again the strange jewel gleamed – 'I cast the drugs which I had prepared into the common well of the Castle. Nay, I did no harm. The more we physicians know, the less do we do. Only the fool says: "I dare." I caused a blotched and itching rash to break out upon their skins, but I knew it would fade in fifteen days. I did not stretch out my hand against their life. They in the Castle

thought it was the Plague, and they ran out, taking with them
their very dogs.

'A Christian physician, seeing that I was a Jew and a stranger,
vowed that I had brought the sickness from London. This is
the one time I have ever heard a Christian leech speak truth of
any disease. Thereupon the people beat me, but a merciful
woman said: "Do not kill him now. Push him into our Castle
with his plague, and if, as he says, it will abate on the fifteenth
day, we can kill him then." Why not? They drove me across the
drawbridge of the Castle, and fled back to their booths. Thus I
came to be alone with the treasure.'

'But did you know this was all going to happen just right?'
said Una.

'My Prophecy was that I should be a Lawgiver to a People of
a strange land and a hard speech. I knew I should not die. I
washed my cuts. I found the tide-well in the wall, and from
Sabbath to Sabbath I dove and dug there in that empty, Chris-
tian-smelling fortress. Hé! I spoiled the Egyptians![15] Hé! If
they had only known! I drew up many good loads of gold,
which I loaded by night into my boat. There had been gold-
dust too, but that had been washed out by the tides.'

'Didn't you ever wonder who had put it there?' said Dan,
stealing a glance at Puck's calm, dark face under the hood of
his gown. Puck shook his head and pursed his lips.

'Often; for the gold was new to me,' Kadmiel replied. 'I
know the Golds. I can judge them in the dark; but this was
heavier and redder than any we deal in. Perhaps it was the
very gold of Parvaim.[16] Eh, why not? It went to my heart to
heave it on to the mud, but I saw well that if the evil thing
remained, or if even the hope of finding it remained, the
King would not sign the New Laws, and the land would
perish.'

'Oh, Marvel!' said Puck, beneath his breath, rustling in the
dead leaves.

'When the boat was loaded I washed my hands seven times,
and pared beneath my nails, for I would not keep one grain. I
went out by the little gate where the Castle's refuse is thrown. I
dared not hoist sail lest men should see me; but the Lord

commanded the tide to bear me carefully, and I was far from land before the morning.'

'Weren't you afraid?' said Una.

'Why? There were no Christians in the boat. At sunrise I made my prayer, and cast the gold – all – all that gold into the deep sea! A King's ransom – no, the ransom of a People! When I had loosed hold of the last bar, the Lord commanded the tide to return me to a haven at the mouth of a river, and thence I walked across a wilderness to Lewes, where I have brethren. They opened the door to me, and they say – I had not eaten for two days – they say that I fell across the threshold, crying, "I have sunk an army with horsemen in the sea!"'[17]

'But you hadn't,' said Una. 'Oh, yes! I see! You meant that King John might have spent it on that?'

'Even so,' said Kadmiel.

The firing broke out again close behind them. The pheasants poured over the top of a belt of tall firs. They could see young Mr Meyer, in his new yellow gaiters, very busy and excited at the end of the line, and they could hear the thud of the falling birds.

'But what did Elias of Bury do?' Puck demanded. 'He had promised money to the King.'

Kadmiel smiled grimly. 'I sent him word from London that the Lord was on my side. When he heard that the Plague had broken out in Pevensey, and that a Jew had been thrust into the Castle to cure it, he understood my word was true. He and Adah hurried to Lewes and asked me for an accounting. He still looked on the gold as his own. I told them where I had laid it, and I gave them full leave to pick it up . . . Eh, well! The curses of a fool and the dust of a journey are two things no wise man can escape . . . But I pitied Elias! The King was wroth to him because he could not lend; the Barons were wroth to him because they heard that he would have lent to the King; and Adah was wroth to him because she was an odious woman. They took ship from Lewes to Spain. That was wise!'

'And you? Did you see the signing of the Law at Runny-mede?' said Puck, as Kadmiel laughed noiselessly.

'Nay. Who am I to meddle with things too high for me? I

returned to Bury, and lent money on the autumn crops. Why not?'

There was a crackle overhead. A cock-pheasant that had sheered aside after being hit spattered down almost on top of them, driving up the dry leaves like a shell. *Flora* and *Folly* threw themselves at it; the children rushed forward, and when they had beaten them off and smoothed down the plumage Kadmiel had disappeared.

'Well,' said Puck, calmly, 'what did you think of it? Weland gave the Sword! The Sword gave the Treasure, and the Treasure gave the Law. It's as natural as an oak growing.'

'I don't understand. Didn't he know it was Sir Richard's old treasure?' said Dan. 'And why did Sir Richard and Brother Hugh leave it lying about? And – and –'

'Never mind,' said Una, politely. 'He'll let us come and go, and look, and know another time. Won't you, Puck?'

'Another time maybe,' Puck answered. 'Brr! It's cold – and late. I'll race you towards home!'

They hurried down into the sheltered valley. The sun had almost sunk behind Cherry Clack, the trodden ground by the cattle-gates was freezing at the edges, and the new-waked north wind blew the night on them from over the hills. They picked up their feet and flew across the browned pastures, and when they halted, panting in the steam of their own breath, the dead leaves whirled up behind them. There was Oak and Ash and Thorn enough in that year-end shower to magic away a thousand memories.

So they trotted to the brook at the bottom of the lawn, wondering why *Flora* and *Folly* had missed the quarry-hole fox.

Old Hobden was just finishing some hedge-work. They saw his white smock glimmer in the twilight where he faggoted the rubbish.

'Winter, he's come, I rackon, Mus' Dan,' he called. 'Hard times now till Heffle Cuckoo Fair.[18] Yes, we'll all be glad to see the Old Woman let the Cuckoo out o' the basket for to start lawful Spring in England.'

They heard a crash, and a stamp and a splash of water as

though a heavy old cow were crossing almost under their noses.

Hobden ran forward angrily to the ford.

'Gleason's bull again, playin' Robin all over the Farm! Oh, look, Mus' Dan – his great footmark as big as a trencher. No bounds to his impidence! He might count himself to be a man or – or Somebody –'

A voice the other side of the brook boomed:

> 'I wonder who his cloak would turn
> When Puck had led him round,
> Or where those walking fires would burn –'[19]

Then the children went in singing 'Farewell Rewards and Fairies' at the tops of their voices. They had forgotten that they had not even said goodnight to Puck.[20]

The Children's Song

Land of our Birth, we pledge to thee
Our love and toil in the years to be;
When we are grown and take our place,
As men and women with our race.

Father in Heaven who lovest all,
Oh help Thy children when they call;
That they may build from age to age,
An undefiled heritage.

Teach us to bear the yoke in youth,
With steadfastness and careful truth;
That, in our time, Thy Grace may give
The Truth whereby the Nations live.

Teach us to rule ourselves always
Controlled and cleanly night and day;
That we may bring, if need arise,
No maimed or worthless sacrifice.

Teach us to look in all our ends,
On Thee for judge, and not our friends;
That we, with Thee, may walk uncowed
By fear or favour of the crowd.

Teach us the Strength that cannot seek,
By deed or thought, to hurt the weak;
That, under Thee, we may possess
Man's strength to comfort man's distress.

Teach us Delight in simple things,
And Mirth that has no bitter springs;
Forgiveness free of evil done,
And Love to all men 'neath the sun!

Land of our Birth, our faith, our pride,
For whose dear sake our fathers died;
O Motherland, we pledge to thee,
Head, heart, and hand through the years to be!

Notes

Puck's Song

1. *Puck's Song*: The version of this poem printed in *Songs from Books* and the definitive *Verse* has three extra stanzas.
2. *King Philip's fleet*: The Armada sent in 1588 by Philip II of Spain to conquer England.
3. *the day that Harold died*: King Harold II of England was killed at the Battle of Hastings in 1066.
4. *the Northmen fled,/When Alfred's ships came by*: The *Anglo-Saxon Chronicle* relates that in 897 there was a running sea-fight between Alfred's navy and the Danes which began round the Isle of Wight. Eventually, three Danish ships escaped eastwards and two were cast up on the Sussex coast.
5. *red oxen*: Kipling wrote of his farming in *Something of Myself* (1937) that, 'After many, and some comic experiences, we fell back on our own county's cattle – the big red Sussex breed who make beef and not milk.'
6. *When Caesar sailed from Gaul*: Julius Caesar landed in Britain in 55 BC, although full Roman occupation of the island did not begin until AD 43.
7. *Gramarye*: Enchantment or magic.

Weland's Sword

1. *called the Long Slip*: The *Strand* text reads, 'which the grown-ups called the Long Slip.'
2. *Bath Oliver biscuits*: A smooth, savoury biscuit made with eggs, milk and butter.
3. *'apricocks, ripe figs, and dewberries'*: See *A Midsummer Night's Dream*, III. 1. 165–6. 'Feed him with apricocks and dewberries/With purple grapes, green figs, and mulberries.'
4. *'What hempen homespuns . . . if I see cause'*: *A Midsummer Night's Dream*, III. 1. 76–9.
5. *Puck's Hill – Pook's Hill*: The place-name Pook Hill, with the

etymology 'pucu healh' – goblin nook – is found in Sussex (*The Place-Names of Sussex*, Cambridge, 1930, vol. II, p. 415). The hill to the south-west of Batemans indicated in the book seems, however, to have originally been known as Perch Hill.

6. *'Farewell Rewards and Fairies'*: The first line of 'The Faeryes Farewell' by Richard Corbet (1582–1635). Puck goes on to quote the first and fourth stanzas of the nine-stanza poem. Kipling subsequently used the first line for the title of his second collection of Puck stories, *Rewards and Fairies* (1910).

7. *Chanctonbury Ring*: Iron-age earthwork on the South Downs, north-west of Brighton.

8. *seizin*: This legal term indicates the possession of land and goods and chattels. Livery of seisin involves the formal transfer of land or goods from one person to another. According to Pollock and Maitland's *The History of English Law* (1898), there is 'no idea more cardinal than that of seisin ... we may almost say that the whole system of our land law was about seisin and its consequences' (II, p. 29). Ceremonies marking livery of seisin probably derive from ancient Germanic law and symbolic transfers such as the one Puck and the children make were still common in Norman times.

9. *quickly*: The *Strand* text reads, 'angrily'.

10. *Arabian Nights*: This collection of Middle Eastern and Indian stories was introduced into Europe in the early eighteenth century and was soon bowdlerized for children. Dan and Una are likely to have read Andrew Lang's edition of 1898.

11. *The People of the Hills ... gauze petticoats*: The *Strand* text reads, 'The People of the Hills would never associate with – unpleasant little buzzflies with butterfly wings and gauze petticoats'.

12. *Sir Huon:* The eponymous hero of a fifteenth-century French prose romance translated into English in the sixteenth century. Sir Huon becomes the constant friend of Oberon, King of the Fairies, and later succeeds him as king of fairyland.

13. *Tintagel Castle*: On the north-east coast of Cornwall. According to Geoffrey of Monmouth's twelfth-century *History of Britain*, King Arthur was adulterously conceived there; his parents, Uther Pendragon and Igerna, Duchess of Cornwall, met together with the help of Merlin's magic.

14. *Hy-Brasil*: The name, in Celtic mythology, of an island paradise in the Western Sea, or Atlantic Ocean.

15. *and I have been mixed up with people all my days*: These words do not appear in the *Strand* text.

16. *People burned in wicker baskets*: Caesar wrote in *Gallic Wars*, VI, 16, that the Gauls 'have regular state sacrifices ... some tribes have colossal images made of wickerwork, the limbs of which they fill with living men; they are then set on fire, and the victims burnt to death.'

17. *Belisama*: Belisama is the name of the river Ribble in Ptolemy's *Geography*, II, 3, 2 (first century AD). It is also the name of a goddess in Gaulish religious inscriptions.

18. *And there were hundreds of other friends of mine:* In the *Strand* text this sentence reads, 'And there were Belus and Ceso and Curon and Rosmert, and oh, hundreds of other friends of mine.' I have not found a source for these names.

19. *Weland*: A metal-worker in Norse mythology. His name has been connected with a chambered long barrow just off the Ridgeway, near Swindon, since the tenth century. The associated legend of the invisible smith shoeing horses in exchange for a penny was first published by an Oxford antiquary, Francis Wise, in 1738.

20. Heroes of Asgard *Thor*: Thor is the god of thunder in Norse mythology. *Heroes of Asgard* is the title of a collection of Norse myths for children, by Annie and Eliza Keary, which was first published in 1857.

21. *Brunanburgh*: Kipling has borrowed the name of a battle fought in 937 between the Danes and the Anglo-Saxons. The site of the battle is unknown but is likely to have been in the north of England.

22. *Andover*: A town in Hampshire, about twenty-five miles from the site of Weland's smithy (see note 19, above).

23. *Willingford Bridge ... Weland's Ford*: A plausible-sounding but false etymology. The name is in fact associated with the family of Wynham of Burwash.

24. *Valhalla*: The hall in Norse mythology where Woden presides over the dead heroes.

25. *lee-long*: The prefix is found in a number of ballads where it has an indefinite intensive force, frequently with the connotation of loneliness.

26. *and Old England after him*: These words do not appear in the *Strand* text.

27. *Runes*: Although runes can mean 'charms', as the text indicates, the primary meaning of the word is to indicate the angular characters

of an old Germanic script which was used mainly for magical and ritual purposes. Anglo-Saxon swords with runic inscriptions have been found by archaeologists.

28. *the garth*: A small piece of enclosed ground; here probably the grass plot surrounded by the cloister.

29. *'Late – late in the evening . . . she could not declare'*: An adaptation of lines 24 and 38–9 of the poem 'Kilmeny' by James Hogg (1770–1835). The poem tells of a girl who visits the land of the fairies for seven years and can say nothing about it when she returns.

A Tree Song

1. *A Tree Song*: *Songs from Books* and *Verse* add a date: AD 1200.
2. *Æneas*: The hero of Virgil's epic poem the *Aeneid* (26–19 BC). Aeneas escapes from fallen Troy and after many vicissitudes founds the city of Rome.
3. *Brut . . . New Troy Town*: Geoffrey of Monmouth, in his twelfth-century *History of Britain* tells the legendary story of Brut or Brutus, supposed great-grandson of Aeneas, who, banished from Italy for unwittingly killing his father, eventually landed in Britain and built a new Troy on the banks of the Thames.
4. *Ellum*: Elm.

Young Men at the Manor

1. *'Sir Isumbras at the Ford'*: Dan has a reproduction of the picture painted by John Everett Millais in 1857 and now in the Walker Art Gallery, Liverpool. It shows a kind and elderly knight who has taken two peasant children on to his horse to give them a lift over a river.
2. *Dalyngridge*: A family of this name lived in Sussex in the four-teenth century. One of them built Bodiam Castle, some eight miles from Burwash.
3. *Engenulf de Aquila*: Engenulf de Laigle was killed at the Battle of Hastings. He was a member of a considerable Norman family who later established themselves in England.
4. *Earl of Mortain*: Robert, Count of Mortain, was a half-brother of William the Conqueror.

5. *Santlache*: This name for the Battle of Hastings is taken from E. A. Freeman's *The Norman Conquest* (1870–76), although Freeman himself usually uses the name Senlac. The *Strand* text uses either the names Senlac or Hastings throughout.

6. *the monastery at Bec ... the Abbot Herluin*: This Norman monastery was founded by Herluin in 1041, and rapidly became a famous centre of learning.

7. *Gilbert de Aquila*: There were two historical figures of this name. The elder was the grandson of Engerrard or Engenulf (see note 3, above) and is recorded in the Domesday Book (1086) as holding land at Witley near Godalming in Surrey. The younger was Warden of Pevensey in 1214 during the reign of King John (see the story 'Old Men at Pevensey').

8. *all the lands by Pevensey*: The Domesday book records that the Rape of Pevensey was granted to Robert, Count of Mortain. Burwash itself, however, was in the Rape of Hastings granted to the Count of Eu.

9. *a sutler*: A petty tradesman, often selling provisions to soldiers.

10. *wastrels*: Good-for-nothings, idle, worthless persons. The Oxford English Dictionary records the first use of this word in 1847. It is thus an example of nineteenth-century medievalizing.

11. *saved our pork*: The *Strand* text continues, 'as well as the swineherd, whom they had tied to an oak.'

12. *hard tack*: Ship's biscuit, the equivalent of bread and water.

13. *seizin*: See note 8 to 'Weland's Sword'.

14. *knight's fee*: Land held on condition of the payment of the feudal obligation of military service owed by a knight to his lord.

15. *yerk*: To strike smartly.

16. *Earl Godwin*: Earl of Wessex (d. 1053), and a powerful figure in the reigns of Cnut or Canute and Edward the Confessor, whose father-in-law he was. His son was King Harold, killed at the Battle of Hastings.

17. *sworn fealty*: Hugh has not taken the oath to fulfil the obligation of fidelity owed by a feudal tenant to his lord.

18. *fretty*: A technical term from heraldry. Interlaced, in a trellis pattern.

Sir Richard's Song

1. *Sir Richard's Song*: *Songs from Books* and *Verse* add a date, A D 1066.
2. *fief*: Synonym of fee; manor or inheritance held by homage to a feudal overlord.

The Knights of the Joyous Venture

1. 'Golden Hind': The name of the ship in which Sir Francis Drake (*c.* 1545–95) circumnavigated the globe between 1577 and 1580.
2. 'Long Serpent': Any Viking ship might be referred to as this.
3. *hiked and howked*: Dialect words, meaning to pull or haul.
4. '*Othere, the old sea-captain*': The first line of 'The Discoverer of the North Cape' by the American poet H. W. Longfellow (1807–82). The poem is based on the voyage of Othere which King Alfred interpolated into his translation of Orosius's *History of the World* (fifth century A D). Dan reads stanzas 1, 8 and 18.
5. *Red William . . . in a forest*: William II, surnamed Rufus because of his red complexion, reigned 1087–1100. He was killed 2 August 1100.
6. *Artois*: The most northerly province of France.
7. *Mantes siege*: In 1087 William the Conqueror attacked the town of Mantes, which stood on the border of Normandy and France, and utterly destroyed it. However, William himself was fatally wounded in a riding accident outside the town.
8. *the Duke of Burgundy against the Moors in Spain*: In 1087 a large army of crusaders was gathered by Duke Eudes of Burgundy, Count Raymond of Toulouse and Viscount Guillaume of Melun to fight the Moslems in Spain, as many Frenchmen were to do in the next century.
9. *Muscovy*: The principality of Moscow, but often applied to Russia in general.
10. *the iron needle pointed continually to the South*: The Chinese were often thought to have invented the magnetic compass as early as 2634 B C and to have believed that it pointed South. It is probable, however, that it was invented independently in China and in Europe in the twelfth century A D.
11. *the North*: The *Strand* text reads, 'the Baltic'.
12. *sweet-smelling grey amber*: Ambergris, the product of the sperm whale, used in the making of perfumes.

13. *Saint Barnabas*: The apostle who accompanied St Paul on his first missionary journey. The *Strand* text reads here 'Saint Bartholomew', to whom Burwash parish church is dedicated.

14. *the Leech-Book of Bald*: No surviving Scandinavian or Anglo-Saxon leech-book, or medicinal hand-book, is attributed to Bald.

15. *the Ship-Book of Hlaf the Woman*: I cannot trace this; Kipling probably invented it.

16. *a mountain . . . pierced the clouds*: Probably Tenerife.

17. *the Great Shoal*: possibly the Bissagos Archipelago, Guinea-Bissau, West Africa.

18. *the Forest in the Sea*: The mangrove swamps at the mouth of the river Volta, in present-day Ghana.

19. *Stavanger Fiord*: In Norway.

20. The Gorilla Hunters . . . Coral Island: Boys' adventure stories by R. M. Ballantyne (1825–94). *Coral Island* was published in 1858 and *The Gorilla Hunters* in 1861.

Thorkild's Song

1. *Thorkild's Song*: The version of this poem printed in *Songs from Books* and *Verse* has two extra stanzas.

Old Men at Pevensey

1. *Henry . . . old laws to our Saxons*: Henry I, younger brother of Robert, Duke of Normandy, and William Rufus, reigned 1100–1135. His first wife was Edith or Matilda, daughter of Malcolm III of Scotland and a descendant of King Alfred of Wessex and Cerdic. (See note 5, below.) His reign is important in the history of English law for the charter drawn up at his coronation, which looked back in some of its details to pre-Conquest law, and also set a precedent for the Magna Charta.

2. *before Odo rebelled*: Odo, Bishop of Bayeux and half-brother to William the Conqueror, led a rebellion against William Rufus to transfer the English crown to Robert, Duke of Normandy, the Conqueror's eldest son. Odo was banished after the defeat of the Norman forces at Pevensey in 1088.

3. *Robert of Normandy*: The *Strand* text reads, 'Robert Shortboots (for so we called Robert of Normandy)'.

4. *those new-fashioned beads for counting of prayers*: It is not known precisely when the rosary was first used. Legend suggests that it was given to Saint Dominic (1170–1221) through a revelation of the Virgin Mary. Certainly the Dominicans later propagated the practice of meditating with its help.

5. *Cerdic's sister, and own cousin to the Lady of Mercia*: According to the *Anglo-Saxon Chronicle*, Cerdic was the Saxon founder of the kingdom of Wessex, who landed in England in 495. The Lady of Mercia is Aethelflaed, the daughter of King Alfred of Wessex (848–?900), who married King Aethelred of Mercia and after his death successfully fought the Danish invaders of her kingdom.

6. *as Odo and Mortain tried to do*: See note 2, above. Count Mortain held Pevensey Castle for the Norman rebels until he and his brother Odo were defeated by William Rufus's troops.

7. *Anselm*: Saint Anselm (1033–1109) was Archbishop of Canterbury from 1093 until his death. He was outspoken in his defence of religion and the church against the policies of both William Rufus and Henry I.

8. *fisk*: To move briskly or scamper about; *flyte*: to contend or to strive.

9. *lizard-mail . . . hauberk*: Lizard-mail is an invention of Kipling's: all medieval armour was made from various kinds of chain-mail. A hauberk is a tunic or coat of chain-mail.

10. *Tours*: A town on the river Loire in France.

11. *the Danes' King*: Canute or Cnut, King of England and Denmark from 1017 until 1035. When flatteringly told by his courtiers that he was all-powerful, he is reputed to have had his throne carried to the shore of the Thames at Westminster where he commanded the tide to stop at his feet. Naturally, it went on rising.

12. *thy good deeds*: The *Strand* text reads, 'thy wickednesses'.

13. *Angevin*: From Anjou, a western province of France. Henry II, who succeeded his uncle Henry I in 1134, was the first of the Angevin Kings of England.

14. *From here to Rome . . . with any sword*: In the *Strand* text this passage reads, '"From here to Rome, Fulke, men will make very merry over that tale, and how Fulke told it, hanging in a well, like a drowned puppy.'
'Fulke hid his face and groaned.
' "Bones of the Saints!" said De Aquila, laughing. "The pen cuts deep. I could never have fetched that grunt out of thee with any sword. Yes, open shame and laughter and scorn in every tongue in

Christendie, Fulke, shall be thy punishment, if ever I find thee
double-dealing with thy King any more. Meantime, the parchments stay here with thy son. Him I will return to thee when thou
hast made my peace with the King. The parchments never."'

15. *dortoirs*: Sleeping rooms, dormitories.

16. *Tenchebrai*: Usually spelt Tinchebrai. A battle fought in 1106
when Henry I defeated his brother, Duke Robert, and finally
captured Normandy.

17. '*The Slave's Dream*': This poem by H. W. Longfellow (see note
4 to 'The Knights of the Joyous Venture') is one of a group
on American slavery. Una reads out the third and fourth
lines.

A Centurion of the Thirtieth

1. Lays of Ancient Rome: A set of four narrative poems about early
Roman history by Thomas Babington Macaulay (1800–59), published in 1842. 'Lordly Volaterrae' is described in the fourth stanza
of the first poem 'Horatius', which celebrates the heroic defence
of Rome by three young men.

2. *Verbenna down to Ostia . . . are slain*: From stanza 17 of 'Horatius'.

3. *Now welcome to thy home . . . to Rome*: From stanza 51 of 'Horatius'.

4. *a Centurion . . . the Ulpia Victrix*: Centurions were the principal
professional officers in the Roman Army. There were six centuries
to a cohort and ten cohorts to a legion or regiment. The Legio
XXX Ulpia was raised by the Emperor Trajan (reigned AD 98–
117). It served in Germany but not in Britain.

5. *Dan's catapult*: The *Strand* text reads, 'Dan's tweaker – catapult, I
mean'.

6. *Our Villa*: Probably the Roman villa at Brading on the Isle of
Wight, which was excavated 1879–81, when Kipling's father
Lockwood was at Osborne arranging the Indian suite for Queen
Victoria. Brading was notable for its mosaics, including the so-
called 'philosopher's pavement'. Parnesius's brother settles 'down
on the estate as a farmer and a philosopher' (p. 123).

7. *Agricola at the Settlement*: Gnaeus Julius Agricola (AD 40–93),
Governor of Britain, extended Roman rule over the island to a line
between the Forth and the Clyde. He encouraged urbanization,
Romanization and the foundation of self-governing communities
in the south, to fill the gap caused by moving garrisons north, but

never made any formal settlement. His life was written by his son-in-law, the historian Tacitus.

8. *Numidian*: A person from North Africa.

9. *the new statue on the Western Road – the Demeter of the Baskets*: The *Strand* text reads, 'the old statue on the Cunetio Road . . .' Demeter was the Greek goddess of fruits and crops and the protectress of marriage; her Roman name was Ceres. Cunetio is Mildenhall, Wiltshire.

10. *Aquae Sulis*: I have followed the Sussex text in emending 'Aquae Solis', found in both the *Strand* and 1906 texts, to the historically correct Aquae Sulis. Bath's waters were named after the Celtic deity Sul rather than after the Roman Sol or sun.

11. *in the west*: The *Strand* text reads, 'at Vindomi'. The modern site of Vindomi is unknown.

12. *the City of the Legions*: Isca Silurum, now Carleon (Casta Legionum) in South Wales.

13. *Antinoe*: A city in Roman Egypt.

14. *Clausentum*: Roman regional capital on the site of modern Bitterne on Southampton Water.

15. *the bow of Ulysses*: Homer's *Odyssey*, book XXI, tells how Odysseus (Ulysses is his Roman name) had a bow which no one except himself could bend.

16. *the Dacian Horse . . . a regular Legion from Rome*: Legionary soldiers were originally recruited from Roman citizens, in contrast to auxiliary troops which were recruited locally in the provinces but served away from their locality. The Dacian Horse would have come from the region around the lower Danube. With the extension of citizenship in the later years of the Roman empire, the distinction between legionary and auxiliary troops gradually broke down.

17. *We split the Eagle*: In AD 364 the Emperor Valentinian I and his brother Valens divided the Roman empire in two, Valens becoming emperor of the east and Valentinian emperor of the west.

18. *Gratian*: Son of Valentinian and emperor of the west, AD 375–83. He had a passion for hunting.

19. *raw-beef-eating Scythian*: The Scythians were a nomadic, central-European tribe of famously war-like and ferocious disposition. They disappeared from the pages of history, but not from myth and legend, in the second century AD.

20. *The great war . . . temples of our Gods were destroyed*: In AD 367 an alliance of Saxons, Picts and Scots overran Britain and almost reached London. Roman rule was restored and the frontier re-

established by Theodosius (see note 23, below). Kipling's refer-
ences to the destruction and rebuilding of the temples of the
Roman gods seem to be suggested by the reign of Julian the
Apostate (AD 361–63). He re-instituted the pagan cults and rebuilt
pagan temples and, while tolerating all religions, preferred and
favoured pagans.

21. *Diocletian*: Roman Emperor (reigned AD 284–305), who authorized
a fierce persecution of the Christians. He was an enthusiast for
old Roman religion, tradition and discipline, which he believed
would reinforce imperial unity.

22. *Hadrian's Wall*: The frontier wall of Roman Britain which runs
from Wallsend-on-Tyne in the east to Bowness-on-Solway in the
west. It was built between AD 122 and 126 during the reign of the
Emperor Hadrian (AD 117–38).

23. *Theodosius*: Roman general (d. 376) sent to Britain by the Emperor
Valentinian to repel the Pict invaders and their allies in 367.

24. *Deucalion*: In Greek mythology he is the son of Prometheus. When
Zeus sent a flood to punish the wickedness of man, Deucalion and
his wife entered an ark prepared on the advice of Prometheus, and
were saved.

25. *Maximus himself, our great General*: Magnus Clemens Maximus
was elevated to imperial status by the army in Britain in AD 383.
He crossed over into Gaul and defeated and executed the Emperor
Gratian (see note 18, above). He then invaded Italy and was
defeated by Theodosius I, the son of the Roman general (see note
23, above), and executed in AD 388.

26. *the Abulci*: A 'Numerus Abulcorum' is known to have made up the
garrison of Pevensey at some point during the Roman occupation.

27. *He wore the Purple*: A purple robe or cloak worn only by emperors.

28. *Tribune*: There were six tribunes to a legion and they were directly
responsible to the commanding officer. The *Strand* text reads,
'Centurion'.

29. *die as Theodosius died*: Theodosius (see note 23, above) was
executed in Carthage, for unknown reasons.

30. *Cyclops*: A one-eyed giant in Homer's *Odyssey*, book IX.

31. *the Road Book*: Itineraries of various land routes, giving distances
and other information, were common in Roman libraries. Only
one, the *Itinerarium Antoninianum*, possibly a late-third-century
collection of routes used for troop movements, survives. There is
no Roman road from Anderida (Pevensey) to Burwash, but Kipling may have used the forged *Chronicle* of Richard of Cirencester which was printed as a reliable authority in *Six Old English*

Chronicles, edited by J. A. Giles in 1863. This was one of the books on Romano-British history recommended to Kipling by Burne-Jones (see Introduction, p. 11). The forgery contains a fictitious expansion of the *Itinerarium Antoninianum*, including an invented Iter XVII from Anderida to London through the forest, the Sylva Anderida.

32. *Mithras*: Mithras was a god of Persian and Zoroastrian origin whose exclusive and demanding cult reached Rome in the first century BC and was at its height in the third and early fourth centuries AD. Mithraism involved secret rites and progress through stages of initiation. It asked for high standards of conduct and courage from its adherents. The cult excluded women and seems to have particularly appealed to soldiers. Three Mithraic temples have been excavated along Hadrian's Wall. Contrary to common belief, Mithraic rites did not involve the sacrificial slaughter of a bull, although reliefs of Mithras himself killing a bull are often found in the temples. Mithras and the sun god were closely connected. The cult had faded by the later part of the fourth century.

33. *Cur mundus militat ... Dic ubi Tullius*: Puck is singing lines 1–4 and 33–5 of an anonymous thirteenth-century Latin poem, which can be translated as follows:

> Why does the world, whose prosperity is fleeting, fight for vain glory? Its power passes as quickly as fragile potters' vessels.

> Where has Caesar gone, lofty in his power, or Dives all splendid at the feast? Tell where Tullius –

A British-Roman Song

1. *A.D. 406*: The Roman garrison was withdrawn from Britain by the imperial pretenders Maximus in 385 and Constantine III in 407. It is unlikely that there was an official Roman military presence in the island after 410, the year in which Alaric the Visigoth sacked Rome. The hopes and wishes of the speaker in this poem are unlikely to be fulfilled.

On the Great Wall

1. *'When I left Rome ... I've lost Lalage!'*: In *Songs from Books* and *Verse* there is a four-stanza version of this poem with the title, 'Rimini (Marching Song of a Roman Legion of the Later Empire)'.
2. *the Eagles*: The legionary standard was a silver eagle carried on a pole.
3. *up North*: The *Strand* text reads, 'near Lindum'; that is, modern Lincoln.
4. *proper respect to Caesar*: See Matthew 22:21: 'Render therefore unto Caesar the things which are Caesar's; and unto God the things that are God's.' The *Strand* text reads, 'proper respect to Rome.' In fact, by the late fourth century the Roman army was largely Christian and Maximus himself was certainly so.
5. *Thirty feet high is the Wall*: Kipling's description of Hadrian's Wall is inaccurate. It was probably around eighteen feet high and between ten and five feet wide. There is no evidence that stakes were used in the ditch, for the wall was not designed as a fighting platform but as a frontier demarcation and a springboard for offensive operations. Civil settlements did grow up behind the wall, but they clustered round the forts rather than stretching out in a snake-like line. The settlements were evacuated during the war with the Picts in AD 367 and never reoccupied.
6. *Ituna ... Segedunum*: Bowness-on-Solway and Wallsend-on-Tyne.
7. *Hunno ... Valentia*: Hunno is Onnum, now Halton Chesters. Dere Street, the road to the north, does not cross the wall at Halton Chesters itself but about half a mile to the west of it. The whereabouts of the province of Valentia is still debated but it did not lie to the north of Hadrian's Wall, although placed there in the forged *Chronicle* of Richard of Cirencester. See note 31 to 'A Centurion of the Thirtieth'.
8. *Roma Dea*: The goddess of the city of Rome, worshipped as part of the official, civic religion.
9. *the Bull Killing*: See note 32 to 'A Centurion of the Thirtieth'.
10. *the Degree of Gryphons*: None of the seven grades of Mithraism was named the Gryphons. However, one of the attributes of the second grade, *krupios*, or 'the hidden one' in Greek, was wrongly transliterated as 'gryphius' in Latin.

11. *Sylvan Pan*: Pan was a Greek rural deity, half man and half goat.
12. *Xenophon*: Greek soldier and writer who lived *c*. 435–354 BC. His writings were popular with the Romans and, among many other works, he wrote the *Cynegeticus*, a treatise on hunting, especially the hare but also wild boar and deer.
13. *the Second Wall*: The Antonine Wall which runs from the Forth to the Clyde. It was built of turf and constructed in AD 142. The Roman frontier was finally withdrawn to Hadrian's Wall in AD 180.
14. *raven-winged ships ... where Rome does not rule*: Saxon pirates began to raid Britain in the late third century, forerunners of the Saxon invaders of the fifth century. The Saxons came from north Germany, although Kipling's mention of 'the North' seems to suggest Scandinavia. The winged helmets also make them sound Viking or Scandinavian. The Saxons did not wear winged helmets, indeed, they probably did not wear helmets at all. Winged helmets are given to the Vikings in popular iconographic tradition, but this is inaccurate; winged helmets are in fact Celtic.
15. *Your fate is fixed*: This sentence is not in the *Strand* text.
16. *Your Gods and my Gods are threatened by strange Gods*: Parnesius and Pertinax worshipped Mithras and the Roman pantheon; Allo worshipped Celtic gods, some of whom had acquired Roman names; the Saxon religion, like the Viking, was Teutonic or Norse.
17. *Cicero*: Roman politician, writer and orator (106–43 BC).
18. *Greek fire*: A liquid incendiary used in siege warfare. It is first spoken of as used by the Greeks against the Arabs in the late seventh century.
19. *She is taking her men out of Britain*: This sentence is not in the *Strand* text.
20. *Duumvir of Divio*: Senior magistrate of present-day Metz, in eastern France.

A Song to Mithras

1. In *Songs from Books* and *Verse* this poem is subtitled 'Hymn of the XXX Legion: circa A.D. 350'.

The Winged Hats

1. *You are the belly*: Kipling is alluding to the fable of the belly in Shakespeare's *Coriolanus*, I. 1.
2. *We, about to die, salute you*: This is the phrase shouted by Roman gladiators, reported by Suetonius in his 'Life of Claudius'.
3. *Nicaea*: Nice, in the south of France.
4. *in a tent by the sea*: The *Strand* text reads, 'at a place called Aquileia'.
5. *Antipolis*: Antibes, in the south of France.
6. *Aquileia*: A Roman city on the Adriatic.

A Pict Song

1. *drag down the Great!*: The text of this poem in *Songs from Books* and *Verse* reads, 'drag down the State!'

'Prophets have honour all over the Earth'

1. *Nineveh Town*: In the Old Testament Book of Jonah, Jonah is sent by God to prophesy doom to the city of Nineveh. After being swallowed and regurgitated by a whale, he does so. The citizens repent and God relents. Jonah is angry at God's change of heart, as it has cast doubt on his own prophetic powers.

Hal o' the Draft

1. *Jack Cade*: The leader of a popular revolt against Henry VI in 1450. After a triumphant march to London and a fight on London Bridge he was abandoned by his followers. He retreated into Sussex, where he was killed near Heathfield.
2. *the ballad of Sir Andrew Barton*: This ballad is found in Thomas Percy's *Reliques of Ancient Poetry* (1765). Barton was a Scottish naval officer turned pirate. The ballad tells of how he was killed by Sir Thomas and Sir Edward Howard in a sea battle in 1511.
3. *swarved*: Swarmed up.
4. *four silver saints . . . Barnabas's head*: The *Strand* text reads, 'four silver apostles round it. Press Luke's head.'

5. *Bramante*: Italian Renaissance architect (1444–1514), commissioned by Pope Julius II to redesign St Peter's in Rome.

6. *St Barnabas' church*: The *Strand* text reads, 'St Bartholomew's church'. Burwash church is dedicated to St Bartholomew. The medieval building was extensively restored in 1856 and not added to in the early sixteenth century, as the story might suggest.

7. *Bristow*: Bristol.

8. *Bruce and his silly old spider*: Robert Bruce, King of Scotland 1306–29, was inspired to persevere in his campaign against the English by watching a spider determinedly building its web in difficult conditions. Eight years later he finally defeated the English at the Battle of Bannockburn in 1314.

9. *a Galilee porch at Lincoln*: This large west porch in the south transept of Lincoln Cathedral was built between 1240 and 1250.

10. *Torrigiano*: Italian sculptor who came to England in 1508 and whose works include the monuments to Henry VII and Elizabeth of York in Westminster Abbey.

11. *the* Sovereign – *our King's ship*: The scrollwork for Henry VII's ship plays a central part in 'The Wrong Thing', the story Harry Dawe tells in *Rewards and Fairies*.

12. *us Dawes*: Dawe is one of the earliest names to occur in the Burwash parish register, which dates back to 1588. According to the former Vicar of Burwash, J. C. Egerton, in his *Sussex Folk and Sussex Ways* (1884), the iron gates in the porch of the church were made by a local blacksmith, Master Daw, and presented to the church on its restoration in 1856. The modern guide to the church, however, maintains the blacksmith was Master Drew.

13. *Master John Collins's foundry*: On the wall to the left of the Lady Chapel in Burwash church is a fourteenth-century cast-iron sepulchral slab – the earliest of its kind in Sussex – bearing the inscription 'Orate p. annema Jhone Coline' (Pray for the soul of Joan Collins). The Collins family are known to have owned the forge at Socknersh, between Burwash and Brightling.

14. *Sir John Pelham*: The Pelham family were connected with the lordship of the manor of Burwash from 1413 until the end of the eighteenth century.

15. *shaw*: A small wood or coppice.

16. *Cabot*: Sebastian Cabot (1474–1557) was the son of the Italian navigator and voyager John Cabot with whom he probably sailed to North America in 1497.

17. *mell*: To meddle or interfere with.

18. *spaulty*: Brittle, chipped or split.

19. *ary one*: Anyone.
20. *hoy*: A coasting vessel.
21. *the Bell Tavern*: The pub opposite Burwash church is still called The Bell.
22. *pure pute*: Thorough-going.
23. *willow-tot*: A clump of willow trees.
24. *lither*: Bad, wicked.
25. *carrack*: A large cargo or war-ship.
26. *his Justice's chair*: The *Strand* text reads, 'his Great Hall'.
27. *stockfish*: A fish preserved by curing it in the air without salt. Used as a term of jocular or contemptuous address.
28. *tod*: A fox, a crafty person.
29. Our King went forth to Normandie: The first line of the ballad 'Victory at Agincourt' and the name of the tune to which it is sung.
30. *timber-tug*: A long cart for carrying tree-trunks.
31. *ary wool-wain*: Any wagon for carting wool.
32. *seely*: Happy, blessed.
33. *vivers*: Small roots, fibres.
34. '*That should be a Hobden by his voice*': This sentence is not in the *Strand* text.

A Smugglers' Song

1. *A Smugglers' Song*: J. C. Egerton, vicar of Burwash from 1867 to 1888, writes in *Sussex Folk and Sussex Ways* (1884): 'A woman has told me that, as a child, she used to say her prayers at night, and then be regularly put to bed with a strict injunction, "Now, mind, if the 'gentlemen' come along, don't you look out o' window." Peeping at smugglers was a heinous offence and was often visited with severe punishment, as it was supposed to give means of identification and detection.'
2. *Valenciennes*: Lace named after the town in which it was made.

The Bee Boy's Song

1. *to us you must tell*: According to Jacqueline Simpson in *Sussex Folklore* (1973), the custom of telling the bees is well attested in

Sussex and it is also said in the county that bees cannot bear angry
voices.

2. *Fanners*: In hot weather bees sometimes gather at the entrance to
the hive and fan with their wings.

3. *dwine*: To fade away, to languish or dwindle.

'Dymchurch Flit'

1. '*Old Mother Laidinwool*': Part of a song sung in hop-gardens in
Burwash in the nineteenth century. A longer version, of six stanzas
and two choruses, is printed in *Songs from Books* and *Verse*.

2. *hem*: A euphemism for the devil.

3. '*Oh I've bin to Plymouth . . . wide world over*': Part of a Sussex
drinking-song associated with harvest homes.

4. *odd-gates*: Peculiar.

5. *the world's divided . . . an' Romney Marsh*: This saying comes from
The Ingoldsby Legends (1840), a collection of comic, mock-medieval
legends and folktales by R. H. Barham (1788–1845), rector of
Snargate, near Old Romney.

6. *see further through a millstone than most*: To be wonderfully or
preternaturally sharpsighted.

7. *nigromancin'*: Necromancy is that kind of magic that aims to reveal
the future by means of communication with the dead.

8. *a passel*: A great deal.

9. *Pharisees*: Fairies. The word derives from the characteristic Sussex
reduplicated plural: fairieses.

10. *out-gate*: Paranormal.

11. *steeples settin' beside churches*: The steeple of Brookland Church on
Romney Marsh stands separately from the church.

12. *grummelin'*: Grumbling.

13. *as ravelly as witch-yarn*: As tangled up as yarn or wool which has
been bewitched.

14. *Reformatories*: The Reformation in England was initiated by Henry
VIII (reigned 1509–47) although the burning of heretics mentioned in the following paragraph was restricted to the reign of his
daughter the Catholic Mary (1553–8).

15. *I dunnamany*: I don't know how many.

16. *the Images*: Many statues of saints and stained-glass images in
churches were damaged or destroyed during the early Reformation.

17. *cruel Canterbury Bells ringin' to Bulverhithe*: Bells were rung at the burning of a heretic. Bulverhithe is the name of a village near Bexhill, swallowed up by the sea between 1500 and the end of the seventeenth century.
18. *a squat*: An infection of the ground caused by keeping too many poultry on it.
19. *stenched up*: Confined.
20. *Old Winchelsea*: A village on the Sussex coast that was washed away by storms in 1287.
21. *a Seeker*: Seekers were seventeenth-century sectaries who sought the truth outside organized religion. They relied on the prompting of the spirit within, which often manifested itself in dreams and visions.
22. *rummelled*: Rumbled.
23. *aps-tree*: Aspen.
24. *hove down dunt*: Heaved down with a bang or a thump.
25. *raklin'*: Rattling.
26. *fretty*: Fretful.

A Three-Part Song

1. *shaw*: A small wood or coppice.
2. *gill*: A narrow valley.

Song of the Fifth River

1. *The Four Great Rivers*: In Genesis 2:10–14 the four rivers which flow out of the Garden of Eden are named as Pison, Gihon, Hiddekel (the Tigris) and Euphrates.
2. *Then He That is Wholly Just*: The text in *Songs from Books* and *Verse* reads, 'Then He Whom the Rivers obey'.

The Treasure and the Law

1. *towling*: Chasing.
2. *sneered up*: The *Strand* text reads, 'went up'.
3. *waily*: The *Strand* text reads, 'whiny'.
4. *King John used to pull out Jews' teeth*: John, always in financial

difficulties, demanded money of the Jews. When one Abraham of Bristol refused to pay his quota, seven of his teeth were forcibly extracted.

5. *Sala-ud-Din*: Saladin, Sultan of Egypt (1137–93), invaded Palestine and captured Jerusalem, where he was attacked by crusaders under Richard I, John's brother.

6. *Bury*: Bury St Edmunds in Suffolk. On 10 March 1190, fifty-seven Jews were murdered at Bury in an outbreak of anti-Semitism at the time of the coronation of the crusader, Richard I. As a result of the massacre the Jews were expelled from the town. See also note 9, below.

7. *In the East . . . dared to learn*: Arab learning flourished in the early middle ages, particularly in medicine and philosophy. This tradition was kept up by the Moslems in twelfth-century Spain.

8. *I have been a brother to Princes and a companion to beggars*: This phrase suggests that Kadmiel belongs to some organization or brotherhood similar to the Freemasons.

9. *A great gathering of Barons*: In November 1214 King John met some of his nobles at Bury St Edmunds to discuss their differences over feudal dues and liberties, difficulties which were to be partially resolved with the signing of Magna Charta in the following year.

10. *'Why of course,' cried Dan . . . who never noticed, went on*: Dan's intervention and Una's, which follow almost immediately, are not in the *Strand* text.

11. *chapman*: A pedlar.

12. *one Langton*: Stephen Langton (1150–1228) became Archbishop of Canterbury in 1207.

13. *'The Morning is come . . . in the land'*: Ezekiel 7:7.

14. *Ahasuerus*: One of the names given to the legendary figure of the Wandering Jew, who is supposed to have been condemned by Christ at the time of the crucifixion to wander the world for the rest of time.

15. *the Egyptians*: In Exodus I: 13–14 it is described how 'the Egyptians made the children of Israel to serve with rigour. And they made their lives bitter with hard bondage, in mortar, and in brick, and in all manner of service in the field; all their service, wherein they made them serve, was with rigour.'

16. *gold of Parvaim*: In 2 Chronicles 3:6 it is related how Solomon, when building the Temple in Jerusalem, 'garnished the house with precious stones for beauty; and the gold was gold of Parvaim'.

17. *I have sunk an army with horsemen in the sea*: A reference to

Exodus 14: 26–27, which tells how God instructed Moses, 'Stretch out thine hand over the sea, that the waters may come again upon the Egyptians, upon their chariots, and upon their horsemen.'

18. *Heffle Cuckoo Fair*: On 14 April a mysterious old woman is supposed to go to Heathfield fair, where she opens her basket and lets out the cuckoos heralding the arrival of spring. This piece of Sussex folklore was first recorded in 1827. I owe this information to Dr Jacqueline Simpson.

19. '*I wonder who . . . fires would burn*': Lines 57–9 of Richard Corbet's 'The Faeryes Farewell'.

20. *They heard a crash . . . goodnight to Puck*: The *Strand* text reads,
    A voice the other side of the brook boomed:

> Oh, it's then, my dears, we'll meet again
> At Heffle Cuckoo Fair.

They heard a crash, and a stamp and a splash of water . . .
    '. . . No bounds to his impidence! I'll go an' hide un a piece with a bat!'
    Then the children went in singing 'Cuckoo Fair' at the tops of their voices without even having said goodbye to Puck.

RUDYARD KIPLING IN PENGUIN CLASSICS

'The most complete man of genius I have ever known' – *Henry James*

THE LIGHT THAT FAILED

A DIVERSITY OF CREATURES

THE DAY'S WORK

DEBITS AND CREDITS

WEE WILLIE WINKIE

JUST SO STORIES

TRAFFICS AND DISCOVERIES

KIM

THE JUNGLE BOOKS

LIFE'S HANDICAP

LIMITS AND RENEWALS

SOMETHING OF MYSELF

PLAIN TALES FROM THE HILLS

PUCK OF POOK'S HILL

REWARDS AND FAIRIES

SELECTED POEMS

SELECTED VERSE

'For my own part I worshipped Kipling at thirteen, loathed him at seventeen, enjoyed him at twenty, despised him at twenty-five, and now again rather admire him. The one thing that was never possible, if one had read him at all, was to forget him' – *George Orwell*

FOR THE BEST IN PAPERBACKS, LOOK FOR THE 🐧

CLASSICS OF THE TWENTIETH CENTURY

The Collected Stories of Elizabeth Bowen

Seventy-nine stories – love stories, ghost stories, stories of childhood and of London during the Blitz – which all prove that 'the instinctive artist is there at the very heart of her work' – Angus Wilson

Look Homeward, Angel   Thomas Wolfe

A lonely idealist in pursuit of 'the great forgotten language, the lost lane-end into heaven', Eugene Gant, the central figure in Wolfe's account of a young boy growing to manhood, scours literature and the world for fresh wonders, until confronted by the intransigent reality of death and disease.

Chéri and The Last of Chéri   Colette

Two novels that 'form the classic analysis of a love-affair between a very young man and a middle-aged woman' – Raymond Mortimer

Selected Poems 1923–1967   Jorge Luis Borges

A magnificent bilingual edition of the poetry of one of the greatest writers of today, conjuring up a unique world of invisible roses, uncaught tigers . . .

Beware of Pity   Stefan Zweig

A cavalry officer becomes involved in the suffering of a young girl; when he attempts to avoid the consequences of his behaviour, the results prove fatal . . .

Valmouth and Other Novels   Ronald Firbank

The world of Ronald Firbank – vibrant, colourful and fantastic – is to be found beneath soft deeps of velvet sky dotted with cognac clouds.

FOR THE BEST IN PAPERBACKS, LOOK FOR THE

CLASSICS OF THE TWENTIETH CENTURY

The Second Sex Simone de Beauvoir

This great study of Woman is a landmark in feminist history, drawing together insights from biology, history and sociology as well as literature, psychoanalysis and mythology to produce one of the supreme classics of the twentieth century.

The Bridge of San Luis Rey Thornton Wilder

On 20 July 1714 the finest bridge in all Peru collapsed, killing 5 people. Why? Did it reveal a latent pattern in human life? In this beautiful, vivid and compassionate investigation, Wilder asks some searching questions in telling the story of the survivors.

Parents and Children Ivy Compton-Burnett

This richly entertaining introduction to the world of a unique novelist brings to light the deadly claustrophobia within a late-Victorian upper-middle-class family . . .

We Yevgeny Zamyatin

Zamyatin's nightmarish vision of the future is both a masterpiece in its own right and the forerunner of Huxley's *Brave New World* and Orwell's *1984*. The story of D-503, who is aroused from acceptance of the totalitarian state by a strange woman, E-330. His revolution is vividly chronicled here in his diary.

Confessions of Zeno Italo Svevo

Zeno, an innocent in a corrupt world, triumphs in the end through his stoic acceptance of his own failings in this extraordinary, experimental novel that fuses memory, obsession and desire.

Southern Mail/Night Flight Antoine de Saint-Exupéry

Both novels in this volume are concerned with the pilot's solitary struggle with the elements, his sensation of insignificance amidst the stars' timelessness and the sky's immensity. Flying and writing were inextricably linked in the author's life and he brought a unique sense of dedication to both.